I0576190

BLOOD
OF
YARUMAYA

KEVIN D. MILLER

WEBMILLER PUBLISHING

BLOOD OF YARUMAYA

By Kevin D. Miller

ISBN: 979-8-9934225-0-3

For more information about the author, or to order autographed copies, visit AuthorKevinMiller.com.

PRINTED IN THE UNITED STATES OF AMERICA

DEDICATION

To my granddaughter, Isabella, for allowing me to use her name as my protagonist. To my daughters Emily and Gracie, who inspire me with their unique and robust personalities, giving depth and a voice to my characters. To my wife Annette, the biggest supporter of my writing.

ACKNOWLEDGEMENTS

Sincere thanks to Katherine Kindred for her insightful suggestions.

Enjoy Other Award-Winning Books by Kevin D. Miller

The Timepiece Series
THE TIMEPIECE LEGACY-Book One
THE TIMEPIECE PARADOX-Book Two
THE TEMPUS GLASS-Book Three
THE TIME TRINITY-Book Four

TAQUOMA

EYES OF MORPHEUS

WHITE SKIES BLACK MINGO

HEART OF STEEL: Based on a True Story

Visit: AuthorKevinMiller.com

Please share this book with friends and family.

ONE

Amazon Delivery

July 28, 2026

The doctor was missing; the radio was dead; the Amazon seized her like a rabbit in a snare.

Isabella Bryn Delgado chose the wrong assignment—one she thought would bolster her master's degree in botany from Stanford University, boost a sagging GPA, and salvage her gymnastics scholarship.

She didn't want to write her thesis from the hushed aisles of a library or her cramped apartment in the city. She wanted to experience it. Live it to the fullest. Conduct research in the field, away from campus life in bustling Palo Alto. Away from the pressures of the balance beam, the nagging injury to her right knee, and away from Teddy, her soon-to-be ex-boyfriend.

In scouring a shortlist of internships, one stood out from the list of lackluster locations. *Dr. Dominic J. Quinn.* A renowned and enigmatic scholar with a Ph.D. in microbiology from Ohio State University—a lone wolf begging for a botanist lab tech to assist him deep in the Amazon rainforest, where he has spent the last decade studying the unusually long lifespan of an isolated indigenous tribe nobody knew existed. Dr. Quinn's photo looked harmless enough—graying beard, mid-forties, round glasses, green eyes, handsome, like so many soccer dads she crushed on growing up.

Insufferable mosquitoes, suffocating humidity, and savage downpours were a daily routine in the rainforest—conditions she thought she understood and blindly accepted before signing up. When people say they could kick themselves, she laughs at how dumb that sounds. But if she could kick herself right now, she'd leave a heavy boot mark in the center of her own khaki shorts.

Isabella pulled her raincoat snug around her shoulders under the heavy tarp of the field lab as a brooding thunderstorm battered the canvas. *The entire tent might literally wash away,* she thought. At least the mosquitoes weren't biting for now.

A musty scent of decaying vegetation filled the damp, warm air. She gazed into the majestic forest toward the river. The stormy scene blurred like snow on a television without an antenna.

The boatman dropped her off six days ago, along with her backpack and a limited supply of food and water. She was two weeks late reporting, and Dr. Quinn was missing. He did, however, leave a soggy note stuck inside a weathered plastic envelope, nailed to a wooden post inside the tent.

Dear Assistant,

Make yourself at home. You'll find an extra cot towards the rear of the tent. There's a limited amount of food in the chest labeled 'Perishables'. I'll be gone for a few days, conducting research among the Kawirén tribe. Please remain inside the field lab for your safety. The Amazon can be treacherous. The field radio is down. I will fix it upon my return. Open the collection barrel when it rains and secure the lid when the rain stops. Also, keep the food chest closed.

PS: If you're bored, connect the DVD player to the solar-powered generator. There's a small collection of DVDs inside a box under the bed.

Welcome to the Amazon. Cheers.

DQ

Isabella plopped into a webbed lawn chair, massaged her knee, and sighed. The humidity seemed to aggravate the joint, and the boredom she thought she'd escaped settled like an uninvited guest.

She sang to entertain herself—songs from the plays she and Teddy attended: *Cats, Chicago, Phantom of the Opera…* The sting from their last conversation lingered as a dull ache, replaying over and over inside her head like a bad 80s song.

We need to take a little break, Izzy-pop … maybe see other people for a while. And hey, time away might be good for us. You're my BFF. You know that, right? That last part cut like a rusted bottle cap on a pristine beach.

For the past two years, she believed she'd found her person—the one guy who could convince her to take a chance and marry him—after college, anyway. It hurt—like being kicked in the stomach. Maybe she didn't fit the mold of his elite circle—didn't deserve to find love so easily, or so quickly. Palo Alto seemed distant now—cut off. Maybe leaving her comfortable life wasn't the best idea. Did her emotions cloud her hasty decision? Probably.

"To hell with Teddy," she whispered, slipping her promise ring off and tossing it into her backpack as several tears dribbled from her cheeks.

Palo Alto represented freedom and independence from her parents' mansion in Malibu. She knew they loved her, but they were always gone—even when she was young. Growing up as an only child was lonely in that enormous house. She swore she'd have a big family someday to fill the gaps. But not until the timing was right, and the person was genuine.

Gymnastics was her only escape, but even the gym had become a tired chore of late.

The rainforest dripped in the aftermath of the heavy deluge. Out of curiosity, Izzy shuffled through Dr. Quinn's small collection of DVDs, half of which were documentaries on the Amazon rainforest, genetics, and microbiology. *Boooring*, she thought.

"Hm, *Indiana Jones*. Uh-uh. I've had enough rainforest for one week. *Braveheart*. Nah, too bloody. *Titanic?* Wow, dude. Really? Looks like he's watched this one a few times."

A smoking pipe made of a hard, rich, golden wood etched with dark amber veins lay at the bottom of the DVD box. She lifted and examined it. The scent of ash and citrus filled her nostrils, the wood hard and smooth. "This is gorge. Wow. The craftsmanship is amazing."

She wove her long, thick chestnut curls into a French braid and closed her eyes as she leaned her head back and stretched her sturdy thighs. Steady trickles plopping into muddy pools, the chirps of insects, the shrills of monkeys, and the whistles of exotic birds were the only sounds keeping her mind stimulated. She couldn't fight it. She missed Teddy, missed Palo Alto, missed her parents, and after nearly a week alone, trapped in the rainforest, all she wanted to do was go home.

A deep, guttural growl shot a surge of adrenaline through her veins. Her heart pounded as she sipped quick breaths. Something was outside the tent, and it wasn't human.

She held her breath as she tiptoed toward the wooden dresser. Tugging on each drawer, she slid them open one by one, shuffling through their contents: a pair of round spectacles, random notes, pencils, vials of liquid, beakers, Petri dishes, rubber tubes, microscope slides, a butane lighter, and a pistol next to a box of .38 caliber bullets.

"Great," she muttered with a quivering voice. "Thanks for never taking me shooting like you promised, Teddy."

The pistol was loaded. She used the tip of the barrel to lift a flap and peeked outside. A thick, spotted tail brushed against the canvas wall. She jerked and pulled the trigger, but the trigger jammed. The tawny, speckled face of an enormous cat glared at her through the opening with unblinking, golden eyes that fixed on her like its next meal. Isabella froze. A sickening sensation tightened her throat and churned inside her stomach. She shrieked and stepped back, fiddling with the pistol. The cat roared like the pull of a chainsaw, sending a charge of adrenaline and primeval terror coursing through her veins.

Isabella unlocked the safety button, stumbled backward, closed her eyes, and fired. The bullet hit the radio, ricocheted, and punched a hole in the tent. Enormous paws were sent splashing in the mud, scampering away, and crashing into the trees before fading.

She braced her hands on her knees, sucked a deep breath, and whimpered. "Oh, my God. What the hell was *that*? Why am I even here?"

She planted herself on the edge of her cot and stared out the front entrance. The pistol trembled in her hand, so she set it on the ground and buried her face in her palms.

"Where is Dr. Quinn?" she sobbed. Isabella trembled uncontrollably for nearly twenty minutes before a deep breath finally settled her nerves.

She slid open the dresser drawer to return the pistol, noticing a brown leather journal at the bottom. She snatched it, flopped onto the webbed lawn chair, and sucked in a quivering yawn.

Rifling through the pages, she skimmed Dr. Quinn's various notes and sketches on the Kawirén tribe's diet, rituals, mythology, and everyday life. As she flipped to the last page, his final note caught her eye.

July 3, 2026, headed to the Kawirén village to observe their ritual of rebirth. I'll be gone for a week. The ritual holds clues to these mysterious people's unusual lifespan and uncanny youthful appearance. My new aide should arrive by the time I return and help me identify the trees and vegetation unique to the region.

"A week?" She mumbled. "That was like … *three* weeks ago. Jeez. I just want to go home."

Izzy tossed the journal onto the dresser and flopped onto the cot, curling into a ball. She zipped the mosquito net, buried her head under a blanket, and screamed.

TWO

Thieves and Bloodsuckers

July 29, 2026

A flash streaked through the sky seconds before a thunderclap exploded, rocking the tent and sending Isabella rolling through the mosquito net and onto the bamboo mat beneath her cot. She shrilled, stumbling in the darkness.

"What the hell?" she shouted as the sky crackled with white light and a steady rain pelted the canvas roof.

Crawling beneath the warmth of her blanket, she tucked her knees to her chest, shivering, but not from the damp night air. Where was Dr. Quinn? Did something happen to him in the village? What if the big cat she chased off earlier ate him? The drone of the rain numbed her mind, forcing her eyes closed. If Quinn wasn't back by tomorrow, she'd find a way out of there. Hell, even if he returned, she's still going home.

The ache in her joints kept her tossing and twisting the entire night. A spasm rippled from her tailbone into her neck, forcing her out of bed. With her blanket snug around her shoulders, she flopped into the webbed chair and gazed at the majestic rainforest coming to life from the dim, amber glow of the morning sun—another day, stranded in the Amazon.

She studied Quinn's journal as a golden glow filled the tent. A rough sketch marked the field lab's location in reference to the Kawirén village—*roughly a three-and-a-half-hour walk through dense, dangerous forest*, his notes read. "Well, that's not an option," she muttered.

The radio. Maybe I can fix the radio. She shook her head and scoffed at the thought. "Yeah, right."

Maybe the boatman will check on her soon. Or deliver supplies. She could only hope as she gnawed on a stale protein bar and continued to read.

…the Kawirén elders appear no older than 30 to 35. Yet their DNA ranges in age from 130 to 150 years. No signs of gray hair, perfect blood pressure, and no signs of disease. Their diets consist of wild berries, fish, turtle eggs, plantains, deer, and tapir meat. On special occasions, they consume acai and honey and drink the blood of monkeys during their ritual of thanksgiving at the end of the rainy season …

"Ew," she whispered.

…every tribe member creates a wooden mask by their 13th birthday, made from the bark of an unusual tree they call Yarumaya. The trees are rare and native to a small section of the rainforest. The mask art is exquisite and creative. After years of learning their language, the elders invited me to create a mask and take part in the rebirth ceremony, to the dismay of the shaman. He said I was 'time-broken'. Unclear what he meant by that.

"Yarumaya tree? Not familiar with that one … Wonder which genus and species it's classified under. Or could it possibly be a new species waiting to be discovered? Hm. Now *there's* a thesis that'd guarantee an A-plus."

Isabella opened the food chest, then realized how thirsty she was. She slid her feet into her flip-flops and stepped outside into the slimy mud. Sweat beaded from every pore in her body, it seemed. The moist air assaulted her face like steam from an open dishwasher, and the mosquitoes were relentless little assholes with no mercy.

"Ow, damn it." Swatting them only intensified their bloodlust. She lifted the lid of the rain barrel, dipped a dented aluminum cup into the clear, cool water, and sipped, the dryness in her throat instantly doused.

"Oh … oh, that's so good."

She dipped her cupped hands in the water and splashed her face, temporarily relieving the sting and the redness in her cheeks and the itch of insect bites.

High-pitched squeaks and whistles from behind caused her to flinch. A family of monkeys sat near the tent entrance and stared—three small creatures with white faces, black crowns, and long tails.

"Aw, you guys are adorable. Wait. Why do you look so suspicious?"

As she stepped towards them, they darted inside the tent.

"Hey … what are you doing? You can't go in there."

Isabella marched inside and realized she'd left the food chest open. The monkeys snatched the last of the power bars and scurried through her legs like a band of merry thieves. She turned, chased after them, and fired one of her flip-flops at them like a throwing axe.

"Get back here. Those don't belong to you. Hey! Ah, come on, man…"

Her sandaled foot slid two feet in front of her, forcing her into perfect but painful front splits, followed by a face-plant into a muddy pool of vegetation and dead insects.

"Ugh! I hate this place! *Oh my God*, why did I come here?"

She rinsed herself with rainwater from the barrel and used an old T-shirt she found on top of the dresser to dab the mud. Rifling through a chest of drawers, she scavenged a bar of soap, a frayed towel, and a small shampoo bottle.

Her pungent scent from days without a bath had reached its limit. She couldn't stand herself anymore. The river seemed to be the only remedy for her situation. "I'm literally dripping sweat from my pits," she whined.

Isabella bundled the towel and toiletries, tucked them under her arm like a football, and hopped on one flip-flop until she recovered the second. She trod down to the river where the boat had left her exactly one week ago and stood on the riverbank, gazing into the easy flow of the opaque water that looked more like black tea and smelled of rotting wood and flora.

She scanned the area, nibbling on her lower lip, and stripped off her clothes, tossing them next to her towel on the rickety boat dock. The warm river flowed around her ankles, stirring a cloud of mud that sent something scurrying into deeper waters.

"Oh, God. I seriously hope I don't regret this…"

She sniffed her armpit and grimaced. "Okay, it's worth the risk."

Moving further into the river, she plunged to her neck and lathered her body at record-breaking speed. As she dipped below her shoulders, a rusty-red pair of reptilian eyes surfaced five feet away. Isabella screeched and rushed to the riverbank, creating swells of olive water around her thighs. Snatching her towel and clothes, she raced back to camp mumbling, "Bad idea, bad idea, stupid idea. Oh, jeez, what was I thinking?"

She dabbed her body with the towel and noticed two gray slugs writhing on her left thigh. She squealed and flicked at them, but they were stuck to her leg. "Oh my God, disgusting! These aren't slugs."

She ransacked the dresser drawers for the butane lighter and flicked it repeatedly until sparks turned into a tiny blue-orange flame. She burned them, watching them coil and flop to the floor, where she smashed them with her flip-flop as if she were putting out a fire. Massaging the two red circles on her thigh, she frowned and sighed.

"Ew. So gross," she muttered.

The day ended like every other day: thunder rumbled in the distance. Sizzling streaks of lightning set boiling clouds afire like Chinese sky lanterns. Darkness consumed the blue sky like a phantom's shadow. The nightly rain was on its way. She secured the tent and poured herself a cup of hot cinnamon tea.

Isabella slid into the webbed chair, opened Dr. Quinn's journal, and continued to skim his notes while sucking tiny fruit-filled puffs on her vape—a habit she hated and swore she was going to kick someday. It's Teddy's fault she even started. Well, that's not entirely true, but blaming him relieved some of the guilt. Her parents would freak if they knew … so would her coach.

…I must leave for the village at dawn. I haven't had time to fix the radio, but I will do so as soon as I return. I think there's a loose wire in the main cable harness…

…my research has led me to the sacred Yarumaya tree. The Kawirén use many parts of the tree in their daily life. Bark for ceremonial masks, juice from a tiny biannual nut-like fruit produced for medicinal purposes, leaves, and the dark amber resin that coats the trees year-round…

…The juice is anti-inflammatory and heals wounds due to its antibiotic properties. Dried leaves create a seasoning for food, similar to turmeric.

…The tree produces a thick, amber-colored resin not used for food or direct medicinal purposes. Instead, the Kawirén use this resin as a fuel to start campfires, and as an adhesive, lacquer, and waterproofing sealant…

"I'm dying to see this Yarumaya tree. I could write my entire thesis on this alone—even name a new species. *Yarumaya Isabellesis.* I really should visit the village at least once before I go home … if Dr. Quinn ever shows his face, that is."

The inside of the tent lit up like Friday night lights at a high school football game. The sky exploded with a booming crash that buckled her knees and muffled the high-pitched screech that left her throat.

"Holy crap, that was close!"

She heaved a breath to calm her racing heart and picked herself off the ground. Tossing the journal on the dresser, she scrounged through the food chest for leftover scraps after today's monkey heist: a broken Slim Jim, a half-melted Snickers bar, and an open bag of stale soup crackers. All she had left in her backpack was a pack of gum and some hard candy she had scooped from a candy dish at a restaurant in downtown Palo Alto. The same restaurant where Teddy dumped her.

Tomorrow was do or die. Find food and a way home, or starve and remain stranded in the rainforest forever. Nobody was coming to rescue her, and Dr. Quinn was probably dead.

Isabella placed the pistol under the cot and curled up in a blanket. Tears streamed as she squeezed her eyes shut and reminisced about her parents in Malibu and college life in Palo Alto. As annoying as her parents were, she missed them terribly. Home had never felt so far-removed. They begged her not to go. She should have listened. Oh, what she'd give to take a hot shower and chomp on a slice of *everything* pizza from Pizzeria Delphina.

The rhythm of the rain and the rumbling of the night sky lulled her into a restless twilight sleep, awakened periodically by the terrifying, primal night chorus of the Amazon.

As the morning light erased the darkness, she stretched her athletic frame, flexing her right hand to ease the tingling tips of her fingers. She refused to open her eyes and begin a new day in the Amazon.

She could sleep until someone came along to give her a ride home. Cut her losses and go back to school and the gym. She'd find a different subject for her thesis, like forensic botany or the effects of climate change on flora, or another overused, vanilla topic.

The shuffling of feet and the clanking of pans shot an electric charge up her spine. She rolled over, snatched the pistol, and leaped to her feet.

"Hey! Who *are* you? What do you think you're doing?"

THREE

A Stranger Calls

July 30, 2026

The dude was handsome. Late 20s. Thick, wavy, coal-black hair with a 3-day stubble beard. He was nearly a foot taller than her, dressed in an apron, a white T-shirt, and khaki trousers. He hovered over a propane stove with a spatula in his right hand and a bright smile framed in dimples. She steadied her hand with the other and pointed the gun directly at him.

"Hellooo … I said, 'Who are you?'".

"Didn't want to disturb your slumber. You hungry?"

"What?" Her quivering hands tightened around the pistol.

"Can you put that down? You're making me nervous. I won't ask if you've ever fired a gun … By the looks of my radio and that gaping hole in my tent."

"Your radio? This lab belongs to Dr. Dominic Quinn, so who the hell are you?"

"I'm Dr. Quinn."

"Seriously, who *are* you?"

"Put the gun down, and I'll introduce myself formally."

She set the gun on the dresser's edge and stood near it. "Okay. Now tell me who you are and what you're doing here … besides making breakfast."

He gazed at her with the most piercing crystal-blue eyes she'd ever seen. "I'm Dr. Dominic Quinn. My friends call me Quinn."

"What? Dr. Quinn? Dr. Quinn *Junior*, you mean? Where's your father?"

"My father died years ago."

Isabella whipped the newspaper ad from her backpack, slapped it on the table, and laid a heavy finger on his picture.

"*That* is Dr. Quinn. He's old. At least 45. You don't have a single gray hair, no wrinkles, and no glasses. You're *my* age, dude. What the heck is this? You think I'm stupid or something?"

He waved a calming hand. "I understand your confusion. But I *am* Dr. Quinn … your employer." He paused and pointed the spatula at her. "And your name is?"

"Ah-ha! You should already know my name."

"Not really. I paid for a service to recruit you. Still haven't looked at the paperwork."

"Oh … well … it's Isabella. Isabella Delgado."

"Pleased to make your acquaintance, Delgado."

"Please don't call me that."

"Why? Isn't that your name?"

"My coach calls me that. You're not my coach."

"Fair enough. What should I call you, then?"

"Hm. How about *Isabella?*" she replied, heavy on the sarcasm.

"It's nice to finally meet you, Izzy."

"Um, my boyfriend … well, my ex-boyfriend called me that. Can you call me *Isabella*, please?"

He shrugged and widened his eyes. "Works for me. Are you going to fix my radio, Delgado?"

"I, uh … don't know how to fix a radio. I'm a botanist."

"Well, ya shot my radio. How the hell am I supposed to use it now?"

"I don't know. Hey, stop changing the subject. Who are you really? What did you do with Dr. Quinn?"

He slapped a pair of over-medium eggs and a slab of meat on a tin plate and set it on the table next to a steaming cup of coffee. "Eat your breakfast, Delgado. We have a lot to discuss."

She placed a hand over her abdomen as it grumbled from the scent of grilled meat. Being deprived of actual food for days had given her a voracious appetite. Warmth flushed across her face. "Excuse my stomach. And stop calling me, Delgado."

She shuffled toward the table and sat. He dropped a second plate and sat across from her, unfazed by her glare. He grinned, nodded, and pointed at her food. "Eat up. Then we'll chat."

She hesitated, then scooped a mix of runny eggs and meat into her mouth. "Mm. This isn't bad—low key, I mean. Thank you. What is it?"

"Turtle eggs and tapir."

Her eyes widened, and her upper lip curled into a half-smirk. "Turtle eggs and tapir? Uh … okay." She swigged her coffee and wiped her tongue with her sleeve.

"You're welcome. I figured you'd be hungry since you left my food chest open. Let me guess. A family of squirrel monkeys showed up and stole all my food."

"How'd you … They did. I'm sorry."

"Yeah, well, it wouldn't be a problem if the radio worked."

"Okay, dude. I'm sorry about your radio, alright? A big freaking leopard was trying to eat me, so I shot at it."

"Well, you missed."

"I'm aware of that. Enough about your radio, Joe Tesla. I want to go home. You left me here all by myself for over a week. I've changed my mind about interning for you … So, when can I go home?" She crossed her arms and glared.

"By the looks of my radio, not for a very long time."

"I can't spend another night in this jungle. It was a mistake to come here. How soon can you have the radio fixed?"

"Look. Delgado. I'll cut to the chase. I need your help to study a very unusual tree, and I'll need you for a week … two weeks tops. Then, I'll fix the radio, and we can send you on your pretty little way. Deal?"

"No deal. I want out of here. I've seen enough of the Amazon to last a lifetime. Once you fix the radio, I'm gone."

"Now, hold on a second. You shot my radio and passed out my food to the critters of the rainforest. You owe me."

"I don't owe you anything, buddy. None of that would have happened had you been here when I arrived."

"According to my calculations, you showed up two weeks late. I didn't think you were coming."

"This wasn't the easiest place to find. I'm sure you can figure it out without me, Bear Grylls."

"I'm not fixing the radio and letting you leave until you come to the village and earn what I've already paid you."

"What? That's blackmail. You can't do that."

"I can and I will. Tomorrow, I'm returning to the village, with or without you. Not sure how long I'll be gone this time." He raised an eyebrow and glowered.

She reached inside her backpack and took a hit from her vape. "I'll stay *one* week. And that's it. After that, I'm out of here."

He pointed at the vape. "You know that shit'll kill ya, right? Ever heard of popcorn lung?"

She scoffed. "After living in the jungle for a week, chased by a big fat leopard, eaten by mosquitoes as big as a house, robbed by monkeys, stalked by crocodiles, and bled by leeches, it's the *least* of my worries."

"Jaguar. It was probably a jaguar. I see her two or three times a month. She usually stays far from the lab. Maybe she's attracted to that fruity little scent you're puffing into the clean air."

She ignored his dig, snatched the newspaper, flared her nostrils, and pointed at his photo.

"Really? Because I didn't see that little factoid written in your ad here."

"Actually, you did. Right there where it says 'Amazon rainforest.' You did your homework before you applied, right?"

She narrowed her eyes and huffed. "You still haven't explained why you look so old in your photo. Very sketch, if you ask me."

"Sketch?"

"Sketch … sketchy, ya know, sus."

"Sus? Are you from California, Delgado?"

"Malibu. Why?"

"Just a wild guess. Come with me to the village tomorrow, and I'll explain everything. Or stay here and wait until I get back. Which might take … weeks … or maybe months."

"Okay, okay … if I go with you, how do we get there? Do you have a Jeep or something?"

"Nope."

She shrugged and leered at him. "Um … then…"

"We hike. I know some shortcuts. Should take us a little under three hours."

"Oh, wow. A three-hour shortcut. Great." She rolled her eyes and shook her head.

"It'll be good for you. You probably need to stretch your legs after being cooped up here all week, handing out my power bars to the natives like trick or treat."

"Funny … when do we leave, *Junior*?"

"Quinn. Call me, Quinn."

"Sure thing, *Junior*."

He chuckled. "We leave first thing in the morning. I need to work on the radio—see how bad the damage is. Unfortunately, they're not built to withstand bullets."

Quinn glanced at the floor and frowned. He snatched a crumpled, muddy T-shirt from the corner of the mat and waved it in the air.

"Did you do this?"

She crossed her arms and shot him a nervous but defiant glance. "I slipped in the mud—"

"And used my favorite T-shirt as a towel?"

"I'm sorry, I…"

"Let's get one thing straight, Malibu: Don't touch my stuff. Don't shoot my radio, and don't leave my food storage open for the jungle critters to raid. Do that, and we'll get along just fine."

"Okay, since we're making up rules … don't lie to me. Never leave me here alone again, and stay on your side of the tent. Oh, and tell me what I'm eating *before* you serve me."

He scowled and stepped toward her with his hand extended. "Deal. Now let me see your passport and shot documents."

"What for?"

"That should go without saying. I'm the only outsider to enter the Kawirén village. You'll be the second. Unbutton your shirt."

She crossed her arms and scowled. "No way. What are you, a perv?"

"I need to give you a medical—"

"You're a microbiologist."

"I'm also a medical doctor. Now, unbutton your shirt."

"When did you have time to earn all these degrees?"

He ignored her question and pulled a flashlight from his pocket.

"Say, ah."

"Ahhh. Are you happy?"

"Look right … now look left."

"You're blinding me."

He massaged the soft area of her neck, then placed a stethoscope over her ribs. "Inhale … again."

"Oh my God, that's cold. Can we be done now?"

He tossed a canvas backpack at her feet. "Fill the plastic bottles from the rain catch."

"The rain what?"

"*Rain catch.*" He pointed outside. "The rain barrel outside the door. Fill 'em up. We'll need lots of water tomorrow."

She sneered. "And … what are *you* going to be doing?"

"I'm going to see if I can fix my damn radio, wash the mud out of my favorite T-shirt, and mend that bullet hole you shot in my tent."

A low growl outside widened her eyes and tightened her throat. "Oh, my God. That cat's back. The big frigging jaguar," she whispered.

"Yeah, well, she probably smelled your fruity vape and wants a hit."

FOUR

River Rats

Isabella grabbed the pistol and wildly pointed it in every direction. Quinn snatched it from her hand.

"Give me that before you shoot somebody."

The jaguar peeked its head inside the entrance—a low growl gyrating in its throat. The rush of blood pulsed inside her ears. She gasped and slid behind Quinn. "Oh, my God … oh, my God. Do something."

"Shhh. Don't freak her out."

"Don't freak *her* out? I'm the one freaking out. Please do something. I don't want to die…"

He set the pistol on the table and knelt, extending his arms and grinning.

"What is wrong with you? Are you a psycho?"

"Come here, Bessie. Aw, that's a good girl."

Quinn hugged her neck as the big cat wrapped its paws around his waist and licked his face.

"What the hell are you doing? She's your fricking pet?"

"Raised her as a cub. Poachers killed her mother and stole her siblings. Bessie escaped. I found her sleeping outside my tent, wet, crying, and hungry. She visits me once or twice a month. This area, including the field lab, has become her territory, and she fiercely protects it like any good predator. Which is good for you and me."

Isabella glared at him. "And you didn't tell me this because …"

"You didn't ask."

"How would I know to ask something like that? Oh, gee, by the way, Quinn, do you have a pet jaguar hanging around? Who are you? Tarzan? Is Cheetah going to show up next?"

He chuckled as he massaged Bessie's ears. "Come here. Slowly. Let her sniff your hand."

"What? No flipping way. I'm fine where I'm at, thank you very much."

"She won't hurt you."

"How do you know that?"

"Trust me."

"I don't know you, and I don't trust you."

"You're in the Amazon rainforest, Malibu. Trust is vital for your survival. I need to know I can trust *you* as well. Now, come closer and let her smell your hand."

Isabella heaved a breath and took a step forward, kneeling next to Quinn, and extending a quivering hand towards Bessie. The cat sniffed and licked her wrist with a tongue that scratched like sandpaper.

"See there. She's curious."

"She's tasting me."

Bessie brushed her cheek against Isabella's shoulder.

"Why is she making that noise? Is she pissed or something?"

"She's chuffing. Big cats can't purr. Chuffing means she likes you. I'm impressed, Malibu. I thought she might turn on you for a second."

"Seriously? Are you being serious right now? You thought she might turn on me?"

Quinn smirked and snickered as he looked away. She punched his arm. "Not funny, buster."

"Rub her ears like this. She loves that."

Quinn stood and went back to work on his radio.

"Wait. Where are you going?"

"I have work to do. You've made a new friend. Get to know each other."

"I-I, uh … Okay."

Bessie plopped next to her, pinning her foot to the floor. When Izzy moved, Bessie held her legs with a gentle paw and chuffed.

"Um, Quinn? I've been petting her for a while now. When is she going to let me up?"

"When she's ready."

"And when is that?"

"Mm … could be anytime. Hard to say."

"Where are you going now?"

"To bed. I need some shut-eye. We're leaving early in the morning. You should get some rest yourself."

"Uh, hello … I would if Tony the Tiger didn't have me pinned to the floor. Seriously, Quinn. When is she going to let me up?"

"Depends."

"On what?"

"Her mood."

"How long, Quinn?" she whimpered.

He rubbed his beard and glanced at the ceiling. "She sometimes stays an hour or two, and every once in a while, spends the night."

"Okay, I'm freaking out here. Can you get her off of me, please?"

"Good night, Malibu. See ya in the morning, kid. Bessie has really taken a liking to you."

He smirked, stretched his body across his cot, and placed a fedora over his eyes.

"Quinn. Come on. This isn't funny. Please. Help me up."

He yawned, rolled toward the wall, and began a chorus of snores.

July 31, 2026

She jerked as a finger poked her shoulder in the dim early light. Every joint in her body locked, and her neck muscles rolled with spasms.

"Wake up. In the words of John Wayne, you're burning daylight, Malibu. Come on. Get dressed."

She peered at him with one eye open. "I hate you," she said with an eyebrow raised and a semi-playful frown.

"Hey, why'd you sleep on the floor all night?"

"You're joking, right? Because Bessie …"

She glanced around the lab. Bessie was gone. Quinn tossed a stick of jerky onto her lap and handed her a water bottle.

"The sun's coming up. We need to go."

"Alright, alright, Jungle Jim. Give me a minute."

She sat upright, groaned, and massaged the kink out of her neck.

"What kind of jerky is this?"

"Don't worry about it. Beggars can't be choosers. Ever heard that old saying? It applies here."

"Dude. Is this tapir?"

"It's deer meat. You'll love it. On your feet."

She stretched her arm, waiting for him to grab her hand. "Uh … help me up. Hello…"

Quinn gnawed on a jerky strip, grabbed her by the wrist, and yanked her to her feet. She rubbed her shoulder and scowled. "Ow-wah. You nearly jerked my arm out of its socket."

He strapped an AK-47 over his shoulder and tucked his pistol into a holster. "I'll wait outside. Get dressed and grab that backpack … please."

The rainforest came alive as sunlight filtered through the thick canopy in shifting golden streaks, illuminating a dense, milky mist. The air was warm and sticky, thick with the scent of damp earth and vegetation. Oxygen-rich air filled her lungs, energizing her, while pesky insects swarmed and buzzed around their heads. Monkeys chittered and whistled, hopping through the treetops and curiously tracking them from above.

The Amazon was timeless. Primordial. It lived and breathed—majestic and unforgiving. A thousand hidden worlds thrived here, waiting to be discovered—a botanist's paradise and a California girl's nightmare.

As they wandered along a small path between mammoth trees and thick ferns, the rustling of leaves startled her.

"No need to be so jumpy, Malibu. It's just Bessie. She usually trails for a couple of miles."

"Why?"

"She's protecting us. This is her territory. Even domestic cats follow you around the house and to the bathroom. Their instinct is to watch over the ones they love. Cats are extremely loyal and loving, unlike a lot of people." He glanced at her with one eyebrow raised, tongue in cheek.

"Can we stop a minute, Quinn? I need water."

He shrugged and grimaced. "We're only fifteen minutes in, kid."

"I'm from California. I'm not used to heat like this, and I'm drenched in sweat."

He stopped, snagged a water bottle, and tossed it to her. "Take small sips. Make it last."

She wiped her brow and chugged big gulps. "Ah. Better."

Izzy pulled her camera from her backpack and snapped a few photos of Bessie peering at them from the bush, then turned the camera on Quinn.

He held his hand over her lens. "No photos, please. I don't like my picture taken."

"A little camera shy, huh? No prob."

"Nah, I just don't want you to steal my soul with that thing. Stick close and watch your step."

"How can you possibly know where you're going, Quinn? I'm already lost."

"Years of making this trip. I could do it with my eyes closed."

"Yeah, well … keep your eyes open, please."

He pointed to a large nail sticking out of a tree painted neon orange. "And I've marked the path with these nails so I can always find my way in and out. Otherwise, it's nearly impossible not to get lost. Take a wrong turn, and no one will ever see you again."

"Please don't take a wrong turn."

He snickered. "What possessed you to want to come down here, Malibu? You don't strike me as the outdoorsy type."

"Hey, I've been camping. Slept on the beach a few times."

"Ooh, wow. That's impressive." He rolled his eyes.

"You're right. I'm not an outdoorsy survival chick. I thought coming down here might be the perfect place to study the problem of deforestation. Take some photos and videos for my Instagram page. Plus, I needed a break from gymnastics."

"You're a gymnast?"

"Yep. Balance beam. I'm a bit tall for the balance beam at five-four. Most girls are three to four inches shorter. I hurt my knee about a month ago, and it hasn't completely healed. Figured time away from the gym and all the chaos would do it some good."

"Well, you have a gymnast's physique for sure. And balance is an excellent skill to have out here, as you'll learn. Doesn't the long hair get in the way?"

"I French-braid it, coil it, and then add lots of bobby pins, hair ties, and a little hairspray."

"Ah, got it."

"You never explained to me why you look so old in your photo. How old are you anyway, Quinn? Truth."

"Not polite to ask someone's age. I'll clear things up for you later, but not right now."

"So, you keep promising … Can I ask where you're from?"

"Can we curb the small talk for a bit and focus on the hike?"

"It's a long walk, dude. Just trying to pass the time. Jeez."

Quinn paused and pointed toward the treetops. "Pass the time with your eyes and your senses, Malibu. Look around you."

Hundreds of vibrant birds filled the rainforest like splashes of multi-colored paint splattered across a green canvas.

"Oh my God, that's amazing. I've never seen so many birds in one place in my life. And they're so loud. Macaws?"

"Yup. It takes my breath away every time I see them," he muttered.

The roar of rushing water grew louder as they exited the dense forest and stepped into a clearing.

"What is that? A river?"

"You're about to find out. Ready to test your balance?"

As they rounded a grove of cocoa trees, they stood on the edge of a cliff. To her right, a powerful waterfall crashed over a craggy ridge and emptied into a pristine river fifty feet below.

Her jaw hung, and her eyes widened like a 12-year-old's. "That's freaking awesome." She grabbed her camera and snapped several shots.

He pointed at the river. "That's where we're headed."

"What? But how are we—"

"We're going to climb down. How's your knee?"

"It's, uh, fine. I think, but … are you serious right now? We're going to climb down *there*?"

"Yes ma'am. Not for the faint of heart."

Quinn pulled a rope from his backpack and threaded it through a metal ring already bolted in the side of a large boulder. He tossed her a harness.

"Put that on. Let me know if it fits."

"Wait, what? I'm not a rock climber."

"Well, Malibu, you're about to get your first lesson."

Isabella hopped from the last section of rock to the ground. She heaved a breath to slow her racing heart and gazed up the side of the cliff, shielding her eyes with her right hand.

"I can't believe you made me do that. I can't believe I actually *did* that."

"You did great. You're a born natural. Balance is essential in life, kid, not just in gymnastics."

"Thanks, *Dad*," she chuckled. "So, how do we get your rope?"

"We don't. We'll have to climb back up on our way back."

"Oh … yeah. That makes total sense."

"Let's keep moving. Only a couple of hours to go."

She took a step and flinched, clutching her knee. "Ah, my leg just tightened up. Sorry."

"Let me take a look at that."

"Um, okay. I guess—you being a doctor and all. You're not going to send me a bill, are you?"

He pressed the tissue around her knee and ran her through a range-of-motion assessment.

"I see some bruising and inflammation here. Looks like you injured your MCL, and the joint seems stressed. You need to take it easy and let this thing heal. My guess is you keep aggravating it by doing too much. Here, take some of this."

"What is it?"

"Cat's claw."

"Oh, Uncaria tomentosa."

"I'll have to take your word for it. Great for inflammation. Let me wrap your knee—to keep it stabilized."

They reentered the rainforest and followed the river for nearly a mile as it snaked through gigantic trees that seemed to stretch forever. Quinn pointed toward the sky.

"What type of trees are these, Malibu?"

"Is this a test, Professor?"

"Eh, maybe."

"They're kapok trees. *Ceiba pentandra.* They can grow up to 200 feet. But wow, seeing them in nature blows me away. I mean, one tree is an entire ecosystem covered in vines and bromeliads. I'm overstimulated with awe. This is so incredible. Nothing like the YouTube videos I've watched."

She ran her fingers over an orchid and grinned. "I hate to admit it, but I'm glad I came along. The air here is so fresh it feels heavy. It's crazy. I'm high on breathing."

Quinn lifted a young green chameleon off a vine and placed it on her shoulder.

"Eek. He's so handsome. Hey, little fella."

"It's an incredible place. If the Mayuma dies, we all die."

"Mayuma?"

"The Kawirén term for Mother Rainforest. I don't think the world appreciates how much our survival depends on her. Or even cares. Okay, enough with the lecture."

He pointed to a narrow section of the river lined with slippery rocks. "We cross here. Wanna go first?"

Isabella darted over the stones like a contestant on American Ninja Warrior. When she hit the other side, she did a perfect cartwheel and stuck the landing. "Your turn."

He shook his head and flashed a crooked smile. "That's why your knee isn't healing properly, Malibu. You're a showoff."

Quinn took his time and leaped from stone to stone. When he hit the bank, he spread his arms, cocked his head, and kept walking.

"No cartwheel, Quinn?"

"Nope. That's all you get."

"Wow, bad form, dude. Can we rest for a minute? I could really use a drink … and I might have tweaked my knee."

"I'm not surprised. Five minutes, then we have to keep moving."

"Why the rush? Has no one ever asked you to stop and smell the roses? My feet hurt."

"You need to trust me on this. We need to keep moving."

"Oh, come on, Professor Pooper. Just two more minutes."

Quinn knelt in front of her and narrowed his eyes. "This is a smuggling lane for drug traffickers and poachers. We're in danger here. Two miles up the river and we're safe. You can rest there. Right now, we need to go. Pronto."

As they rounded a bend, the voices of several men echoed through the trees. "They're speaking Spanish," she whispered.

Quinn pressed his index finger to his lips and shook his head. He crouched and crept along the riverbank, hiding in the reeds, waving for her to follow. To their right, the river widened to over 50 yards. Six armed men formed a human chain and passed taped bundles from the riverbank to a ten-foot speedboat.

"River rats," he whispered.

"What do we do?" she mouthed.

"Wait for them to leave. I guess you can rest now."

She rolled her eyes and frowned. "Great."

Hours passed. The river rats sat on the bank smoking, drinking, and growing rowdy. The sun loomed directly overhead, and dark clouds gathered in the distance, rumbling and lighting up the sky.

Quinn whispered, "We can't wait any longer. The last thing we need is to be caught in that storm and spend the night here."

She shadowed Quinn as he crawled along the reeds and led her to a six-foot aluminum boat tucked beneath branches, grasses, and leaves. He flipped it over and pushed it into the water.

"Get in." He handed her an oar and steered the boat with another.

"Where are we going?"

"We have to make it to the other side without being noticed."

"Oh, crap. Shouldn't we wait until they pass out or something?"

"Looks like the party is only getting started. The white powder they're snorting is going to keep them up all night. If they spot us, row for your life, kid."

As they reached the middle of the river, a voice shouted. "Oye, amigo! Trae ese barco aquí."

"Oh, God. He's telling us to steer the boat over there," she said.

"Row, Izzy. As fast as you can. Don't look back!"

A boat engine fired as all six men jumped aboard, hollering and cat-calling in Spanish. The nose of their boat rose out of the water, turned, and headed straight for them.

"Quinn! Are we going to make it?"

"We're almost there. Keep paddling and keep your eyes on the prize. As soon as we hit the riverbank, follow me."

Ten feet from shore, a shower of bullets ker-plunked in the surrounding water.

Quinn shouted, "Jump! And run!"

Mud and tree bark exploded around them from a barrage of bullets zinging past their heads to the raucous laughter of the smugglers. They darted into the forest as the smugglers hit the shore. Quinn grabbed her hand and led her down a slope and over a felled tree. He kicked a camouflaged wooden lid aside and shoved her inside a three-foot-wide hole. He wriggled his body next to hers and sealed them inside.

"Stay quiet," he whispered as he flipped on a lantern next to them.

Isabella shivered. Her heart pounded into her throat. She couldn't breathe—couldn't think. Squeezing her eyes shut, she prayed and gripped Quinn's forearm. He pulled her close and wrapped his arms around her shoulders. "It's going to be okay, I promise. Take slow, deep breaths. That's it. You're doing great."

The shouting and footsteps subsided. Half an hour later, an engine fired and faded into the distance.

"Are they gone?" Her voice quivered.

"Possibly. But we'll wait here a little while longer to be sure. They may leave a couple of rats behind to trick us into showing ourselves. We may need to spend the night here. I'm sorry."

"I knew I should have gone home."

"We're safe. I won't let anything bad happen to you. Besides, I've paid you a lot of money, so I have to protect my investment."

"I didn't sign up for this, Quinn. I really just want to go home."

"You can go home in a few days, I promise. Just hang in there a little while longer. Hey, this is the adventure of a lifetime. Right?"

"No. It's definitely not. And I'm going to hold you to your promise. I don't know how much more drama I can stand. This place is turning into my worst nightmare. Look at my hands. I-I can't stop shaking."

"Tell me about gymnastics. How'd you learn to jump around like that? You looked like a rabbit hopping over those rocks and a spider monkey shimmying down that cliff."

She nibbled on her lip, a slight smile creasing her lips. "My mom started me young. I was five. I hated going to practice, but she never allowed me to miss. So, I cried, threw fits, but I could never break her. After a while, I fell in love with the sport—loved competing and all the attention that came with it. It became my passion. My escape."

"Do you still love it?"

"M-hm. I finished second on the balance beam at our state championships in high school, which disappointed my mom. But … I got a full-ride scholarship to Stanford thanks to a little help from my dad. College was tougher than high school. It didn't come as easily. In college, everyone was the star of their high school team, so the competition is fierce."

"Well, I was genuinely impressed by how you skipped over that river and landed that cartwheel."

She tittered. "Thanks. But you're obviously patronizing me."

"Well, you're not shaking nearly as much. I'm going to check outside. See if the old coast is clear, as they say."

Quinn pulled the pistol from the holster and handed it to her. "Just in case. Make sure you aim *before* you shoot and keep your eyes open. And if you have to shoot, make sure it isn't me you're shooting at."

"What? No, don't leave me here alone. I-I don't know where I am or what to do if you don't come back."

"I'll come back when I'm sure they're gone. Worst-case scenario, follow the orange markers back to base camp."

He cracked the lid several inches, scanned the area for movement, then slipped outside and sealed the opening. She was alone in the dim light. Panic rose in her throat, and her stomach churned. "God, please come back … please, please, come back," she murmured.

A constant drizzle tapped the lid like a bongo as five, then ten minutes crept by. A few seconds later, the lid moved and then flew open as if a gust of wind sucked it from its hole.

"Amiga! Come outside and join the party, Chica."

A short, heavyset smuggler dressed in Army fatigues, a boonie hat, with an assault rifle strapped to his shoulder, grabbed her ankle and yanked. She screamed and kicked. "No! Let go of me! Quinn! Help!"

"I'm not going to hurt you, Chica. I just want to introduce myself and have a little fun."

FIVE

The Betrothed

The smuggler clenched his teeth and sneered as he latched onto her calves and tugged. Her vision blurred. She sucked in so much air she nearly fainted. Adrenaline surged through her veins, and her mind went blank, like on the balance beam, where she blocked out the crowd noise and focused on her performance. *In the zone*, they called it. Her fear subsided, and her mind slowed, running on the disciplined instinct of a skilled athlete.

Isabella snatched the pistol, aimed at his chest, and fired. The man's eyes widened as he stumbled backward and lay sprawled on his back. She crawled from the hole, gripping the pistol with quivering hands, aiming at the dying smuggler's face.

She pointed at him. "You made me do that … I-I didn't want to do that. This is *your* fault…"

He reached for her, his hand curling like a claw. Blood bubbled over his lips as he gurgled and choked. His gaze widened, his eyes unblinking—seconds later, his stare turned empty.

The rainforest was quiet except for the steady drizzle and the chirping of birds. "Quinn?" She whispered. "Quinn?"

POP, POP, POP echoed through the trees. She ducked behind dense ferns and peeked toward the source of the gunshots. Sounds of crunching leaves and broken branches rushed towards her. She raised the pistol and held her breath.

It was Quinn. Thank God, it was Quinn.

He rushed toward the shelter, aiming his AK-47 at the dead body. Lifting the shelter lid off the ground, he flipped it like a Frisbee and shone a flashlight into the opening of the small grotto. "Izzy?"

"I'm here." She rushed out of the brush and into his arms.

"Are you alright? What happened here?"

Tears filled her eyes. "I thought you were dead. He … he grabbed me … so I shot him. He's dead, Quinn. I-I killed him … I killed him."

"Well, you must have kept your eye on the target this time. Nice shoot'n, Tex."

"I killed somebody … I've never shot anyone before in my life. Oh, my God."

"Well, I would hope not. It's okay. He was a piece of shit. Probably killed lots of innocent people. Think of all the kids he's murdered with the drugs he's smuggled."

"It's not okay, Quinn. I really need to go home."

"Well, we can't stay here, and it's getting late in the afternoon. I knocked off the other river rats, so no one will follow us. There's a tree shelter about three miles from here. We'll spend the night there. You good?"

"I think so," she whispered, staring at the ground as if the answers to her trauma were written in the mud.

"You're going to be fine, Izzy. Let's move before the skies let loose or more river rats crawl out of a hole."

He pointed at a Brazil-nut tree. "See the orange marker, Izzy? We go this way. Pay close attention to the markers and the path. It's important."

❧❧❧

The shelter was twenty feet off the forest floor, set between the sturdy limbs of a mahogany tree and well-hidden amongst its thick leaves and branches. Quinn scaled the tree and dropped a rope ladder as the sky unleashed a torrent, pelting her face and soaking her to the bone.

"Climb, Malibu. Get your butt up that ladder before the rain washes you away."

The shelter reminded her of a childhood friend's treehouse, where she spent many nights having sleepovers. Wooden planks built around tree limbs, a single door, no windows, and a tin roof. Quinn spread a wool rug across the floor and tossed her a cotton blanket. He lit a fire inside a homemade stovepipe oven.

"Best bed-and-breakfast in the Amazon, Malibu. Minus the breakfast, of course."

"Oh, now it's *Malibu* again. A little while ago, it was Izzy."

He shrugged. "I don't know what you're talking about. Make yourself at home. We'll sleep here tonight. Tomorrow, we have about an hour's hike to reach the village."

She sat across from him, stretching the blanket around her shoulders as the rain intensified and pinged off the metal roof. Thunder rattled the floor as if the entire shelter might splinter any second. Rain dripped through a crack in the ceiling, creating a small puddle near her feet. Quinn pulled a small wooden case from his backpack, took his hand knife, and smeared a sticky, golden substance in the crack, sealing it instantly. He scraped the excess off onto the edge of the case.

"Jeez, what *is* that? We could market that stuff to Home Depot and make a killing."

"Resin from the Yarumaya tree. Best glue I've ever seen. They use it for everything. The citrusy scent lasts until it dries. You can plug a hole and freshen the air at the same time. I used it as fuel to light the fire. Highly combustible."

She nibbled on deer jerky and narrowed her eyes. "Quinn? Doesn't the murder of six people bother you at all?"

"We didn't murder them. More like self-defense. Huge difference."

"I know they deserved it, but it doesn't bother you?"

"Why should it?"

"I don't know … maybe they had families. People who loved them. Couldn't we have wounded them instead? Tied them up."

"Ugh. I forgot. You're from California."

"What's that supposed to mean?"

"It means that's a stupid thing to say. Are you opposed to guns? 'Cause a gun saved us both today."

"No, I'm not against guns, for your information. My ex-boyfriend was big into guns. Promised to take me shooting. Never did."

"Well, I can believe that," he snickered. "First lesson in firing a weapon in self-defense, Malibu: Shoot to kill. You did that today. Remember that lesson."

"Fine. How about we talk about you, Mr. Mystery Man? Why the heck are you so old in your photo? Yet, we look the same age. So, is that a photo of your dad? Or did you dress up to look like a harmless middle-aged man to fool potential young assistants like me?"

"It's just a grainy photo. Besides the rainforest has been good for my health."

"Hm, because something feels very sketch in all of this. I mean, how can you have a doctorate from Ohio State and be so young? Were you some kind of child prodigy or something?"

"I'm not as young as I look." He lit his pipe and blew a cloud of blue smoke.

"See. That's what I mean. You're not making sense, and you're hiding something. I think I deserve an explanation." She crossed her arms and glared.

"Well, you're wasting your time. Nothing more to tell."

She removed her vape from her backpack and took a hit, filling the air with the sweet scent of watermelon.

"That shit's bad for you. An athlete like yourself should know better."

"You're not my dad. Well, your photo looks like my dad, but you're not him, so mind your own business, buddy. And besides, what's that thing hanging off your lip? Tobacco is just as bad as a vape."

"Suit yourself, but that's going to catch up with you someday. And for your information, this is pure homegrown tobacco. No pesticides, no herbicides, just organically grown tobacco. None of that fruity chemical crap coming out of your silly little pipe. That thing looks ridiculous—more like a pencil than a pipe."

He rested his head against his backpack, stretched his long legs, and closed his eyes. "Nighty-night, Malibu. Get some rest. You're gonna need it."

She sat in the dark listening to the crackle of the fire and the rhythm of raindrops pinging off the tin roof. The air was damp but cool, filled with a citrusy scent from the resin in the fire. It was a tremendous relief to be high in a tree, away from the river rats and all the pesky insects. Just thinking about those little vampires made her itch. Those little suckers weren't feasting tonight. Not on her anyway.

The soft amber light flickered across Quinn's face as he snored. How can he look so young yet act like such an old fart? Hair thick and black as a raven's feathers, nothing like the salt and pepper gray in the photo ad. Strong jawline, perfect complexion, great teeth—it's disgusting. He's handsome, she hates to admit. But his ears stick out like satellite dishes, messing up the symmetry.

"You should grow your hair out," she mumbled as he wheezed.

She likes that he's tall—over six feet. None of her boyfriends was over five-eight. Teddy was five-seven but swore he was five-ten—not the only thing he lied about.

She curled into a ball, closed her eyes, and exhaled a shivering breath. As horrible as the day was, she was safe. Safe from the storm, safe from the smugglers, and safe inside the treehouse with Quinn.

August 1, 2026

Her eyes popped open, inhaling a screech as she sat upright, scrambling to remember where she was. A gentle voice broke the tranquility of the early morning.

"Bad dreams?"

"I-I was drowning in the river. That creepy man's body was floating next to me … trying to grab my foot."

"Well, did you kick him this time?"

She stretched her legs and twisted her torso, creating a series of satisfying pops along her spine.

"No. I'm so tired. Can we sleep a while longer? Please?"

"This isn't the Ritz, Malibu. We need to go. We're already behind schedule."

He tossed her a small container and nodded. "Drink that. It'll wake you up."

"What is it? I don't trust you."

"Yoco bark. Better than coffee and easier on the stomach."

"Yuck." Her face contorted. "So bitter. Tastes like a dirty shoe."

"How many dirty shoes have you tasted?" he chuckled.

"Funny."

"It's going to put a spring in your step. You'll thank me later."

He opened the door and unrolled the rope ladder. She scurried down the rope like a Vegas acrobat and hollered, "I think it's kicking in. I feel like I drank ten cups of coffee. Wow, can I have another shot of that? It's amazing … what a beautiful morning. Jeez, can I find some of this at the health store? What's in this again?"

"Can you turn down your volume a notch, Malibu? The entire rainforest knows we're here now."

"Uh … rude."

They moved along the river to the edge of a placid creek where a felled tree formed a natural bridge.

"Oh wow, look. Giant water lilies. *Victoria amazonica.* Aw, those itty-bitty frogs are so darn cute … and colorful. Don't you think?"

"And poisonous," he grunted.

"We don't have frogs like that in America. Or do we? I'll have to Google it. I once had a friend who had a colorful lizard."

He snatched the yoco bark from her hand and replaced the cap. "I think you've had enough. This is still the Amazon, and my ears are starting to hurt."

Isabella snickered, leaped onto the tree bridge, and began a series of dance moves, cartwheels, 180 splits, a salto, and a shaky dismount. She turned and bowed from the other side, giggling like a schoolgirl at recess.

"A perfect ten, Malibu. I guess you didn't notice that 20-foot anaconda snoozing beneath your impressive routine."

"What? Are you joking?"

He nudged the snake with a stick, prompting it to slither further down the creek.

"Oh, my God. Why didn't you tell me?"

"I just noticed her. They're masters of camouflage, and she's big enough to swallow a gimpy gymnast whole. You should stay close … tone it down a bit."

The dense forest gave way to an open, desolate area littered with logs, splintered wood, dried fronds, and scattered leaves and branches.

She gasped. "Holy crap. What happened here? Quinn? Who did this?"

"Wood poachers."

"Oh, my God. How do they get away with it? This is horrible."

"No laws to stop them. Where there's money, there's crime."

"Why can't anyone stop them?"

"The laws are weak, and there aren't enough folks to enforce them. It's sad to watch. They rape the land, steal the trees, and waste the rest. To add to the heartbreak, they kill the wildlife that make these trees their homes."

She narrowed her eyes and shook her head. "It makes me so angry. Reading about it doesn't compare to actually seeing it. It's disgusting."

"I agree. If it continues, your grandkids will never have this experience."

"I can't believe how greedy and cruel people can be."

She lifted her camera from around her neck and photographed the devastation.

He pointed. "We're almost there. The village is up that mountain and through a hidden valley."

Her eyes widened. "Up *that* mountain?"

"Yep. How's your knee?"

"Okay, I guess." She snatched the yoco bark from his backpack and took a swig.

"Let's do this."

He shot her a suspicious glare, then glanced at his backpack, securing the vial of yoco bark.

She shrugged innocently. "What?"

As they reentered the forest, a group of Amazon parrots scattered—their lime-green feathers blending into the massive trees. The canopy was dense, blotting out the sun and casting an ominous gray shadow around them. The warm, moist air was woody, filled with an earthy scent and a faint hint of sweet vanilla.

"Plumeria Frangipani," she whispered.

"Okay, Malibu, see if you can locate the marked trees that will lead us to the village. It's vital that you learn how to navigate the forest in case something happens to me."

Izzy pointed. "There's one. So, we go this way."

Quinn chuckled. "Good eye. Lead the way."

"Ooh. Over there. This is fun. Like Easter egg hunting."

"Not if you don't find the 'Easter eggs', Malibu. That wouldn't be *fun*."

After a few hundred yards, she plopped onto a rotting log, dropped her backpack on the ground, and blew a sharp breath. "Quinn. I need to rest a minute. My sock slid down my boot. It's like, wrapped around my toes and bugging the crap out of me."

"I wouldn't set my backpack on the ground, Malibu. Not a good idea."

She scoffed and waved him off. "It's only for a minute. Jeez. Why do you sound like somebody's dad all the time?"

She stood, slid her backpack around her shoulders, and grinned.

"There. Good as new. Lead the way, Tarzan."

Her shoulder burned like fire. A stabbing, blistering sting sent goosebumps across the back of her neck.

"Ow, ow, ow … shit! Quinn! Something bit me."

He yanked her backpack off her shoulders and tore the back of her sleeve. A five-inch brown spider with black bands around its legs dropped from her backpack to the ground like a fleeing assassin. Quinn stomped on it, wiping the creamy guts from his boot onto the edge of a sharp stone.

"I can't breathe. Oh God, am I going to die? What was *that*? Quinn!"

"Calm down. It was a spider. I told you not to leave your backpack on the ground. Hopefully, one of these days you'll learn to trust me."

"My shoulder's spasming. What do we do? Oh God, I need to sit…"

Her knees wobbled as she collapsed into his arms. Quinn's face blurred, and his voice muffled.

"Stay with me, Malibu. Izzy? Look at me. Breathe, come on, breathe…"

Children's voices tittered. Raindrops thrummed. Muffled conversations in a language she didn't understand roused and confused her. Her right shoulder ached; her body drenched in sweat.

Quinn's velvety voice broke the silence. "You're going to be fine, Malibu. A banana spider bit ya. Maybe next time you'll follow instructions."

"Ugh. Enough with the lectures. How long am I going to be like this, *Mr. I Told You So*?"

"A day or two. You're lucky I had the antivenom. A Brazilian Wanderer is no joke, kid. It's serious. You rest. When you feel better, I have something to show you."

"I think I'm fine." She pushed herself upright. Lights flashed in her eyes, and her stomach cramped. She grabbed his sleeve. "Give me something … quick."

"What do you mean?"

She snatched a wooden bowl, knocking over everything on the table, and vomited. "Oh, my gosh … disgusting. I'm so sorry," she said as she wiped her mouth with her sleeve.

"I don't think you're fine. You need to rest," he said as he handed her a water bottle.

"No, I'm good. I puked and rallied."

She glanced around the room. "What is this place? You have another field lab in the village?"

"Yep. And as the only doctor in the village, I insist you rest."

She clenched his wrist. "Help me up."

As she stood, she clutched her throbbing groin and frowned. "Oh … oh, crap. Ouch."

Quinn stifled a smirk. "Yeah. There's that effect, too. That might last another hour or so until the swelling goes down … which is another reason I think you should lie down for a bit."

She crossed her legs and grimaced. "Okay," she muttered in a meek, squeaky voice.

Ninety minutes later, Isabella emerged, paused at the edge of the porch, and heaved a quivering breath.

The Kawirén village spread before her in a mosaic of color and movement. Sunlight slipped through the canopy, casting dappled patterns over wooden huts crowned with thick, thatched roofs. Children raced between them, their innocent laughter ringing through the trees.

"Oh, my God," she whispered as her jaw slackened.

Their eyes were striking. The children's eyes were like black coffee. But every adult, male and female, bore bright crystal-blue eyes, almost neon-like—a curiosity she couldn't ignore and didn't expect.

It was one thing to read about tribal life in journals, memorize the customs, and prepare herself with YouTube videos. It was another to feel the warmth radiating from sunbaked earth, and smell the wood smoke mixed with a sweet and spicy scent unlike any other she'd ever encountered. The sounds of the thriving rainforest never let up, setting her senses on fire.

Under a large shelter woven from leaves and grass, women gathered, their voices rising and falling in a soft rhythm. They gossiped as they stirred a steaming mixture inside a heavy stone cauldron. Isabella caught a whiff—earthy, sharp, unfamiliar.

Teenage girls wove colorful tapestries, fingers moving so quickly they blurred. Men knelt in circles, carefully shaping spears and arrowheads, only pausing long enough to pass around a carved wooden jug.

Women and girls wore grass skirts, their torsos and breasts bare, adorned with colorful beads, shells, and bright feathers. Men wore vivid loincloths, faces painted in sharp patterns of black and white, their noses pierced by slender wooden needles, and feathered headdresses that shook as they moved.

The forest seemed to hold its breath, watching her. A flicker of guilt rippled through her soul. She was an outsider—a scientist. A stranger peering into lives older and deeper than any she could have ever imagined.

She swallowed, heart racing, both humbled and electrified. She had come in search of a thesis. Instead, she stood at the threshold of a world more alive, extraordinary, and sacred than anything she'd ever dreamed of.

The mass destruction of the rainforest from the tree poachers broke her heart as she gazed over these amazing people and the essence of their daily lives. They were as much a part of the rainforest as the trees, the birds, and the rivers.

She was small in comparison. Insignificant in the presence of the majestic rainforest, its people, and all the creatures who call it home. She couldn't feel it, see it, or taste it on a computer screen in Palo Alto. But here she breathed it, and it filled her soul with its presence the way a mist fills a forest. The way a storm fills a river. It consumed her, erasing every misconception she had of its magnificent beauty. The Amazon was a living, breathing being. Fantastic in its unique beauty, yet utterly terrifying. *Mayuma.* Mother Rainforest.

Quinn sat with a group of four men, passing a large wooden cup between them. They laughed it up like good old boys in a locker room. When he noticed her, he leaped to his feet and marched towards her, waving his hands to prevent her from stepping any closer.

"Whoa, hold up, Malibu. I have to introduce you to the people before you can walk around the village."

He took her by the hand and led her into the center of the village, where he shouted something in Kawirénian. The people stopped what they were doing and gathered.

Quinn continued to speak. All she could do was flash a nervous smile and fidget like a teenager introduced to a new school by the teacher. When he finished, the crowd went silent for several seconds. Isabella glanced at Quinn, awaiting his response. He frowned and shook his head, taking her by the hand and facing the crowd, speaking with authority and passion. She had no idea what he was saying, but his words inspired and energized her, anyway.

Moments later, the tribal women shrieked and chanted. They gathered around her, took her by the arms, and led her to a small private pool, where they bathed her in sweet salts and lathered her in something oily, washing her hair and massaging her neck. The young girls braided her long, dark hair with orchids and tiny white flowers. The teenage girls dabbed her skin dry with a thick cloth and painted her face and full lips with a russet-colored dye that smelled of clay.

They dressed her in a bright red grass skirt and draped flowered necklaces over her bare breasts. When they finished, they led her back to the center of the village and presented her to Quinn like a prize.

"Uh, what are they doing, Quinn? Why am I dressed like this?"

"They're presenting you … to me." He wouldn't make eye contact despite her efforts to lock eyes with him.

"What? Why?"

"You don't want to know."

"Are you kidding? What is going on?" she hissed.

He winced. "You're my betrothed. You've been prepared to offer yourself to me."

"WHAT? Are you insane? Not happening, dude. Keep dreaming."

"Don't worry, Malibu. I have no interest in … well, you know. Our betrothal has nothing to do with sex. It was the only way I could get them to accept you into the tribe. But the good news is, now that you're connected to me, you can complete the ritual that connects you to Mayuma and the tribe."

"The good news? Why don't I believe you? You set this up. I know you did."

"Not true." He reached for her hand, but she slapped it away. Murmurs rumbled through the crowd.

"Look. If you don't go with me, they'll excommunicate you, and you'll be all alone in the rainforest. Work with me here."

She glared at him and sneered. "Unbelievable. This is like, major creepy."

He led her inside and tossed her backpack onto the bed. "Get dressed."

She shot red-hot laser beams at him and shooed him away. "Turn around. Look over there. Were you peeking earlier?"

"I was *not* peeking." He squatted on a stool and faced the wall. "We'll need to wait about twenty minutes."

"Ooh. Wow. A twenty-minute man."

He snickered and pinched the bridge of his nose. "Can I turn around now?"

"Yes, you may."

"Okay, look, Izzy. As my betrothed, you are safe in the village. A member of the tribe. There was no other way to keep you here. We wait inside for a while, then reemerge as partners. You'll complete the ritual of Mayuma to be forever connected to the rainforest and the Kawirén people. Do you understand?"

"Okay, I totally get it. Just don't get any crazy ideas."

"I wouldn't think of it. Take my hand."

"Why?"

"We have to step outside holding hands and greet the crowd so they can give us their blessing. Seal the deal before your bonding ritual to the rainforest."

"Seriously, when is this going to be over?"

"Soon." Quinn slid a leather bracelet with the tooth of a jaguar as a pendant over her wrist. He strapped a similar bracelet, with a thicker leather band, around his own wrist.

"What's this for?"

"It represents our bond. Similar to wedding rings. You need to wear it when you're in the village. I'm sorry."

"No, it's actually kind of cool. I like it."

The second they emerged, the crowd cheered. The women lined up, took swigs from a fat wooden pitcher, and spat on them.

"Ew," she whispered.

"They're blessing us. Just smile and go with it."

The women moved behind the men as the men lined up to share their blessings.

"Oh, God. What are *they* going to do? Pee on us?"

"I dunno. But if they do, just roll with it."

The men took turns kissing Isabella on her right hand and slapping Quinn on the left cheek. When they finished, Quinn's cheek was so red it was nearly purple. She glanced at him and beamed.

"Oh, that was *so* worth it," she chuckled. "Where's your smile, Quinny? Way to roll with the punches, buddy. Not so funny now, I bet."

He frowned at her, rubbing his cheek.

A cacophony of spices and sweet scents filled her nostrils. Beyond the crowd, several of the women had organized a smorgasbord while they were inside "bonding", awaiting for them to emerge.

"Now what?" she asked.

"We eat, drink, and celebrate. Then you undergo a brief ceremony, and bam, you're in the club. Afterward, you'll start earning your paycheck, Malibu."

SIX

The Sacred Grove

The women led Izzy into the center of the Circle, where a small fire of Yarumaya wood crackled and billowed a sweet, citrusy smoke. They guided her onto a decorated ceremonial Yarumaya stump. The entire village circled them, chanting in low tones. Quinn kneeled behind her and remained silent.

Drums vibrated in low, soft rhythms, while shaker sticks rattled a hypnotizing melody. Izzy gulped and sucked in a nervous breath, anticipating whatever came next.

A woman dressed in a bright red grass skirt, sandals that tinkled with tiny shells as she danced, a mauve-feathered headdress, and her face and bare breasts painted white, knelt in front of her and offered a gourd, painted green, and filled with a milky brown liquid that smelled of orange blossoms. The woman nodded, encouraging her to drink—so she did.

The liquid was sweet and tart. It had the consistency of eggnog and numbed her tongue and throat as she swallowed. The moment Izzy handed the gourd back to the woman, the drums, shaker sticks, and villagers exploded into an orchestra of rhythmic music and chants.

Everything around her blurred—the sounds muffled. Warmth coursed through her veins to every inch of her body. Izzy relaxed and allowed the effect of the drink to override her inhibitions. Sweat streamed off her body as the flames leaped from the fire and licked her skin without burning.

Without warning, Izzy's spirit left her body and soared over the rainforest. The Amazon filled her with its glorious presence as she witnessed the soft bluish-green glow of its dynamic life force.

Spirits surrounded her like angels of light, cradling her and bathing her in the purest love she'd ever experienced. Below, the ancient spirits of the Kawirén ancestors sang a song so powerful it filled her with a terrifying vibration. She panicked, tumbling back into her body like falling from the balance beam to the soft mat.

Her wrist burned like fire. Tarenu sat in front of her, chanting, etching a tattoo of the Yarumaya into her skin—like a silhouette of the tree. The long history of the Kawirén flashed through her mind like a movie reel on fast-forward. She understood. Felt their struggles. Felt their bond and the unconditional love they had for each other. The emotions crushed her as unstoppable tears cascaded down her cheeks.

As quickly as they had come, the visions vanished. Izzy sat alone in the Circle. Everyone gone. She glanced around the village, confused and still tingling from her experience. What seemed like minutes was actually hours. Quinn approached, remaining silent and extending his hand to her.

"Quinn?"

He raised his finger to his lips and shook his head. "Shh."

He led her back to the field lab and carried her inside.

"Oh my God, Quinn. What happened to me out there? I was out of my body … I-I could see the entire rainforest. I've heard about out-of-body experiences, but wow, it was like—"

"Nothing you ever experienced, Izz. I know."

He rolled up his sleeve and showed her the same tattoo on his wrist.

"Welcome to the Amazon and to the Kawirén tribe. You're official. You can move through the village freely."

She sighed. "Brief ceremony, my ass. My head is still spinning."

He chuckled. "Take a quick nap, and when you wake up, I have something to show you."

⁂

They entered a dense area of rainforest north of the village, led by the Chief Shaman, Tarenu. He wielded a walking stick carved from a solid branch of the Yarumaya tree and wore a cloak of woven leaves. Beads rattled softly across his chest, his face covered with streaks of red, white, and black paint. Tarenu led them to an ancient stone archway etched with mystical glyphs, hidden beneath thick vines, spiderwebs, moss, and plants with inverted trumpet-shaped flowers. Beyond lay a small grove of trees about the area of a gymnasium floor that towered above the canopy.

Before they could enter, Tarenu waved his staff over them, mumbling prayers and rattling a decorative gourd. He dipped a large feather into a wooden flask and sprinkled them with a deep red, sticky substance.

"Quinn … what's he doing?"

"We can't enter the sacred grove until he blesses us and binds the evil spirits from following us. Have some respect for their customs, Malibu."

"Okay, well, that's terrifying." She dabbed the substance with her pinky and curled her upper lip. "Is this blood?"

"It'll dry. Don't worry about it."

"Well, whose blood is it?"

"Nobody's. Probably animal blood."

"Ugh, gross," she whispered.

Tarenu directed them toward the entrance, then sat in the archway, legs folded, as they entered.

"Isn't he coming with us?" she asked.

"He'll guard the entrance from demons and devious spirits."

Izzy grabbed a stick and lifted the heavy branches with the inverted cream-colored flowers dangling like tiny trumpets. "You know what this is, Quinn?"

"Um, a bunch of dangling flowers?"

"Ha, I'm surprised you don't know. This is Angel's Trumpet. Brugmansia suaveolens. Very toxic. Every inch of the plant is deadly. People think they're extinct in the wild, but here they are."

"Yeah, well, those flowers are all over the place around the village. I've seen Tarenu pluck them, but never knew what he used them for, and I never asked."

"They have a strong hallucinogenic effect if given in the right dose. Fatal if given in the wrong dose. A couple of these flowers ground up in your coffee, and you'll be talking to the Mad Hatter the rest of the night."

Quinn reached for a flower, but she quickly slapped his hand.

"Dude! Don't do that. They're toxic, even to the touch."

As they entered the sacred grove through the archway, the unusual, massive trees struck a chord of curiosity.

"Okay, this place is vibing *Indian burial grounds*."

"Probably because it is."

"Are you serious? This is a graveyard?"

"It's the most sacred place on earth to the Kawirén. When the Kawirén Indians die, they give their bodies to the trees for nourishment, opening the door to the spirit world, where their souls dwell within the grove eternally."

"Quinn, I feel nauseous about entering here. Why would they allow us inside such a sacred place? It's kind of spooky. And so quiet."

"Normally, they wouldn't. This is only my second time being here. Trees are dying, Izzy. They have no answers, and their survival depends on the health of the grove. It wasn't hard to convince them to let us help."

Isabella lost her breath as she gazed skyward at the majestic Yarumaya trees soaring 130 feet into the sky—trunks ten feet thick, flaring out into huge buttress roots at the base. Rich amber-brown bark with subtle golden veins sheened in the filtered light, oozing a sticky, golden resin that carried a sweet, citrusy scent. Leaf clusters about the size of a dinner plate topped the canopy. The leaves had an elongated oval shape with a pointed tip. She recalled the shape being similar to a species in the Dipterocarpaceae family common in Southeast Asia.

When she laid her hand on the trunk of one of the sick trees, she was stricken. The veil of the spirit world seemed to unravel. Unseen centuries and ancient souls weighed on her as she witnessed the grief of the dying tree and the spirits inhabiting it. After taking two steps backward, she slumped to her knees and gasped. Quinn knelt beside her and rested his hand on her shoulder.

"You alright? You're as pale as goat's milk, kid."

"I-I don't know … I have this overwhelming sadness in my heart. Like I sense their pain. It feels like I've been here before. I've never experienced anything like it. Quinn? What's happening to me? Why am I crying? I feel broken. Completely wrecked."

"It's a place of spirituality. Beliefs in all cultures originate somewhere. You could be sensing that…"

"What's *that* have to do with it?"

"I'm just thinking you're having some kind of religious experience. Or you're caught up in the moment, or it's a residual effect from the ritual you experienced earlier. I mean, it *is* a sacred sanctuary. You're only the second outsider in the history of the world to walk on these hallowed grounds. More people have walked on the moon."

He helped her to her feet. "I need your help to save these trees and the people whose lives depend on them. Will you help me?"

She nodded. "Yeah … I'm good. Um, let me get my test kit … take some soil samples."

Her jaws tensed as she repeatedly tested the soil, with the same results. She shook her head and sighed.

"What'd you find?" he asked.

"The pH levels around the sick trees are low. Acidic. That's not good. We need to figure out why."

She scooped a handful of leaves and examined them under a magnifying glass. "See how these leaves are malformed and yellow? Chlorosis."

She tossed him a few of the nut-like fruits she plucked from the ground. "Look at how small and hard these are compared to the fruit from the healthier trees."

He watched as she squeezed one between her fingers until it crumbled and burst into dry powder. "There's something seriously wrong with this soil. We need to take samples back to the lab to do more tests."

Quinn rubbed his chin and nodded. "I'm not surprised. I've observed damage to the tree's DNA from the samples I took last week."

"Quinn, I need soil, leaves, bark, and some of this sticky resin from both the sick and healthier trees." She pulled an insect from the root of a dying tree with a pair of tweezers and glanced at him. "Wood borers. They feed on dying trees." She dropped several of the insects into a test tube and capped it.

He glanced at his pocket watch. "It's getting late. Do you have all the samples you need? Anything else?"

"I have everything I need except one thing, Dr. Quinn."

"Name it. I'll help you get it."

"Answers to my questions. The answers you've been promising me since I got here."

He grimaced and squatted on a round boulder. "Fair enough. What do you want to know?"

"Have you figured out why the Kawirén live so long? I mean, how do they look so freaking young and vibrant? It's mind-blowing."

He heaved a breath and pinched the bridge of his nose. "I'm working on it."

She shrugged and widened her eyes. "You're working on it? Any, uh, hunches? Clues? Wild guesses in the past *decade*?"

"Their longevity involves these trees—the Yarumaya. Each question I answer spawns three more. That's why, after ten years, I'm taking a risk by hiring my first lab partner."

She placed her hands on her hips and glared at him. "Why do you look so young, Dr. Quinn? How is it that the photo in your ad shows a man in his mid-forties, yet the man in front of me isn't much older than I am? What are you hiding, huh? What am I missing here?"

"Alright, Malibu … the truth. The man in the photo was my father. He died ten years ago. I took over his research."

"Ten years ago? So, you earned your doctorate at fifteen or sixteen years old? Quite impressive, dude. A young genius, eh?"

"Hey, it's just good living. Clean air … what can I say? Like I said before, I'm older than I look. Okay?"

She inhaled and rolled her eyes. "Why don't I believe you? Maybe because you're the spitting image of your *dad*? Same smile, same big ears, and this…" She brushed his hair aside and ran her finger over a scar on his left eyebrow. "Your 'dad' has the exact same scar in his photo."

He rose and brushed the dirt and vegetation off his knees, his face flushing. "We have more important things to worry about. I hired you for your knowledge of botany, not your detective skills, Nancy Drew. Can you please focus on the job?"

"I'm trying to focus on the job, but you're lying to me, and I don't trust you."

"The work doesn't require that you do. Just do the fucking job and I'll make sure you get home on time for summer break with the valley boys."

"Ooh, feeling a little salty, are we? I must be on to something."

He pointed a stern finger at her face and sneered. "Do the job I'm paying you for and stay the hell out of my personal life. Maybe you don't give a crap about these people and their livelihood, but I do."

He wagged his finger at her backpack and narrowed his eyes. "Do your tests, give me the results, and you can catch the next boat out of here and never give this place a second thought … enjoy your privileged life safe on the coast sleeping on the beach."

He marched toward the archway and tapped Tarenu on the shoulder, stirring him from a deep meditation. Isabella chased after him.

"Hey! We need to finish this conversation, Quinn. Don't walk away from me."

"No, we don't."

"If I'm going to help you figure out why the Yarumaya are dying, I need to know the truth. You owe me that much."

"I don't owe you a damn thing. But you owe me results. The results I paid for."

"Okay, fine … lead the way. I'll give you your frigging results. Then I *am* out of here."

"Good. That's all I'm asking."

"Ugh." She sneered at him. "Why are their eyes so blue, Quinn, huh? The adults—why are they so blue when the children's eyes are brown?"

"Damn it, can you cease with the inquisition? The trees, Malibu. It's a side-effect of the resin. Alright? The resin contains a precursor compound I call resindopa. It's activated by an unknown process in adults and migrates to ocular tissues and binds with melanin. It slowly replaces or alters the iris structure to a luminous blue pigment."

She crossed her arms and narrowed her eyes. "And why are *your* eyes so blue?"

He glared at her, his jaw tightening. "Because I'm Irish. It's in my genes. The OCA2 gene you learned about in Biology 101. You're here one day and you've got everything figured out, don't you, Malibu?"

Tarenu paused and pressed the tip of his staff into Quinn's chest. He glared at Quinn and slowly shook his head, then turned toward Isabella and took her hand, mumbling in his language.

"What's he saying? Quinn? What is he saying?"

"He says you're an idiot."

Isabella cut him off and grabbed two handfuls of his shirt.

"You're an arrogant jackass, and I don't need to put up with your little bitch fits anymore." She drilled her index finger into his sternum and sneered. "Tell me what he said. Right now, or I'm not helping you."

Quinn's eyes darkened, and his jawline rippled. "Bitch fit? Really?"

He glanced at the sky and crossed his arms.

"You wanna know what he said?"

"Yeah, I wanna know what he said."

"You wanna know?"

"Yeah, I wanna know!"

"Alright. He said he felt your pain. Saw the ancestors embrace and accept you. He called you Nahuari."

"Who's Nahuari?"

"A shaman. From long ago. The only woman shaman in their history. He said the ancestors told him you came to heal the trees. That you felt their sadness."

He shrugged and flashed a fake grin. "Ya happy now?"

Her anger cooled. "No. I'm not happy. I'm confused. How did he know that? I'm not this Nahuari person. I haven't even graduated yet."

He paused, turned, and raised his eyebrows. "You're damn right you're not Nahuari," he grumbled. "Wait a minute? You haven't graduated? Your application said you're a botanist."

"Uh, a botanist in need of a thesis. Hellooo."

"You *lied* on your application? And after calling me a liar every day since the moment you got here? You, entitled little brat."

"I didn't lie, actually. I have my bachelor's in botany, and I'm a thesis away from my master's.

He pointed at her and scowled. "You lied. Now we *both* have trust issues, Malibu."

As they strolled into the village, Isabella stormed off toward the lab while Quinn marched toward the Circle—a place where the men drank lakira made from bananas, women's saliva, yeast, and fermented Yarumaya fruit.

"Yeah, go cry in your beer with the boys, *Junior*," she muttered.

Hours later, Quinn stumbled into the tent and plopped onto his bed. The sapphire glint in his stare narrowed as he glared at her. "What d'ya find, Malibu?"

"You're drunk. Sleep it off. We'll talk later … when you sober up."

"I'm not drunk. I'm relaxed. What did you learn?"

She spun in her chair, crossed her arms, and sneered. "Glyphosate."

"Glyphosate? An herbicide?"

"Exactly. The soil beneath the dying trees shows traces of it. The question is, where did it come from?"

He rose and paced. "The villagers know nothing about herbicides or pesticides. They've been isolated from the outside world for centuries."

"Quinn. Take me to the logging area. The one we passed on our way here."

He paused and stroked his beard. "You think the soil is contaminated there?"

"We need to find out. We should at least start there, don't you think? It seems the Yarumaya is vulnerable to glyphosate. If a small amount like this can cause such severe damage, I don't even want to think what a larger exposure might do."

"Alright then. First thing in the morning, we visit the logging area."

"Also, we should collect the fruit from the healthy trees and store them in a sterile environment to protect the species," she insisted.

"I'm already a step ahead of you on that."

She sighed and lowered her eyes. "Quinn, I want to apologize for calling you a liar. It was unprofessional and rude. I'm here as your assistant, and I should have respected that fact."

He nodded and pursed his lips. "Apology accepted."

She sat in silence for a few seconds, then huffed and crossed her arms. "Well, don't *you* have something to add?"

"Um, nope. I mean, you also called me a jackass."

She scoffed and rolled her eyes. "You're unbelievable."

Quinn extended his arm and offered her a wooden flask.

"What are you doing? What is that?"

"A peace offering."

"What's in it?"

"Don't ask. Just take a hit."

She sniffed it and scowled. "Ew, gross."

"Come on, Malibu, don't be such a wuss."

She scoffed, popped the cork, and swigged. "Oh … oh God. That's disgusting."

He grinned, swigged, and handed it back to her.

"No. No more for me, thank you. There's probably monkey pee mixed in there, or worse."

His chuckle was guttural. "It'll help you sleep. We have a long day tomorrow … thanks for helping me, Malibu. For caring."

"Are you getting soft on me, Quinn?" She grabbed the flask and chugged, wiping her lips with her sleeve and grimacing as if she had bitten into an unripe persimmon.

"Blah! Nasty. It does have a kick, though. Not that bad once you get past the putrid taste of a dead carcass."

He snickered and took her by the hand. "Come with me."

"Where?"

"Just … come with me."

"I still don't trust you."

"Come with me anyway."

He led her out of the lab and into the Circle, where men and women relaxed, drank lakira, gossiped, sang, and embraced the night beneath a thatched roof around a blazing fire.

"You're part of the tribe now, Malibu. Join the Circle. Let your hair down a little."

The Kawirén cheered as she took her place in the Circle, and a woman shared lakira with her. The spray of rain was cool on her face, and with each sip, her anxieties, worries, and fears dissipated. Being accepted and engaged by these people warmed her heart. The tribe was a huge, loving family. Descendants of an ancient people. Guardians of the rainforest and all its creatures. For the moment, she belonged to a big family.

The women chanted. One by one, they offered gifts of polished stone, carved bone trinkets, and beaded necklaces.

The tribe chanted softly, "Nahuari, Nahuari, Nahuari…"

She turned to Quinn. "Why are they doing this? I'm not this Nahuari person."

"They believe you're here to save the Yarumaya. To save their village. You're now officially a VIP member of the Kawirén tribe. That tattoo is permanent, by the way."

He pointed at his wrist. "Like mine."

"I don't know what to say."

"There's nothing *to* say. They've welcomed you into the rainforest. Into their family."

The women formed a circle, danced, and sang, passing lakira from person to person as the men pounded an intoxicating rhythm on their drums and shaker sticks. One woman tugged at her arm, smiled, and nodded. She kept pointing at Isabella's shirt, repeating the same phrase. Isabella glanced at Quinn and grimaced, shielding her face with her hand. "What is she asking?"

"They want you to dance with them. It's tradition. Oh, and she's asking you to remove your top." He chuckled and raised his gourd. "Now it's a party."

SEVEN

Wood Poachers

August 2, 2026

Descending the mountain from the village was quicker than the ascent when they had arrived days ago. Especially since Quinn didn't have to carry her this time after that nasty banana spider bite. They pushed through the sweltering mist and into a bright clearing. The area of deforestation they passed on the way to the village lay a hundred yards in front of them, like a timber graveyard.

After her paranormal experience in the sacred grove along with the Mayuma ritual, she swore she could hear the rainforest whispering to her this morning. She's either lost her mind or her imagination was playing tricks on her.

They stepped over the "broken bones" and decomposing bodies of a piece of the rainforest slaughtered by the greed of evil men. Acres of damaged wood lay rotting from harsh sunlight and insect damage. Wildlife that once called this area of the forest home had retreated into the safety of Mayuma.

Isabella crouched on one knee next to a tree stump infested with termites. Quinn swung the assault rifle from his shoulder and did a 360-degree sweep of the area with a pair of binoculars.

She scooped soil and tested it, then retested it, and glanced up at him, shielding her eyes with her left hand. "Quinn, this isn't good."

"What's the verdict?"

"This soil contains dangerously high levels of glyphosate. It's in the wood too. It's like they're poisoning the trees before they cut them down."

"So, how do you think the chemical made its way up the mountain to the Yarumaya grove?"

"If I had to guess, I'd say the wind carried it when they sprayed. Or contaminated animals or birds found their way into the grove and left remnants in their droppings. The Yarumaya appear to be extremely vulnerable even to the slightest exposure. This is so sad."

Quinn grabbed her wrist. "Sh. You hear that?"

"No, what?" Her eyes widened as the rumble of an engine and the crunch of tires echoed in the distance. "What *is* that?"

"Poachers. Back for more lumber."

"What do we do?"

"We hide and observe their operation. Hopefully, get some answers."

They raced to the edge of the forest and hid within the heavy brush and ferns. Quinn handed her the binoculars and used the scope on his rifle to monitor the poachers as their vehicle approached.

The logging truck pulled next to the killing field and parked. Several workers hopped off the truck bed and used chainsaws to section dead trees. Other workers used hooks and chains to load the poached logs onto the flatbed, while a man with an AK-47 and a radio observed the operation as he paced and barked orders. When the truck was full, he shouted commands into the radio and climbed into the cab.

As the truck swung back around and drove off, a small aircraft appeared out of nowhere, headed straight for them.

"Quinn? What's that plane doing? Why's it flying so low? Is the pilot drunk or something? Or is he trying to land?"

"Ah, shit. I think we should move."

"Why?"

"Move!"

The aircraft dumped a white cloud of spray over the trees above them. They scampered deep into the forest to escape, but the cloud drenched them with a vinegary scent of chemicals, stinging her eyes and nostrils.

"Son of a bitch! Are you okay, Izzy?"

"I've been better. We're soaked in glyphosate, Quinn. We need to wash it off our skin, and fast. Those idiots, ugh."

"Follow me. I know a place."

Quinn led her down a ravine, across a shallow creek, to a pristine pond fed by a series of 10-foot waterfalls.

"Oh, my God. This place is *gorge*. It'd be a sin to pollute this water."

"We have no choice, I'm afraid."

Quinn pulled a bar of soap from his backpack and winked. He pulled his T-shirt over his head, removed his boots, and unbuckled his trousers. He glanced at her with a wrinkled brow—a look of impatience in his eyes. "What are you waiting for?"

Quinn's body was lean, his stomach flat and rippled, solid, round shoulders, muscled thighs. *Oh, God. Stop staring at him*, she thought.

"I, uh. Close your eyes and turn around. Look over there or something," she demanded.

"There's no time for modesty. Get in. Keep your panties on and don't piss in the water."

"Why not? The chemicals are far worse than my pee."

"A little fish called the candiru. It's said to be attracted to urine, and when it swims up your urethra, it opens its spines, making it difficult to remove. Especially in the middle of the rainforest."

"That's a myth. You're trying to scare me."

"The story may be … but the fish is real. You want to test the myth?"

Isabella removed her clothes, leaving her panties intact, and stepped into the cool water, arms crossed to shield her breasts. Quinn dropped his trousers and dove into the water wearing only boxers.

He surfaced next to her, running his fingers through his wet locks and shaking out the water. "Turn around," he said.

"Why? You're shy all of a sudden?"

"Not a shy bone in my body, Malibu."

The silky slime of soap caressed her shoulders and the back of her neck, sending chills along her spine. His firm hands massaged deep into her muscles, easing her tension. He slid the bar of soap along the small of her back and gently guided it to the groove between her shoulders. It had been months since a man had touched her so intimately.

He tugged her hand and guided her under the waterfall, where he lathered her hair. Her knees weakened from the strokes of his fingertips massaging deep into her scalp. She melted into his arms, hating how good it felt.

"I don't know if I'm comfortable with you touching me like this, Dr. Quinn."

"I'm removing chemicals from your skin and hair, Malibu. I'm not hitting on you. If that makes you uncomfortable, then maybe check yourself."

She turned and faced him. "How dare you insinuate—"

"Insinuate what? That you like me touching you?"

"No … well, yes."

Quinn raised an eyebrow, his lips forming a half-grin. He grabbed her hand, planted the bar of soap in her palm, then turned his back on her.

"Oh, now you want me to lather *you* up?"

"I can't reach. It's your turn."

She scoffed, then lathered his broad shoulders, running her fingers along the stiff contours of his back. His skin was flawless. Not a single blemish. His light-blue boxers clung to his firm buttocks, becoming transparent from the water. A whimper rose in her throat, and she sighed.

"Did you say something, Malibu?"

"No … nothing. Hold still. And you better not be smiling," she said with a slight quiver in her voice.

He rinsed in the waterfall, suds rolling along the contours of his sculpted back and shoulders, then turned and faced her. Sipping shallow breaths, with her heart pounding, she raised her eyes to meet his.

His grin curled into two symmetrical dimples noticeable inside his light beard. "I'd offer to do your front, but I think you can handle it from here."

She looked away. "So kind of you." Warmth flushed her face, and the back of her neck prickled.

Isabella dipped to her shoulders and pushed away from him before he could notice her embarrassment, assuming he hadn't already. She turned and scrubbed the rest of her body as Quinn submerged their clothes, rubbing them against a boulder, and wringing them out one by one.

"Toss me the—"

The bar of soap bounced off the side of his head and hit the water.

"…Soap. Thanks." He frowned and snatched the slimy white bar.

She swam beneath the waterfall, allowing the cool water to rinse the remaining suds from her skin. Her eyes closed. The soft, warm breeze caressed her face, raising goosebumps along her arms. Did Eden feel like this? Paradise was both breathtaking and treacherous—the devil hidden in every detail. Did Adam get under Eve's skin the way Quinn had gotten under hers? Probably. He was a man. God's first and only mistake.

Quinn spread their laundry over dry, warm rocks beneath the few rays of sunlight that penetrated the canopy. He sat on the shore, cleaning his fingernails with the tip of his pocketknife.

"Quinn? Have you ever been married? Ever had a girlfriend or been in love?"

"Once. It didn't work out."

"What happened?"

"Long story."

She turned her head and glared at him. "It'll be a while before our clothes dry. We have time. Come on. Share."

He heaved a breath and exhaled slowly. "We met in college. Got engaged, had a big wedding. It ended."

"What was her name, if you don't mind my asking?"

"Aubrey. I called her, Brey."

"Aw, how cute. That's a beautiful name. Continue."

"It's not a story I like to talk about."

"Why not? Did she cheat on you or something?"

He lowered his eyes and sighed. "She died."

Isabella covered her mouth and gasped.

"Oh, my God. I am so sorry. I didn't mean to—"

"It was a long time ago. I'm married to my work now. To the rainforest."

"That's so sad, Quinn."

"I don't need your pity, Malibu. I love my life. The Kawirén people are my family now. The rainforest is the Heart of the Earth. I want to keep her safe, the way I tried to…" He paused and swallowed.

"The way you tried to … what?"

"Never mind."

"Have you ever considered having a relationship with another woman someday? No one in the village interests you?"

"I'm not allowed to marry or have a relationship with any of the women. It's forbidden in their culture."

"Sounds a bit racist."

"It's not. And besides, in their eyes, you and I are married."

"That's going to be awkward when I leave you next week."

He lowered his head and nibbled the inside of his cheek. "I'll find a way to explain it to them. All that matters now is that we save the Yarumaya and the Kawirén people."

She glided towards him, shielding her nakedness beneath the cover of the shimmering ripples.

"Get dressed, Malibu. I think our clothes are dry now."

She reached for his hand while covering her breasts with the other. "Help me out."

His grip was tender this time and lasted several seconds longer than she expected. He narrowed his eyes and looked right through her as if he wanted to speak, but hesitated.

"What? Why are you looking at me like that?"

An ultramarine sparkle softened in his eyes as he glanced away. "We should go."

She moved in front of him and locked eyes, forcing him to return her stare. "I guess we should. Wouldn't want to get caught out here in the rain now, would we?"

"Nah, we wouldn't. A person could get swept away like that."

"Right. Swept away." She sighed. "Lead the way, Dr. Quinn."

As they entered the village, Tarenu intercepted them—his voice animated, and his eyes wide and glistening.

"What's he saying?" she asked.

Quinn was visibly shaken. He squinted and curled his lips over his teeth. "More trees are sick, and Tarenu says the hunters are having a harder time finding wild game. A few of the animals they bagged seem ill."

"The glyphosate. They're spraying it from a hundred feet above the canopy. The wind is carrying it up the mountain to the grove. We need to test the soil in the village, Quinn. And the water sources."

"Yeah, it's taking a toll on the village. You test the soil and the river. I need to take some blood samples. I'll catch up with you later."

Isabella spent the afternoon analyzing soil sample after sample of resin, bark, and leaves for chemical contamination. She set her glasses on the table next to her, rubbed her temples, and closed her eyes for a moment.

"Malibu?"

"Oh, crap." She jerked, knocking her glasses off the table.

CRUNCH. Quinn froze, eyes wide and mouth agape. "Oops."

"Dang it. That's my only pair, dude."

He pulled the Yarumaya resin from his backpack. "No worries. I can fix 'em. Best glue on earth. Here you go."

She scanned the repaired nosepiece and pursed her lips. "I guess that works. Thanks. At least I can enjoy the smell of citrus while I work."

"Enjoy it while it lasts. You'll lose the scent after it dries…"

"It's actually kind of pleasant … Quinn, the soil samples from the village show trace amounts of glyphosate. I found traces in the river, too. I'm afraid these poachers are going to poison the entire village in addition to the Yarumaya if we don't do something. So, what do we do? What do we tell them?"

He rubbed the back of his neck and grimaced. “I don’t know what to tell them. They’ve lived in this village for centuries.”

“Can’t we relocate them? Plant a new grove?”

He glared at her for several seconds as if she had food in her teeth. He opened his mouth to speak, but no words came. Quinn shook his head and paced.

“I’m sorry; that was a dumb question,” she confessed.

“It’s okay. I know you’re just trying to help.”

“Oh, so it *was* a dumb question.”

“No question is dumb, Izzy.”

“I have an idea of how to save the trees, Quinn.”

His eyes widened as he sat across from her. “I’m all ears.”

“First, we remove a couple of feet of earth around the contaminated roots and replace it with a mixture of clean soil and activated charcoal to absorb the herbicide. The heavy rains will help dilute the remaining glyphosate.”

“And where do we get activated charcoal? No Walmarts for thousands of miles, and my radio has a bullet hole, so I can’t place an order.”

She lowered her brow and pressed her tongue against her cheek. “Can we get past the bullet hole in the radio, dude?”

He nodded and rolled his eyes. “Fine. Continue, please.”

“We make our own. We gather hardwood, some buckets, and a nice big fire.”

“That’s great. But how do you activate it?”

“Lemons and heat.”

“We don’t have lemons in the Amazon.”

“True. But you do have the camu camu tree. The fruit is similar to a lemon and should work. We char the wood, clean it with the fruit juice, heat it until it dries, then pulverize it. If we can make enough, it should help neutralize the herbicide."

"Well, we're going to need a lot of it, Malibu."

"Which is why we teach the villagers how to make it, Junior. We have an army at our disposal. I'm sure everyone in the village will be eager to pitch in."

"That borders on genius, kid."

She crossed her arms, tilted her head, and squinted. "It *is* genius."

He placed his hand on her shoulder and nodded. "This is going to work. It's a brilliant plan."

"It will be when the trees recover."

"I'll explain our plan to the village. You're finally giving me my money's worth, Malibu. I might just give you that raise."

EIGHT

Saving the Yarumaya

August 3, 2026

They converted the village into a charcoal and soil factory overnight. Morale was high among the Kawirén. The men charred the wood blocks, while the women cleaned them with camu camu juice, baked, and pulverized them into powder. They sent the teenage boys to collect baskets of clean soil near the river, while the teenage girls mixed the fresh soil with the activated charcoal in a large pit using their feet. It reminded her of old photos of winemaking in Northern California. They danced, sang, and made a game of it, as was so common in their culture. Tarenu led several men to the Yarumaya grove with the right tools to remove two feet of contaminated soil.

"Quinn, I think we have enough of the charcoal-soil mixture in the pit."

He instructed the villagers to fill their baskets and head to the grove. Everyone in the village who could carry a basket lined up. The village danced and chanted, "Nahuari, Nahuari," and marched with enthusiasm and faith.

Isabella's face flushed. She grabbed Quinn's wrist and whispered, "Tell them to stop. I'm not Nahuari."

"That's like asking the birds not to crap on the statue they're going to erect to you. Let them have their fun, Malibu. This is a special day for the village. I haven't seen this much hope in months. *You* did that."

Quinn fell in line behind the last villager and grasped Isabella's hand.

"Grab a basket, kid. We've got a train to catch."

They replaced the soil and tamped it with their feet. One by one, the villagers exited the grove and returned to the village. Tears filled Isabella's eyes as the last of the villagers departed.

Tarenu blessed the grounds and sat cross-legged in the archway, meditating while he waited for Isabella and Quinn.

Isabella planted herself on a smooth boulder and buried her face in her hands, sobbing. Quinn sat next to her, folding his hands in his lap and resting his elbows on his thighs.

"Why are you crying, Izzy?"

"I'm sorry. I'm just a bit overwhelmed, and I can't fight it. I've never felt like this before…"

She wiped her cheeks and glanced at him through blurry eyes.

"What if it doesn't work? They believe in me, Quinn. I don't want to disappoint them. They looked so happy. I'm so afraid of disappointing them."

"You gave them the only chance they had, Izzy. They're united and full of optimism. We've done all we could do. Now we wait."

"I just don't want to let them down, Quinn."

Quinn's hug was warm and comforting. It gave her permission to lay her head on his shoulder and allow her tears to flow.

"Can I tell you something, Izzy?"

She nodded.

"What you did today has nothing to do with gymnastics. Your mom isn't here to disappoint. They trust you. Believe in you. Win or lose, we gave it our best shot. I know you have to leave in a few days, but the Kawirén will never forget what you did for them today. And neither will I."

Isabella pulled away from him and stood, arms crossed, keeping her back to him.

"I don't need to be psychoanalyzed, Dr. Quinn. Did you earn a degree in psychology to add to your storied list of diplomas?"

He rose and stood behind her. "No. No psych degrees. That was all me. Just my opinion."

"I don't need your opinion when it comes to my personal life."

He lowered his head and nodded. "Fair enough. I'll take you back to the village."

"Quinn, I'm sorry. It's just that I'd had my fill of therapists growing up. Anytime I spoke up for myself, my mother would send me to therapy. I hated being treated as if I weren't allowed to feel emotions or get angry, or speak my mind."

"Nah, I understand. I had an overbearing father, so I can relate to the frustration of not being seen or heard. We'd best head back."

The sky rumbled, spitting a steady drizzle as he tapped Tarenu on the shoulder and led the way back to the village. Boiling clouds dropped a deluge upon them as they entered.

Quinn huddled beneath the thatched roof of the Circle and swigged lakira with the men.

Isabella dashed into the field lab, crawled into a hammock, and wrapped herself in her childhood blanket she kept hidden in her backpack.

He was right. She was exposed and vulnerable and didn't know how to respond. She built her entire life around her fear of disappointing the ones she loved. Her mother, Teddy, and now the Kawirén and Quinn. Only time will tell if her actions will save the sacred Yarumaya. And now she had more than enough data to finish her thesis and introduce a new species to the world. But in doing so, will she compromise her work here? Endanger the Kawirén people and the rare and fragile Yarumaya tree?

There was still work to be done. The question of why the Kawirén live so long and enjoy vibrant health and extended youth remained unanswered. And Quinn had yet to share his research with her. Izzy's relationship with the Amazon and the Kawirén deepened, forcing her to reevaluate her purpose here.

Isabella woke before dawn, analyzing the samples she and Quinn had taken from the grove. Quinn sprawled across his bed, snoring and drooling, holding a corked gourd of lakira in his right hand.

She noticed that the resin from the healthier trees had a more robust amber color, a thicker viscosity, and a strong citrusy odor. Resin from the sick trees was pale with a light viscosity and only a hint of a citrusy scent. She guessed Quinn had older samples of resin hidden somewhere, along with his research notes. But his reason for keeping it from her was confounding.

She removed the empty gourd from his hand and nudged him.

"Hey. Hey you. I need your notes and your samples. I'm sure you have them here somewhere. Hey buddy. Wake up."

He glared at her with one reddened eye. "What are you doing, Malibu?"

"What you're paying me to do, Junior."

"You've already done what I asked. We know why the trees are sick. Thank you. I'll take you back today, fix the radio, and send you home."

"We're just getting started, Quinn. I want to see your research notes and older resin samples. You still haven't figured out why the Kawirén live so long. Why they're so healthy."

"I'm … working on it."

"Yeah, you said that. You need help, Quinn. Let me help you."

He sat upright and planted his bare feet on the straw mat.

"I don't need your help, Malibu. You can go home now."

"I'm not leaving until we figure this out together."

"It's complicated. I can't risk—"

"Can't risk what? Sharing the discovery of the century?"

"No. I can't risk my research falling into the wrong hands of scientists and corporations who will use it to create their next billion-dollar pharmaceutical. They'll destroy the Yarumaya and the lives that depend on it."

"Quinn, I want to help you save the Yarumaya. Save the village. I'm not interested in making a name for myself."

"How do I know I can trust you?"

"You're in the Amazon rainforest, Quinn. Your survival depends on trust."

He shook his head and sighed. "Touché."

"The clock is ticking, Dr. Quinn. We need answers right now, not weeks, months, or years from now. Let me help."

Quinn slid a metal locker off the top of a cabinet and unlocked it. He tossed a thick journal onto the table and pointed at the locker.

"All the samples you need are in there, along with my notes and data."

"Okay." She pointed at the cabinet. "What's in the other locker with the red X?"

"Never mind that one. It's something I've been working on. It's not related. Don't worry about it."

"Um, sure. Okay," she said. "Now, go away and let me work. I'll call you if I find anything interesting."

Two hours later, Quinn returned and squatted on the edge of his bed.

"Anything jump out at you, Malibu?"

"Yeah, buddy. Some strange inconsistencies. The chemical profiles of the new samples and your old samples are remarkably different."

"How do you mean?"

"Your old resin samples have a high concentration of a unique compound. The new resin samples from the semi-healthy trees and the sick ones have the same precursor compound, but the active molecule is missing. We need to figure out what's providing that molecule in the old samples and why it's missing in the new."

"That's a good start."

He heaved a deep sigh and rested his palms on the table in front of her. "Izzy, I diagnosed a five-year-old boy with non-Hodgkin lymphoma two days ago. There were two more cases last night."

"Oh, my God."

"I believe exposure to glyphosate and the change in the Yarumaya resin are responsible. There hasn't been an illness in the village in over a century."

"What am I missing, Quinn?"

"My theory is they absorb an unknown compound by inhaling the smoke from the resin during the Rebirth Festival of the Half Moon each month. They breathe it while wearing their tribal masks made from Yarumaya bark. *The breath of life*, they call it."

She narrowed her eyes and rubbed her temples. "But now it's missing the active longevity molecule, and they're getting sick. When's the next rebirth ritual?"

"In two days. August 5th. You're going to need a ceremonial mask to partake. In the meantime, stay after it. We need answers."

NINE

Dawn of Microbe X

August 4, 2026

Her eyes itched, and her temples throbbed. She stretched her arms in the air and arched her back, inhaling a deep yawn. Quinn slouched in a chair across from her, snoring. She kicked him under the table.

"Hey, sleeping beauty. Wake up. I have something to show you."

He grunted and glared at her with bloodshot eyes while grabbing his knee and grimacing.

"Ow … you want a cup of coffee, Malibu?"

"Mm, nah, but I'll take some of that yoco bark."

He raised an eyebrow and hesitated before handing it to her. "Go easy on that stuff. My head already hurts."

She swigged and frowned. "Stop being rude and come look at this."

He squinted through the microscope. "What am I looking at?"

"You tell me. I'm a botanist, not a microbiologist."

"Well, I see a colonization of microbes. One I haven't been able to identify."

"You've seen this before?"

"Yep. They're present in my older samples and missing in the latest samples."

"Well, you could have shared that tidbit with me and saved me a couple of hours of research."

"I wanted to test your methods."

"Seriously? Can we get on the same team here?"

"What else you got, Malibu?"

"Look what happens when I introduce the microbes."

His eyes widened. "I'll be damned. It changed color … and the scent is more pungent. It's almost immediate."

"Right? But it's not quite there. The color and scent are slightly off compared to your old samples."

He rubbed his beard and frowned. "What's your conclusion? Any theories?"

"Microbe X metabolizes the sterile resin into the active longevity molecule. But there's still a catalyst missing for it to work. The newly metabolized sample here doesn't fully recreate the chemical fingerprint of your older samples. Quinn, I think the glyphosate is killing microbe X in the resin."

"Is that what you're calling it? Microbe X? Get some rest. I'll wake you up in a couple of hours. Let's visit the grove and take more samples. See if we can find your catalyst. Great work, Izzy. I think we're on the same page now."

Tarenu meditated outside the archway as Isabella and Quinn entered the sacred grove.

"Does he have to spatter us with blood every time we visit?"

He chuckled and hung his backpack on a vine attached to a semi-healthy tree as she dabbed away the blood with a tissue and took soil samples.

"Oh, wow, the pH has improved significantly. Almost normal in most areas. We still have a few borderline spots, but nothing near what it was. I need a collection of healthy fruit and two or three saplings to take back to the lab."

Isabella kicked something buried beneath the floor vegetation and stumbled to her knees. "Ouch… crap."

"What the heck you doing over there, Malibu?"

"Nothing. Just falling on my butt and playing in the dirt, I guess."

She brushed away the vegetation, revealing a large tree stump that rose several inches above the forest floor and spread twelve feet across.

"Quinn? Come look at this."

He scratched the back of his neck and pressed his tongue to his cheek.

"Looks like you discovered a tree stump, Malibu. Congrats. There's more over there, so watch your step."

She rolled her eyes and scoffed. "Thanks for the heads-up, Junior."

"Your knee is bleeding. Let me get the first-aid kit and take a look at that."

"I'm fine. Look closer, Quinn. The growth rings."

"Okay. What am I missing?"

"These trees are thousands of years old. I'm guessing between two and three thousand years. They're ancient."

"I imagine they are."

"How did they manage to cut down such a large tree with no tools?"

"The process is a well-kept secret. A ritual only a select few get access to. The wood from one tree lasts for years."

"Interesting. How long have the … Ow, that stings."

"Hold still. This needs a couple of stitches."

She dug her nails into his knee. "Oh, my God … can you find a duller needle?"

"Don't be a crybaby."

"Easy for you to … say."

"What was your question?"

"I was going to ask, 'How long have the Kawirén lived here?' Before you started sticking me with your blunt needle."

He pointed two fingers at his eyes. "Look at me."

She shook her hand as if it were on fire, bit her lower lip, and glanced up at him. The gentleness in his eyes was calming. It distracted her from the nagging sting.

Isabella plucked a hair from his head and snickered. "A gray hair. So, the flawless Dr. Quinn isn't so flawless … wait, hold still. Here's another one."

He bandaged her knee and removed a syringe from his kit and smirked. "Stand up and pull your shorts down to your hips."

"Why? What are you going to do with that?"

"I'm going to inject you with a tetanus vaccine."

"Quinn, I hate needles. Can we not?"

"I'm not asking. Pull 'em down."

"Oh, I bet you're enjoying this part, aren't you?" she said, more like a statement than a question.

"Don't flatter yourself, Malibu. You'll feel a slight pinch."

"That's what you *all* say right before … Ow-wah. God, you suck at this."

"There. All better. You can, uh … pull 'em up now."

She grabbed his wrist and locked eyes with him.

"I know I'm a terrible patient, but I appreciate it."

He held her stare for several seconds longer than felt normal.

"Anytime, Malibu … all part of my Hippocratic Oath. Or hypocritical oath, depending on your point of view."

His hands on her shoulders were gentle, his lips parted, ready to speak, but he hesitated. Again. Her heart raced. What was happening? Quinn lowered his eyes, ran his fingers through his hair, and nonchalantly walked off.

"Finish your work, Malibu, and we'll head back."

She rolled her eyes and blew a soft sigh. "Right."

Isabella worked throughout the night trying to duplicate Quinn's old resin samples by adding different compounds, salts, and enzymes, but nothing worked.

In the wee hours of the morning, her eyes burned, and her head pounded. *Just five minutes*, she thought as the drone of rain pattered against the thatched roof of the lab. The second her head hit the table, her eyes shut, and she faded.

The rain had stopped. It was quiet. Sunlight filtered through a window, illuminating the inside of her eyelids. She squinted and glanced at the Petri dish next to her, glittering with morning sunlight. She gasped and sat upright. The resin inside the Petri dish had turned a darker amber, matching Quinn's older samples.

Her temples throbbed as she scrambled to test the sample against the gold standard. It matched! Perfectly. She shrieked and fist-pumped the air. "Oh, my God!"

Quinn leaped out of bed and grabbed his rifle. "What the hell? What happened?"

"It's photo-sensitive, Quinn! The morning sunlight activates the molecule and creates the chemical change. I need to rerun test samples to prove it, but I'm sure we got it."

Quinn lifted the Petri dish and narrowed his eyes. "Remarkable," he mumbled. He hugged her and then pointed a stern finger. "Run three more trials. I'm going to get a blood sample from the sick boy. We'll see what effect the samples have on diseased blood cells."

Her head tilted as she pressed her tongue to her cheek. "I want that raise, by the way."

Quinn lifted his index finger and started to speak, then shook his head and rushed out of the lab.

When he returned, he glared at her expectantly as he planted himself in a chair.

"What's the verdict, Malibu?"

"One-hundred percent confirmed. The resin needs filtered sunlight to activate the molecule. The new samples match the chemical fingerprint of your old samples precisely."

"Spectacular." He raised a test tube filled with blood. "Take a break. My turn."

Thunder boomed, and a flash of light lit up the lab. She screeched and sat upright. How long had she slept? Quinn puffed on his pipe in the corner, his legs crossed and feet resting on a tree stump, staring out the front of the lab into the darkness and the rabid torrent flooding the village. She wrapped a blanket snugly around her waist and sat next to him in the dark.

"How long was I asleep?" She asked.

"All day." He swigged a gourd of lakira, wiped his lips with his sleeve, and handed it to her.

She waved it off. "No thanks, buddy … So?"

"So what?"

"So, how did it go? Any news you want to share with your lab partner?"

"The resin has no effect on the blood samples. I tried using the old samples with the same result. Nothing."

"Then we're still missing a variable."

"We are … or two, or three…"

Quinn threw the empty gourd out the door and watched as it skipped and tumbled through the mud into the darkness.

"Oh, my God. You're drunk. We'll figure it out, Quinn."

"We're not going to figure it out, Izzy. And three people are going to die because of it, including a child."

"Quinn. We'll figure it out. The answer is here somewhere. We're just not looking in the right place."

"It'll be too late when we do."

"What is wrong with you? We can't give up now."

"That's easy for you to say. You can go back to your life in sunny California, enjoy your college parties and boyfriends, while precious lives are lost in the Amazon. Lives that don't mean a damn thing to the outside world, but mean the world to me. They *matter* to me, Izz!"

He stood and threw a wooden bowl across the room. "All this research. All these years … and I'm going to lose them. My incompetence is going to cost them their lives, their home. Everything."

Isabella stood and exposed her palms to him. "Okay, let's stop throwing things. That doesn't help. We're not going to lose them, Quinn."

He threw up his arms and shook his head. "Ah, get back on your boat and go home, Malibu."

"What's the truth here, Quinn? What aren't you telling me?"

His words slurred. "There is no truth here. I've failed. I've failed everyone I ever loved. They believed in me. Believed I always had the answers. But I didn't."

"Who are we talking about here?"

"Everyone. You'd do best to stay the hell away from me. Go home."

"Oh, my God. You're talking about your wife. What happened to her? Quinn, what happened to Brey?"

"It's none of your damn concern. Leave me be."

"No. It *is* my concern. I'm your goddamn lab partner. I'm 100 percent invested in helping these people and the Yarumaya. You pulled me into this mess. You can't just kick me out or send me home when things get difficult."

She grabbed fistfuls of his shirt. "I want to help, Quinn. But you have to tell me what is going on here. I can't help you unless you tell me."

He lowered his head and sobbed. "I lost her, Izz. I lost her because she trusted me. The doctors had other plans, other treatments. But I knew the right one. Oh, I was sure of it. The one that would cure her and bring her home to me. Guess what? I was wrong."

"You can't blame yourself for someone getting sick."

"I do blame myself, just like I blame myself for all of this. Their future depends on me, and I can't figure it out. I don't have the answers."

"You're not alone in this, Quinn. Their future depends on *us*. I'm not going home. I'm staying until we find the answer. When we do, I'll leave if you like. But not until then."

She took him by the hand and led him to his bed. He stumbled and swayed, then collapsed on the mattress. She lay next to him and ran her fingers through his hair until his sobs lengthened into deep snores. Her heart ached for Quinn, the village, and the Yarumaya. She needed answers. *They* needed answers.

TEN

The Rebirth of the Halfmoon

August 5, 2026

Her eyes opened to Quinn hovering over her with a plate of food in his hand. Children's voices and the chirps of birds echoed outside, and a peculiar spicy aroma filled the sticky air.

"Breakfast time, Malibu. Uh, boiled fish, passion fruit, and plantains."

"Thank you for letting me know *before* I eat."

"Just trying to keep up with your rules of engagement."

He plopped next to her and sipped coffee from an aluminum cup.

"I apologize for my behavior last night." He lowered his head.

"What behavior? I don't recall."

He chuckled. "Thanks."

"What's on our agenda for today, Dr. Quinn?"

"A celebration mask for you. Tonight is the Ritual of the Rebirth of the Halfmoon."

"Why is it the half moon and not the full moon, or the new moon?"

"From what I understand, the half-moon represents the light and the darkness. Good and Evil. The dual nature of mankind. Sort of ying and yang thing, I suppose."

"Your breakfast was bomb, by the way."

"I assume that means palatable."

"Yeah, dude, you totally slayed it. I'd hire you."

"Alright, well, cool, man. I have something for you."

"Seriously? What? Wait. I don't trust you."

He laid an oval, curved, one-inch-thick Yarumaya board the size of a medium frying pan next to her. "I already carved holes for the eyes."

"Oh, my God. Is this my mask?"

"Yep."

"Is it finished?"

"It will be when you're done." He laid a hand knife and three cups of paint next to the mask—one red, one white, and one black.

"What do I do? I have no clue what I'm supposed to do. Where are the instructions?"

He pointed at her chest. "Right there. In your heart. Create the face that you see within the wood grains. Then paint it. I'll be outside helping set up for tonight's festival."

"Quinn? Quinn? What am I supposed to do? Okay, big yikes here. Not good."

An hour later, Quinn returned. She hid the mask behind her back.

"Let me see what you did, Malibu."

"No."

"Oh, come on. It can't be that bad."

She heaved a breath and rolled her eyes. "It is."

"Let me be the judge of that."

She bit her lower lip, her eyebrows forming a sharp peak. "Don't laugh."

"I promise."

"I'm serious. You better not laugh."

He crisscrossed his heart. "Scout's honor."

She laid her mask on the table, crossed her arms, and glared at him, searching for any sign of a smirk.

His eyes widened as he lit his pipe and puffed. "Well. Now that's interesting."

"It sucks. Go ahead. Say it."

"It's, uh … colorful. Points for originality…"

"Come on, Quinn. I did the best I could. I had trouble with the knife."

She opened her palm. "Look, I cut my finger."

Quinn's face flushed, and he couldn't contain himself anymore. He snorted and turned away.

"I knew it! It sucks." She puffed out her lower lip and tossed it onto the bed.

He sucked on his pipe and wiped tears of laughter from his eyes. Isabella flopped on the bed next to her mask and pouted. "It's so embarrassing. If I wear this monstrosity, the entire village is going to make fun of me."

Quinn nodded. "Probably. Let's see what we can do to doctor it up a wee bit."

"There's no fixing this, Quinn. It looks like a bloody Halloween mask spit out by a wood chipper, and I've got paint all over me. This is so annoying."

"I didn't realize you needed supervision."

"I've never been artistic. Let me see *your* mask."

"Sure." Quinn slid open a cabinet and removed a cloth bag. He untied the pull string, revealing his mask.

"Oh my God, that's beautiful. It belongs in a museum."

"Eh, it turned out nice. Yours isn't that bad, Izzy."

"You're such a liar. Stop patronizing me. Ugh. What am I going to do? I'm so humiliated."

"Let me see your mask for a few minutes. I'll be right back."

"No. Where're you going with that? Quinn. Give it back."

He glanced over his shoulder on his way out the door. "Trust me."

"Quinn!"

Fifteen minutes later, he returned with a large purple sack.

"Hope you had fun, buddy. I'm sure that joke of a mask earned you a lot of laughs."

"The tribe does have a great sense of humor, but only Tarenu saw it."

"And?"

"In the ten-plus years I've spent in the village, I've never seen him laugh so hard. He couldn't stop."

"Bruh … are you serious? I'm a laughingstock?"

Quinn presented the purple sack. "Tarenu wanted me to give this to you. But only on one condition."

"I'm afraid to ask…"

"He wants to keep your mask."

"No flipping way. What the heck for?"

"No idea, but he was adamant about it."

"I hate you both." She crossed her arms and plopped onto the bed.

"Well, you might change your mind when you see Tarenu's gift."

"Okay … I'm waiting." She narrowed her eyes and frowned.

He placed the object on the bed next to her. "Open it."

She pulled the cloth aside and gasped. "This is gorge. It makes your mask look like a third grader's."

"Well, I wouldn't go that far, but…"

"Whose mask is this?"

"It's the mask of Nahuari."

"Nahuari? The shaman?"

"Yes, it's an enormous honor. Hundreds of years old. He believes it belongs to you already … that you're Nahuari reincarnated."

"I don't know what to say. I feel so unworthy. This is crazy."

"Well, the ceremonies begin in less than an hour. There are clothes inside that go with the mask. I'm sorry, but there's no top."

"Oh, I'll bet you're real sorry. What Kawirén man came up with that tradition, anyway?"

"I can bring you body paint. It's acceptable to paint your body for this ritual."

"Yes, to the body paint. It'll cover these paint splotches." She squinted and pointed at him. "I'd better not catch you staring tonight."

"Absolutely not. I wouldn't think of it."

"Where are you going?"

"To get dressed in the men's hut."

"Oh, I see. Like a bunch of good ole boys."

"I'll send someone with the body paint. When you hear the drums, meet me at the center of the Circle."

"Hey, you're forgetting something." She handed him his mask.

He nodded and pointed at her. "Don't be late."

Drums vibrated through the air with electricity. The Ritual of the Halfmoon began with a robust feast of deer and tapir meat, plantains, passion fruit, boiled turtle eggs, fish, and candied insects beneath the huge thatched roof of the Circle.

They coated the firewood for the Grand Fire with Yarumaya resin as the sunlight faded. When the fire was lit, it erupted with a whoosh like a mini volcano, prompting murmurs from the crowd and the onset of powerful drums.

All the villagers wore masks of fantastic design and creativity. Isabella sighed, thinking about her cringy mask compared to the beautiful one she was wearing. And what the hell did Tarenu want with her mask, anyway?

Smoke billowed and filled the Circle with a sweet scent of citrus. The *Breath of Life*, the Kawirén called it. A tall man approached. No doubt it was Quinn, since the average male height in the tribe was five feet five inches. His inability to see her grinning behind the mask was a relief.

Quinn was a presence in his tribal dress. *Tarzan*, she thought, not wanting to admit how darn sexy he looked. A grass skirt with no shirt. Rippled abs and etched pecs painted in reds and blacks. A silver armband, beaded necklaces, and his awesome mask.

"Malibu? Is that you?"

"Funny." She crossed her arms to cover her bare breasts.

"Thanks for saving my seat," he chuckled.

"Quinn, is it possible the resin smoke is how the Kawirén absorbs the longevity molecule? Their blood must be full of it."

"I've suspected it for a long time. They use the resin for everything. It's lipid-soluble. Stored in their fat cells. I just don't know how it's activated."

The drums stopped. Tarenu entered the Circle with a ceremonial cup carved from Yarumaya wood and decorated with paint and shells. He stood next to a stone cauldron filled with a steaming brew. One by one, the adults rose and formed a line. Tarenu filled the cup with the brew as each adult villager sipped, one by one, before returning to their seats.

"Anquawnie se parabwana e antiquanta," he chanted after each villager took a drink.

"What does that mean? She whispered.

"It roughly translates *the smoke blesses the body, and the tea ignites the spirit.*"

"Uh, Quinn. What's the tea made of?"

"The Piritayá flower that grows atop the Yarumaya. It blooms once every five years, and only the chief shaman can harvest it. It has some narcotic effects associated with it, so they only allow adults, 13 and up, to sip. But just a heads up … it's extremely bitter."

"Hello … have you tested this tea in the lab?"

"What? No, only Tarenu has access to it. It's brewed for this specific ritual, then it's stored in a secret location."

"We need to test it."

"Not possible."

"If they've given us access to the sacred grove, why wouldn't they allow us to test the flower or the tea?"

"I've asked. They believe only the chief shaman can touch the petals. Others would contaminate the brew and condemn the tribe to eternal hell … you know, screaming, lava, bodies torn apart…"

"Well, that's a great way to keep people's hands off it, but we need a sample. It's probably the only thing in the entire village we haven't tested."

"I hate to admit it, but I think you're right. We should get our hands on a sample. I'd given up trying."

"I say we sip and don't swallow, Quinn. Spit it into a cup."

"As crude as that sounds, that's actually not a bad idea," he said.

"Okay." She shoved him. "It's our turn to get in line. Go."

When Isabella reached the front of the line, she lowered her mask. The crowd chanted, "Nahuari, Nahuari…"

Tarenu guided her and Quinn to the front of the quieted crowd and spoke. Quinn whispered, "You're not allowed to drink tonight. Don't ask me why." He extended his arm. "Tarenu wants us to hold hands."

The shaman filled the cup and offered it to Quinn. He sipped and pretended to swallow. Tarenu frowned and glared suspiciously, nodding at Quinn and gesturing for him to swallow. Quinn faked confusion, then cradled Isabella's face and pressed his lips to hers, filling her mouth with the warm brew. Her eyes widened as she stepped backward, stunned.

Tarenu shook his head and scolded Quinn, ordering him to swallow and open his mouth. Quinn exaggerated a nod, pretended to swallow, and stuck out his tongue.

Tarenu smiled and gestured for Quinn and Isabella to kneel so he could bless them by drawing a circle around them in salt and sprinkling them with blessed rainwater. The drums resumed. Young girls dropped flowers outside the salt ring, and young boys offered polished stone.

Quinn whispered, "They're thanking us for saving the Yarumaya."

Tarenu approached with an offering of fish eggs.

"Izzy. Spit the tea in my shoe. Quick," he muttered.

Quinn stood while Tarenu fed him the fish eggs on a wooden spoon. Before Isabella could spit the tea in Quinn's shoe, Tarenu grabbed her by the elbow and stood her up. He cradled her chin and offered her the fish eggs. She glanced at Quinn, swallowed the tea, and gagged on the pungent jungle caviar.

As the ritual continued with dancing, drinking, and games, Quinn and Isabella weaved their way back to their seats. Torches ignited, illuminating the night and casting flickering shadows over the crowd.

Quinn grabbed her hand. "Let's get back to the lab."

"What? Why? The party is just getting started, dude. I wanna dance."

"Ah, shit. You drank the tea."

She pressed her finger to her lips, widened her eyes, and hiccupped. "Oopsy." Then the giggles began.

"Izzy, you were supposed to spit it into my shoe. What happened?"

She shrugged and made a face like a kid caught stealing from the tip jar. She jammed her finger into his chest and grinned, her words slurring. "You're hot … for an old fart … a rickety old fart." She belly-laughed, amused at herself.

"Okay. We need to get you back to the lab."

"Are you looking at my boobies? You better not be looking at my boobies."

"I swear I'm not. Come on. Let's go."

"Quinny? Why'd you *kiss* me tonight?" She frowned as if she had forgotten something. "*Did* you kiss me?"

"I didn't kiss you. I was giving you the tea to hold in your mouth. But you blew that one."

"He didn't let me."

"Who didn't let you?"

"Tarenu. He didn't let me spit it in your shoe. I really wanted to spit in your shoe, dude." She doubled over, stuck in a silent laugh before a shrill rose in her throat.

"You had one job…"

Her eyes welled, and her eyebrows formed a peak. "I'm sorry … are you mad at me?"

"No, I'm not mad."

"Don't be mad, Quinny. I tried my best. I didn't mean to let you down," she burst into tears.

"Okay, phase two of the tea effects just kicked in."

Isabella staggered and fell on one knee. Quinn scooped her into his arms and marched towards the lab.

"Hang on to your mask, kid. We're almost there."

His face blurred, and her body relaxed as she cuddled into his muscular arms, sniffed his neck, and closed her eyes.

ELEVEN

A Tainted Sample

August 6, 2026

Quinn's face was the first thing she saw when her eyes popped open. He stared without blinking, stoic like a statue, with a cup in his hand.

"Ow … my head is pounding. I need an aspirin or something, Doc."

"You've been asleep all morning. That was powerful stuff you drank last night."

She gasped. "Quinn. I'm so sorry. I swallowed it. What do we do now?"

She pointed at the cup in his hand. "Is that coffee? Can I have some?"

"No, it's not coffee."

"Well, can I have some coffee, please? Wait. I've gotta pee first."

He handed her the cup.

She glanced inside and frowned. "It's empty."

"Not for long."

"Why?"

Her eyes lit up. "Oooh, I get it. You think the alkaloids in the tea are now in my pee?" She giggled. "That sort of rhymed.

"Yup."

"Oh, that's so smart. This just might work. I'll be back."

"Watch your step. That tea stays in your system for twenty-four hours."

Five minutes later, she returned, beaming, with a slight sway in her step. "I might have, uh, filled it up too much … I didn't want to waste any."

Izzy stepped towards him as he peered into the microscope. Her knee buckled, sending her crashing into the table. She shrieked. Quinn caught her by the arm and snatched the cup from her grasp.

"Oh my God, no!" she screeched.

"There's enough left, Izzy. It's okay. I warned you to be careful. You should lie down for a while until the tea is out of your system."

"I'm so, so sorry. Did we lose it?"

"No, there's enough." He heaved a breath, wiped his hand with a rag, and gazed at her.

"The moment of truth, Izzy…"

Quinn introduced several drops of the urine specimen into a Petri dish of one of his older resin samples.

Her stomach tightened as he leaned in, looking for a reaction to the tea alkaloids.

"Oh God, please work," she whispered. "How do we test it, Quinn?"

"There it is … I see the reaction I was hoping for. I'm going to inject our three cancer patients. If our theory is correct, this should go far in reversing the cancer."

"This totally has to work. Please, please."

Quinn filled three syringes with the cocktail and wrapped them in a sterile towel. He handed her a small bottle, several gauze pads, and sucked in a nervous breath.

"Well, this is all we have. We'll know in a few days if we're on to something. Let's go, Izzy."

They entered the makeshift infirmary Quinn had set up several days ago. The base of her throat tightened, and her heart ached seeing a young mother tending to her child, and families gathered around their loved ones.

Family members cooled the children's fevers with dampened cloths as the group chanted prayers. Quinn handed Isabella a journal and a pen. "Take notes for me."

August 6, 2026-Approximately 11 a.m.

Patient B, a 22-year-old male, and patient C, a 16-year-old female, are in stage I of Non-Hodgkin lymphoma. Patient B has a swollen anterior cervical lymph node on the right side of his neck, 2.1 cm in size. Patient C suffers from a swollen submental lymph node beneath the right side of her chin, 1.8 cm in size.

Patient A, a 5-year-old male, is now in stage IV, affecting his liver, with no lymph nodes affected. The patient has lost over 10% of his body weight and struggles to breathe, unable to hold food down.

All three patients are receiving a 10mg injection of the 'YaruTea' solution.

Quinn injected each child and hugged them one by one. He whispered something in the mother's ear, placed his hand on Isabella's shoulder, and said, "Now we wait."

Isabella whispered, "Quinn. Look at the older kids' eyes."

"I know. They've lost the blue tint."

Izzy wrapped her arms around Quinn's waist and rested her cheek on his chest. "There's nothing more we can do now, Izzy."

He took her by the hand and led her from the infirmary back to the field lab.

August 9, 2026

Three painfully slow days of resin analysis, soil specimens, and blood tests passed the time while they waited for the results. On the fourth day, Patient B and Patient C were in full remission and returned to their families in good health. A light shade of blue outlined their brown irises.

Patient A showed remarkable improvement, gaining 2.9 pounds of body weight, but remained bedridden—too weak to leave the infirmary.

The look on Quinn's face told her all she needed to know.

"He needs another dose, doesn't he?"

He nodded and lit his pipe, sucking in a deep drag. "Unfortunately, none of your recent urine samples contain the alkaloids. We need a new tea sample, and Tarenu won't allow it."

"Why not? Explain to him that the boy needs it to live, Quinn."

"In his eyes, the welfare of the village outweighs the needs of a single tribal member."

She crossed her arms and scowled. "Well, you need to make him listen. That little boy will die if you don't."

"That's true … he will. Aye, I'll try to talk to Tarenu. No guarantees."

"Not without me. I'm a *shaman,* after all, right?"

"Shaman or not, you can't enter the smoke hut. It's the best place for me to persuade him to understand how dire the situation is. Wish me luck, Izzy. We're going to need it."

"What? Another boy's club?"

Isabella watched from the field lab as Quinn approached, his shoulders slouched, and his head down. As he neared the porch, he glanced up with misty eyes.

"So, how'd it go?" she asked, already seeing the answer written on his face.

He shook his head, plopped into a chair, and took a shot of lakira.

"That bad, huh?" she said.

He nodded and wiped his chin.

"What do we do?" she asked.

Quinn widened his eyes and wrung his hands. "I can't save him, Izz."

"How about we climb the Yarumaya and harvest our own flowers?"

"Bad idea. For one thing, the next bloom isn't for another two years. Second, doing so would get us excommunicated and possibly executed."

"Oh."

"There's nothing we can do. I'll drug the boy to numb his pain and help him die." He leaned back and closed his eyes. "I need you there, Izzy."

The boy's family gathered around him. His mother held his hand and wept. The child was frail, his eyes sunken. Tears streamed down his cheeks. Wails echoed inside the infirmary as the family hugged each other, kissed the child, and said their goodbyes.

Quinn's eyes were wet, and his jaw clenched as he removed a syringe from his bag and tapped the needle, removing the remaining air bubbles. He whispered something in the boy's ear and kissed his forehead.

"Wait, Quinn! This is not happening. Not today."

"What are you doing?"

"Playing the only ace in my hand. Call a meeting of the village and make sure Tarenu attends. Then interpret for me."

"Are you out of your mind? What are you planning, Izzy?"

"I'm Nahuari, not Izzy. Get me an audience."

He spoke to the family and pointed at Isabella. The mother's eyes lit up as she wiped her tears. She stepped towards Isabella and kissed her hand.

Quinn pounded the gong inside the Circle and shouted in Kawirénian. The elders of the tribe slowly gathered, confused. Tarenu was the last to arrive, scolding Quinn for calling for a gathering at such a sacred time.

Isabella emerged from the field lab fully dressed in the ceremonial garb and mask of Nahuari. Murmurs traveled through the crowd as she stepped in front of them.

"Quinn," she whispered, waving her hand frantically. "Stand next to me … and stop staring."

Public speaking wasn't her forte. She barely passed the only speech class she ever took. So many faces fixed on her made her heart thump and her ears buzz. Thank God she could hide behind the mask, having no idea what she was about to say.

A warm, gentle hand squeezed hers. "I'm ready when you are, *Nahuari*."

"Okay. I'm ready, Quinn. Whew. Here we go."

She raised her hands to the crowd and said, "Greetings, everyone. I am Nahuari, the ancient shaman. I'm here today to plead for the life of a young boy. So young, he hasn't had time to experience the world, the rainforest, the pains of growing up, and growing old. He won't be able to love, or marry, or have children of his own.

"I'm saddened. My heart breaks for him and his mother. I am here to save the Yarumaya, but I am also here to rescue this boy. The medicine to save his young life exists in the village."

The crowd mumbled and gasped. One elder shouted.

Quinn whispered, "He demands you tell them where the medicine is."

She pointed at Tarenu. "He possesses the medicine but will not share it. The boy will die because Tarenu refuses to allow us to give him the cure."

The elders grew restless and argued with each other. Tarenu rose and shouted at the elders, pointing at Isabella.

"What's he saying, Quinn?"

"He says you don't speak for the village. That Tarenu is the Chief Shaman."

"Mayuma sent me, and she is a greater authority than Tarenu. Greater than me, and greater than all the elders in the village. Mayuma told me to save the boy. To do that, I need the sacred tea from the half-moon ritual."

The crowd moaned, and arguments broke out. Tarenu pleaded his case, reminding them of the sacred vow to protect the flowers from contamination.

"Mayuma told me she would protect the flowers and make an exception to save the boy's life. If you do not obey, many plagues will fall upon this village."

"Man, you sound like Moses. You're doing great," he whispered.

The elders turned on Tarenu, shouting and crowding around him. Tarenu raised his hands and bowed his head.

"I'll be damned … You did it, Izzy. Holy shit, you actually did it."

"I did? … Oh, my gosh … I did it."

"Tarenu will make a special batch of tea and provide us with as much as we need."

Isabella raised her palm. "Don't leave me hanging, Quinn. High five, buddy."

He smacked her hand and hugged her. "Thank you, Izzy. You may have saved a life today."

Quinn and Isabella wasted no time in preparing the cocktail. They raced to the infirmary only to find the family preparing the child's body for burial in the sacred Yarumaya grove. It was too late. The child had passed.

Isabella gasped. Her lungs deflated. Her stomach twisted into knots, and her throat tightened. She darted outside, hit her hands and knees, and vomited, her spirit crushed.

"Oh God, we're too late. We took too long … I took too long."

Tears spilled over her cheeks, and her body shook with grief.

Quinn gently took her hand and lifted her to her feet. "Izzy. Izzy, it's all right. He was beyond saving. His liver failed."

She buried her face in his chest and blubbered, "It's my fault for taking so long…"

"It's nobody's fault. He was barely hanging on."

"We failed him, Quinn. That poor little baby."

"But we have the tea now, thanks to you. We have old samples of the resin to buy us time until the trees heal. Izz, we saved two lives and lost one. I know it isn't fair, but his sacrifice won't be in vain."

She lowered her head and sniffled. "I'm just so sad. Seeing so much pain in that mother's eyes breaks my heart. I wish we could have saved him."

"I do too, Izzy. There's nothing we can do now. Put your boots on and come with me. I have something I want to show you."

He led her beyond the sacred Yarumaya grove, following a pristine creek until they were deep in the rainforest, where the land and trees were untouched by humans. She shadowed him for nearly an hour until they reached a small opening in the forest.

She covered her mouth with both hands and shrieked. "Is that what I think it is?"

"I planted them several years ago. There are 25 in all. I'm the only one who knows they're here … until now."

"It's amazing how fast they grow. How many years, Quinn?"

"Just over three."

"Oh, my God. They grow twice as fast as a kapok tree. They must be 60 or 70 feet high."

"Some near 80. I originally planted them in secret to study, since at the time I had no access to the sacred grove. Now I'm thankful I did."

"Have you sampled the resin?"

"Yeah. It's thin, sticky, and almost clear, with a slight citrusy scent. I really don't know how long it takes for them to mature and produce fertile resin. I was hoping you could tell me. Or at least give me an idea."

"It's hard to say. The trees in the grove are thousands of years old. It could take decades, or even hundreds or thousands of years. And there's the possibility that the conditions in the grove are unique and cannot be replicated in this section of the forest. They might not produce the same chemical footprint in the resin."

Quinn's chest deflated as he planted himself on a smooth log. "I was afraid you were going to say that."

"How many more secrets are you keeping from me, Quinn?"

He chuckled. "You have no idea."

She punched his shoulder. "You are such a pain in the butt."

"You're not the first to make that claim."

"Quinn, I need to go home and turn in my thesis so I can graduate. I'll come back as soon as I can."

"Your thesis? When did you have time to write a thesis, Malibu?"

"You underestimate women, Junior. We can multitask in any situation. I have all my notes and my outline. But I haven't actually written it yet. I need my laptop and an internet connection for that."

His grin couldn't disguise his genuine surprise. "And what is your thesis, Malibu?"

"Well, the title is, '*Ecological Indicators of Forest Health in Remote Amazonian Groves: An Analysis of Decline in Endemic Tree Species Due to*

Disruption of Symbiotic Pathways'. I'm not naming the species, or the location, or our work here, Quinn."

"Thank you for that. I was afraid the temptation to claim the discovery of a new species of tree might be too much to pass up."

"You taught me that trust is vital for survival here in the rainforest, Dr. Quinn. It's also vital in the outside world. You don't need to worry."

He nodded and hugged her. "I'll take you back to base camp and fix the radio, so you can go home. You are always welcome here, Izzy."

Quinn gazed at her in silence. There were words behind his eyes, left unsaid. He appeared tired. The stress of the past few days must have weighed heavily on him. Isabella plucked another gray hair from his head.

"Ow. Can you stop doing that?"

"I think you need to take a sabbatical, Doctor. Take some time off and go fishing or something."

"I'll consider it. Let's pack your things and get you on the next boat out of here."

TWELVE

Ticket to Palo Alto

August 10, 2026

The base camp field lab remained unchanged as they arrived just before noon. Storm clouds roiled in the west, and the rumblings of an evening storm were headed their way.

Isabella dropped her backpack on the floor and plopped into the webbed chair, blowing out a long sigh of exhaustion. Quinn immediately went to work on the radio.

"I can't believe I made it up the side of that cliff. I can add rock climbing to my resume now, I guess."

"You scaled it like a pro, Malibu. I'm quite impressed, actually. How's the knee?"

"The knee is healing. Slight pain, but not bad. It was a much nicer hike without the creepy smugglers and the cringy banana spiders."

Minutes later, the squelch of static filled the tent. Quinn snatched the mic and glanced at her. "Testing one, two, three. Chucho? You out there?"

Static pops and crackles continued. "Señor Quinn? Where the hell have you been, muchacho?"

"I was at the village, my friend."

"I thought you were dead, amigo, so I stopped by a couple of days ago to check on you and your guest, but no one was home. Saw the radio was still busted, so I left the special part you ordered. Sounds like you found it."

"Yes, I did. Thanks. It's fixed now, as you can tell." He heaved a breath. "Listen, I need you to swing by and pick up my partner. She needs to catch a plane home." He glanced at Izzy, forced a half-smile, and winked.

"Sí, Señor. I can be there in a couple of hours, amigo. I have some supplies for you, so I'll bring them along."

"Gracias, mi amigo. I hope that includes more tobacco."

Chucho snickered. "Always, my friend."

Quinn laid the mic on top of the radio and turned to face her, folding his arms and crossing one leg over the other as he leaned on the table.

"Promise kept."

"That took you like five minutes to fix, dude. Are you serious?"

"The bullet only damaged the casing. Didn't hurt the electronics. I had a faulty wire. Chucho left the new wire harness I ordered. Piece of cake."

"So, a wire harness was all you needed to fix the radio?"

"Yepper."

She chuckled and shook her head in disbelief. "Okay, then. I don't feel guilty about shooting your damn radio anymore. So never bring it up again."

He chuckled, his lips forming a smug grin. "Can I fix you some turtle eggs and tapir before you go?"

"Um, I'll pass. I think I'll eat on the plane."

"Your loss."

"It is my loss, Quinn … leaving here, I mean."

"Ah, so you enjoyed your stay?"

"I could never have imagined such an insane experience in my life. It's changed me, I think. Seriously, the world looks different, Quinn. The Amazon has opened my eyes to so many things I never realized."

"Mayuma. Don't forget about her, Izz. Write your congressman."

"I will. I promise. And hey, I *am* coming back, you know."

"Yeah, well, I'll believe that when I see it."

They sat, chatted, and drank lakira for a couple of hours, waiting for Chucho. An unexpected ache tightened her throat as she locked eyes with him. Was it her imagination, or was his stare filled with longing? Or was it regret? Her eyes blurred, but she quickly wiped them before he noticed. Their eyes remained locked for several moments in silence, neither of them yielding.

The hum of a boat engine in the distance stripped the moment away like ripping off a band-aid. Quinn stepped forward, and Isabella sprang to her feet from the webbed chair. She slung her backpack over her shoulder and forced a smile—a sickening pit developing in her stomach.

"Can you walk with me?"

"Uh, of course."

They strolled shoulder to shoulder to the edge of the river as the boat made a final turn towards the dock. She turned towards him and stuck out her hand.

"Thank you for everything, Dr. Quinn. Give my best to our tribe."

He nodded and squeezed her hand. "I'll do that. You take care. I want to read your thesis. You'd better get an 'A', Malibu, or I'll be very disappointed."

"I plan to, Junior." She shrugged and grinned—stalling. "Well … I guess this is it."

His head tilted, and his eyes narrowed. "I guess it is. Safe travels, kid."

Chucho wrapped a rope around a pole at the end of the dock and waved. "¡Ándale! Chiquita! That storm is coming in fast."

She waved back. "Coming!" She hesitated, turned toward Quinn, and hugged his neck. He squeezed her tight, his hand resting a couple of seconds longer than it should have on the small of her back and brushing gently against her shoulders as he released her.

"I'm going to miss you, Quinn."

"I'll miss you too, Isabella. Thanks for all your help. And for caring."

Izzy's heart sank as she turned and strolled along the dock towards the boat. She couldn't understand why it hurt so badly to leave. There was so much more she wanted to say, but…

Firm hands grabbed her by the shoulders and spun her around. Quinn cradled her face and planted a firm, gentle, wet kiss across her lips. Her backpack slid from her shoulders and hit the dock with a thud. Izzy wrapped her arms around his neck and kissed him back with an intense passion that surprised her. Never in her life had she experienced a more sensual and emotionally charged kiss than this one.

He placed his hand on her shoulders and beamed—his boyish dimples making another appearance and his crystal blue eyes piercing her soul.

"Goodbye, Izzy," he whispered in a voice as gentle as a warm breeze.

Quinn turned and marched towards the field lab without looking back. Isabella stood at the rear of the boat, stunned at what had just taken place—tingling from head to toe—waiting for him to turn and wave. Waiting for him to do something. When he reached the lab, he stood and watched as the boat turned and sped away. He hesitated, then raised his hand slowly to wave goodbye.

August 11, 2026-Palo Alto

The trip home was long. Grueling. The kink in her neck wouldn't go away. Neither did the wound in her heart. She had no idea Quinn felt that way, and until the moment his lips pressed against hers, she hadn't acknowledged her feelings for him either. At least that's what she told herself.

The Uber dropped her off in front of her apartment and sped off. She fumbled with her keys but finally opened the door. The air was stale and quiet. She tossed her backpack on the sofa and poked her head inside her miniature fridge, looking for anything edible from the modern world. The fridge was empty except for a couple of water bottles, a jar of raspberry jam, and a block of moldy cheese she lifted with two fingers and tossed in the garbage.

"Ew."

She reached into her pantry and snatched a box of instant mac and cheese and a package of chicken-flavored Top Ramen.

This'll have to do for now, she thought.

Izzy unplugged her iPhone from the charger next to her bed. She didn't take it with her when she left for the Amazon as part of her *disconnect from civilization* pact with herself. She literally had hundreds of text messages awaiting her return, most of them from her mom and dad. Only one from Teddy.

MOMMY DEAREST–Izzy, please call us when you get home, dear. We've been worried ever since you left. Not having any means of contacting you has been hard on your father and me. Please call when you get this message! Love, Mom.

BIG DADDY–Izz, please call your mom, Mija. She's worried about you. Me too.

TEDDY–Hey, girl. I've been giving our last convo some major thought, dude. Was thinking we should talk it over. Hit me when you get this message. Miss you, Izzy-pop. Heart emoji, fist emoji.

She collapsed onto her bed, heaved a breath, and tapped her phone.

"Mom? I'm home."

"Izzy dear! Oh, my Lord! You've been gone for weeks. You were supposed to be gone for only a few days. I've been worried sick."

"It's a long story, Mom. I'm fine. You and Dad can come up and have dinner with me, and I'll give you all the tea. Okay?"

"How about Saturday night?"

"Perfect. Tell Dad I love him. I love you too, Mom."

Hissing and gurgling drew her attention to the kitchen. She leaped out of bed and raced to the stove, where her noodles boiled over.

"Ugh, seriously?"

The MSG packet dissolved into her noodles, and she slurped them down in record time. Ramon noodles never tasted so good. She tapped Teddy's number at least fifteen times before she finally called.

"Izzy-pop-pop! What's up, girlie? Where you been?"

"What do you want, Teddy?"

"Wow. Hostile. I just wanted to talk, bruh."

"We have nothing to talk about. You said it all at dinner. The dinner I paid for, by the way."

"Hey, I said I'd pay you back. I forgot my wallet. Dude, chill."

"You know what, Teddy? Lose my number. Don't call or text me. Have a nice life. I'm over it."

"Whoa, hang on, Izz. It's me. I just want to talk. I think we made a mistake in taking a break. Break's over, man. Great news, right?"

"Ugh. You're so annoying. Get a clue, buddy. I'm not interested. I've moved on. You should too."

"I don't believe that. How about I come over? Spend the night. We can—"

"No, we can't. You disgust me. I wasted my time on you, Teddy. I was stupid, and I'll never make that mistake again. Goodbye. I'm blocking your number."

"Wait … Izzy … come on, I'm sorry. I love you, and I've missed you. I made a big mistake. Please give me another chance. I know I'm an idiot. I should have never let you go. Can we talk? Please?"

"We have nothing to talk about. You wanted to take a break from me, and you did. You don't get to come back when things don't work out or go your way. Life doesn't work like that, Teddy. And I'm worth more than that."

"I know, I know. That's what I'm saying. Just let me come over so we can talk about it. I made the biggest mistake of my life, Izz. Give me another chance to fix it. Please."

"No. I don't want to talk about it anymore. Move on, Teddy. I'm sorry, but I don't have any feelings left for you. There's nothing. Like you said, we can still be friends."

"I don't want to be friends, Izz. Please."

"Yeah, I know the feeling. I'm sorry. I have to go, Teddy. Take care of yourself. I'm sorry things didn't work out with your other girl."

"Wait, Izz!"

CLICK.

She wiped a tear and snickered. "That felt so good," she whispered.

She spent the rest of the day knocking out her thesis. It was going to be late, but hey, better late than never was the cliché of the day. Izzy changed into black leggings, a sports bra, and a baggy Stanford Cardinal T-shirt. She tied her hair in a ponytail and ran downstairs to the apartment gym and blasted out a workout. It had been too long since she had tasted an acai smoothie from the Zester Jungle up the street, so she jogged to the corner, ordered, and sat in the back, scanning her iPhone.

Quinn's kiss haunted her. His gentle touch at the waterfall, massaging her scalp, lingered in her mind. Catching his glances at the Ritual of the Rebirth of the Halfmoon, where she wore only body paint from the waist up, was intoxicating, and the way he took care of her when she swallowed the narcotic-laced tea warmed her heart. How could she not see what was happening? There's only one conclusion. She'd never truly been in love. Nor had anyone ever shown her genuine love.

She narrowed her eyes and stalked him on her iPhone, opening Google and searching for his name. Nothing came up except the ad looking for an assistant with the photo of who he swore was his dad.

Izzy accessed the Ohio State Online Alumni Association Directory for his name, but nothing popped up. She skimmed the library catalog for all the theses written in microbiology in the past 20 years. Nothing.

"What the heck?" she mumbled. "Is he a fraudster?"

She nibbled on the inside of her cheek and glanced around the store. The phone number of the Department of Microbiology jumped off the screen. She clicked the link and watched as her cell auto-dialed. After waiting on hold for nearly five minutes, a voice broke on the line.

"Department of Microbiology, Cathy speaking. May I help you?"

"Yes … uh, I'm wondering if you can help me locate an alum. An old professor of mine."

"Sure. What's the name?"

"Um, Dr. Quinn. Dr. Dominic J. Quinn. Not sure when he graduated or taught class there."

"Let me see. Nothing recent."

"He has a PhD in microbiology, and I think he has a medical degree as well."

"Not seeing him ... Wait. There *is* a D. J. Quinn who graduated in May 1963. His date of birth is January 25th, 1935."

She gasped. "That would make him like 91 years old. That can't be him."

"He's the only Quinn in our database with those degrees. Graduated Magna Cum Laude. He taught for a while, from 1970 until 1975, and earned a Selman A. Waksman Award in Microbiology in 1973."

"Thank you, but I don't think it's him. I appreciate your time."

Izzy sat and stared at her screen for several minutes, then shook her head to snap herself out of her trance. She exited the Zester Jungle and hoofed it to the Stanford Library to research winners of the Selman A. Waksman Award in the 1970s. There's no way it's Quinn, but her curiosity was eating her alive. Maybe it was a relative.

She scanned dozens of microfiche articles before coming across a list of publications by the National Academy of Sciences from 1973. Her pulse jumped, and her stomach fluttered. She sifted through them one by one until she found an article that mentioned the winner of the 1973 Selman A. Waksman Award. *Dominic J. Quinn.* Her heart was racing now. "Page 43," she whispered.

She slowly spun the dial and adjusted the focus until page 43 came into focus.

Dr. Dominic J. Quinn is the Winner of the 1973 Selman A. Waksman Award for his pioneering research in microbial symbiosis and bacterial genome evolution in the Amazon Rainforest.

She ignored the article and zoomed in on the grainy color photo of Dr. Quinn. Izzy covered her mouth and gasped. A 28-year-old Dominic Quinn was an uncanny match for her Quinny. Her heart was in her throat. It was difficult to make out, but she could swear the scar over his left eye was there. Or was it a blemish on the screen? His eyes were green, not blue. Maybe it isn't him. And how could it be anyway?

"It can't be; that's impossible," she mumbled.

Impossible only if she denied what she's always suspected—that Dr. Quinn, Junior, and Dr. Quinn, Senior, are the same man.

Izzy ran an obituary search for "Aubrey Quinn" between 1955 and 1985. She got a hit within five minutes.

Aubrey Lane Quinn, formerly Aubrey Lane O'Malley, died on March 12, 1975. She was 38 years old and left behind her husband of 12 years, Dr. D.J. Quinn. The couple had no children. Brey, as she was called, graduated from Ohio State University with her PhD in psychology in 1965. She was born and grew up in Lubbock, Texas, where her parents, Rob and Linda May O'Malley, continue to reside on their 12-acre ranch. She loved camping, fly-fishing, and spending time with her husband in the Amazon rainforest in Brazil, where he was conducting research.

The article below the obituary stunned her like a slap in the face.

Doctor Charged with Gross Negligence in the Death of His Wife.

A 40-year-old physician was charged with gross negligence in the death of his wife, Wednesday afternoon. Dr. Dominic J. Quinn was charged when his wife, Brey, who had been battling Stage IV non-Hodgkin lymphoma for over nine months, succumbed to the disease.

Dr. Quinn refused conventional treatment for his wife and is said to have been administering a controversial treatment, comprising an elixir made of tree resin and various herbs derived from the Amazon rainforest. He pleaded no contest to the charges.

"Oh my God," she whispered.

Izzy printed all the articles, stuffed them into her backpack, and raced home.

THIRTEEN

Return to the Amazon

August 16, 2026

When Izzy returned from a quick jog, her parents were sitting on a bench outside the apartment security entrance.

"Mom. Dad. You're um early."

"Yes, dear. Traffic was light from the airport."

"Have you two been sitting out here long?"

"Ten minutes, dear. We were tracking you on GPS, so we waited."

"Great. Where do you guys want to eat?"

"Surprise us, Mija," her dad said as he pulled her in for a quick hug.

"How about you take me to Madera?"

"Excellent choice, my dear. I can't wait to hear your … tea," her mom said with a tinge of sarcasm.

They sat near the fireplace overlooking rolling green hills, cypress trees, and a grand swimming pool beyond the bay windows. Izzy tapped the floor and fidgeted, staring blankly at the crackling fire. Her father downed expensive beers, while her mother sipped wine from a $3,500 bottle of Sauvignon Blanc.

"Izzy? What are you drinking, dear? The help wants to take your order. Where are you right now?"

"Oh. Sorry. I'll have an iced tea. Passion fruit. And some stevia."

Her dad scanned his cellphone, mumbling to himself and shaking his head. "Damn it."

"Frederico. Can you put that down? We're ready to order dinner."

"Go ahead and order. I need to sell these shares within the hour. I'm doing this for you, Flo. And Isabella. Give me a minute."

Her mother rolled her eyes and glanced at Izzy. "Dreadful business. And it's so unnecessary. Your father loves to play on that thing all day. It's an addiction, you know. I keep telling him that, but…"

Her mother's voice faded as Izzy's mind reverted to the rainforest.

"Izzy. Izzy? Snap out of it, dear. It's your turn to order. Never mind, I'll order for you."

"No. No, Mom, I can order for myself, thank you."

She glanced at the server and smiled. "A Caesar salad, please."

Her mother scowled. "That's all you're having? Your dad is paying, dear. Order whatever you want."

"That's all I want, Mom. Really."

"You need more sustenance than that if you're going to compete in the next Olympics. A salad doesn't have enough protein."

"I'm not going to compete in the next Olympics or any Olympics for that matter. I've told you that a hundred times. That was *your* dream, not mine."

"How are your workouts coming along?"

"They're not. My knee still hurts."

"I'll make an appointment with Dr. Craig this week—"

"I don't need an appointment."

Her dad interjected. "Flo. Can you give the girl a break? I want to hear about her Amazon trip."

"Thanks, Dad."

Izzy spent the next fifteen minutes summarizing her adventure in the rainforest, filtering many of the details as her mother glared with boredom. Her dad threw out a few token questions, then returned to his day trading.

"Have you finished your thesis, dear? I want to read it."

"I turned it in, but I can email you a copy. Mom … Dad. I'm going back.

"Back where, dear?"

"To the Amazon. There's more work to do."

"Out of the question, Isabella Bryn."

"Mom, I'm 25 years old. You can't control my life. I don't need your permission. I'm going."

Her mother feigned a look of shock, resting her hand over her heart. "What has gotten into you? And after all I've done for you."

"Mom, stop. Please. I'm going back. I've finished my Master's degree, and after I graduate next week, I'm leaving."

"What on earth for? Your father has arranged a wonderful career for you in one of his businesses."

"I appreciate all you've done for me all my life. I love you, Mom, and I love you too, Dad. But I'm going where I'm needed. Where I have to earn my way. I don't want the world handed to me on the proverbial silver platter. The rainforest is dying. Thieves and poachers are destroying it. I want to help save it. Do something with my life that matters. I'm going to write my congressman for our district."

Flo glared at her husband and huffed. "Do you hear your daughter? Say something, Frederico. Be a father for once in your life."

Her dad frowned and narrowed his eyes, laying his phone on the table. "Alright, Flo, I will." He turned toward Izzy and took her by the hand. "You go back to the Amazon with my blessing, sweetheart. You're Daddy's little girl, but I see the grown woman before me. And I'm proud of this young woman. Go chase your dreams. Fight for what you believe is right. And when you're ready, I'll introduce you to your congressman. He's a friend of mine. We play golf on the weekends. If you need anything, I'm here. Just a phone call away, Mija."

She leaped from her chair and hugged him. "Aw, thank you, Daddy."

"Frederico!"

"Ah, put a sock in it, Flo." He pointed at a lone shrimp on her plate with his fork. "Are you going to eat that?"

Izzy kissed her mom on the forehead. "I have an Uber waiting. Goodbye, Mom. Bye Daddy. I'll call you when I get back."

Flo's eyes widened. "But … but we haven't ordered dessert yet, Izzy."

Her mother chased after her and tugged on her elbow. She turned Izzy around and hugged her tight, like when she was six.

"I'm so sorry, Izzy. I don't mean to control your life, dear. It's just … it's just that I'm so afraid for you. The Amazon, Izzy … what a dreadful place for you to spend so much time in. Dr. Craig prescribed sleeping pills for me because I worry so much. I lose sleep. What if something happens? How would we know?"

"I'm fine, Mom. I appreciate your concern, but I need to do this."

"Oh, Izzy." Flo caressed Izzy's cheek, her glistening eyes widening.

"Please be careful, dear. I don't know what I'd do if anything terrible happened to you in that frightful jungle."

Izzy kissed her mother on the cheek. "I will. Stop worrying so much. I love you, Mom."

"I love you too, Izzy." Her mother covered her mouth with both hands and watched as Izzy darted out the front door of the restaurant and climbed into the Uber. Izzy waved and blew her a kiss, a lump cramping her throat, seeing her mom so vulnerable for the first time in her life.

❧❧❧

The flight from San Francisco to Manaus was eleven hours. One benefit of being five-feet-four is that it's easier to sleep on a plane in first class. She had an hour flight on a small hopper to reach Rio Negro, where she caught Chucho's boat for a two-hour ride back to Quinn's remote field lab.

As Chucho pulled up to the dock at base camp two hours later, a wave of emotion crashed over her. The Amazon was calling her home. It embraced and welcomed her through the songs of birds, the earthy scent of the thick, humid air, and the lush greenery enveloping her.

"Give my regards to Dr. Quinn, Chica. He's a good hombre."

"I will, Chucho. Thank you for the ride. Although it was a little choppier than usual."

He tossed her a small package wrapped in newspaper and bound with masking tape. "Give this to the doctor. Tell him to savor it this time."

"These aren't drugs, are they?"

Chucho ignored her question and roared with laughter as he flipped a 180 and headed back to civilization. She could still hear him laughing in the distance as he faded out of sight. The sun blazed overhead, radiating across a barren blue sky dotted with wisps of clouds, intensifying the sweltering heat and smothering humidity.

Nervous flutters tickled her stomach as she wandered up the dock toward the lab. She wanted to surprise him. More than that, she wanted to know if something was going on between them. In her heart, she knew there was, but she wanted him to say it.

As she entered the tent, her backpack slipped from her hands and hit the ground. Someone ransacked the place. Scattered papers lay across the floor. Beakers and test tubes lay broken. The microscope was in pieces.

Insects swarmed the open food crate, and outside, the rain catch lay on its side, empty.

"Quinn? Quinn, are you here? Anyone?"

She lifted the webbed chair from its side and plopped. "Oh, my God. What happened here? Who did this?"

She lowered her head and massaged the back of her neck. "The village. I need to get to the village," she muttered.

She heaved a deep sigh and pinched the bridge of her nose. "Ugh, I'm too tired for a 3-hour hike, and it's too late in the day. I don't even know if I can find my way back."

She shuffled through the dresser drawers—the ones that weren't splintered and strewn across the ground, that is—looking for Quinn's journal. The one with the map. But it was missing—just like Quinn.

She lifted a water bottle from her backpack and swigged, splashing her face for a few seconds of relief. The mosquitoes were sucking her dry, but she needed to rest. In the morning, she'd try to find her way back to the village. For now, she could barely keep her eyes open.

The storm was fierce last night and finally broke just before dawn. Her clothes clung to her like another layer of skin. She slipped her feet into her hiking boots, then slid her arms into the straps of her backpack. Izzy pulled her braided ponytail through the back of her Stanford Cardinal ball cap and headed for the village.

A crash of leaves and branches through the brush almost made her pee her pants.

"Oh, my God, Bessie. You scared the holy crap out of me. Never do that again."

The cat rubbed its thick, solid neck across her thigh and chuffed as they walked side-by-side. Izzy rubbed the fur behind the big cat's ears and heaved a breath.

"I have to admit I'm glad to see you, girl. I could use a friend right now."

Bessie trailed Izzy for five miles before darting off into the forest, leaving her alone with her memories and her instincts. Quinn always said, "Navigating the primal required a primal mentality."

She glanced skyward, where hundreds of macaws covered the trees in a rainbow of color. "Okay. I remember this place." She pointed. "That way … I think."

The rush of a waterfall put a spring in her step. Despite bringing a climbing rope in her backpack, she was relieved when she saw Quinn's rope already attached. Quinn hid harnesses in the brush, so she wasted no time finding one that fit. Izzy talked herself through the climb and jumped the last two feet, not nearly as nimble as she was when Quinn was watching. She loved to show off and basked in the attention of an audience. Her confidence waned when she competed against herself.

"Aha. The rocks." She tightened her knee brace and then darted over the rocks, forgoing the stunt this time, then followed the water past the large bend where the river widened.

Izzy sneaked past the area where they had encountered the smugglers and dug through the brush searching for Quinn's boat. It wasn't there. Quinn must have used it to cross recently, so it must be on the other side.

"Oh, God. How do I get across? Crap. Gotta be another way, right?" she mumbled.

The river was wide in this area, and the water deep and swift. Swimming would be out of the question even if there weren't crocs, snakes, leeches, and God only knows what else in there, waiting to devour her.

Maybe there's an easier place to cross up ahead. I'll keep going, she thought.

She worked her way up the river for over a mile when she spotted a logging boat anchored by the shore with a raft in tow, loaded with logs. Three cargo boats sat beached next to the larger logging boat, and two small canoes rested on the shore, half-filled with select pieces of rare wood.

"Bastards," she whispered.

A light crew of men and women loaded and unloaded cargo, fueled boats, and tended to the busy decks. She could steal a canoe and sail upriver to the crossing point, but risk being spotted. The wooden pieces would certainly weigh her down, she pondered.

Izzy crawled through the reeds and ferns towards the canoes, spying on the crew and workers, oblivious to her presence. She belly-crawled and hid next to the closest canoe, peeking over the top. No one noticed.

One by one, she emptied the canoe of the wood blocks and gently slid the craft into the water. Having laid her backpack inside, she lifted an oar and steered herself into the river's swift current. Four hundred yards into her journey, shouts echoed through the trees, and an engine fired.

"Oh, my God. Oh, my God." Adrenaline surged through her veins as she turned the vessel toward the opposite shore and paddled ferociously without looking back.

The sound of the engine grew louder, with shouts in Spanish commanding her to stop and return the canoe. Izzy was shocked by her urge to giggle before leaping from the canoe five feet from shore and sprinting into the dense brush and trees. The chase somehow ignited her competitive nature, and the danger she was in never entered her mind. *They should be happy just to have recovered the canoe. I mean, I left them the wood.*

She didn't wait around to find out, darting through the trees and using the river as a guide until she reached Quinn's landing point. The throbbing in her MCL caused her to limp, so she rested her hands on her knees, lowered her head, and sucked deep breaths to slow her heart. The engine seemed to follow along the river, so Izzy turned inward into the forest until she reached Quinn's shelter. She slid the lid open and sealed herself inside. She slowed her breathing, allowing her to relax within the cool clay walls of the shelter.

"Safe. Oh my God, I made it." She chuckled. "I made it. That was freaking awesome. I can't believe I did that. Okay, okay. I'll stay here for a while … then look for the treehouse. I got this … dude, you totally got this."

Izzy stretched her legs in the pitch darkness and massaged her throbbing knee. The rainforest was quiet once again, but she waited a while longer before venturing outside. She fished around in her backpack for a bottle of water and a banana and sang to pass the time.

Rumbles in the sky roused her. "Oh, gosh. I'd better get moving."

Peeking out of the shelter, she made her move and scurried stealthily through the brush, darting behind mammoth kapok trees and gliding through the dense thickets. She was terrified, but high on adrenaline—her senses alive and focused. The exhilaration far exceeded any charge she got out of her gymnastics performances. She was surviving in the Amazon rainforest, and it was amazing.

Ahead in the distance, she could make out the treehouse, confirming she was on the correct path. Surprised and pleased with her instincts, Izzy heaved a breath of relief and slowed her pace.

Continuing past the treehouse, she crept along the river until she found the natural bridge, tossing rocks into the water to see if the giant snake was loitering and waiting for its next meal. With no movement beneath the surface, she scurried over the bridge and continued up the river to the large bend. The rainforest was alive with motion. Chirps and whistles surrounded her in stereo. The annoying buzz of insects around her head urged her forward. She swatted at them, but that only seemed to piss them off and intensify their resolve.

Twenty minutes later, the rainforest looked the same in every direction she turned. The dense trees and bushes closed in on her as if she were being swallowed by a giant green beast. She was lost. Disoriented. Confused.

"Oh, my God. Where'd the path go? Was it this way? It has to be this way, right?"

Izzy wandered for another hour as the skies rumbled, and sparkling, jeweled droplets pelted her face. She huddled beneath a kapok tree and rested, keeping her backpack strapped to her shoulders.

What did Quinn teach her if she ever got lost? To navigate using the sun. But that doesn't apply in this weather. To look for the tree markers, but as she scanned the trees of the forest, there were none.

His warning about getting lost in the rainforest haunted and terrified her now. She swallowed her panic and noticed her footprints in the mud.

"Okay. I'll follow them back the way I came. Yeah? I totally got this," she whispered, trying to convince herself she wasn't frightened out of her mind.

She retraced her steps for miles as the sky unleashed a feral downpour. The rain flooded her tracks and soaked through every layer of clothing she wore. Izzy crawled into the tree hollow of a mammoth kapok, drawing her knees into her chest and shivering. She sucked on her vape, slowly inhaling and blowing white fruity puffs into the misty air.

A small canvas tarp she yanked from her backpack repelled the rain, but she had to climb to avoid getting stuck in the swirling flood headed her way. Izzy waited out the storm for over an hour before it turned into light sprinkles.

She gazed towards the sky, noticing the kapok tree had low, reachable branches. *Climb*, she thought. Get high enough to see the surrounding forest and find a landmark.

She adjusted her knee brace, clutched a thick branch above her head, and climbed. Her stomach fluttered at the alarming height as she slithered from branch to branch, reaching higher and higher until she could see the top of the canopy spread out for miles. Miles of green vegetation enveloped her. Quinn never taught her this tactic. No, this was all her idea. She sighed, taking in the vast ocean of greenery.

But there in the distance, about half a mile north, was the open timber yard created by the wood poachers, with the mountain leading to the village perched behind it.

"Oh, thank God. Thank you, thank you."

She blew out an enormous sigh of relief as she shimmied down the tree with a renewed spirit and her confidence restored.

Emerging from the forest, she gazed over acres of the lumber graveyard, where the wood poachers continued to ravage the rainforest and its inhabitants.

"They're not going to stop until they take it all."

Someone had left a logging truck parked on the other side of the wooded field unattended. Izzy glided through the damp debris, stepping over felled logs, and crept next to the rig, making certain no one was inside or guarding the vehicle. Pulling a small hunting knife from its sheath, she slashed the tires, listening to their protests as they hissed and flattened. Crawling beneath the vehicle, she cut every rubber hose and line she could get her hands on, then bolted for the cover of the mountainside leading to the village.

"I can't stop you idiots, but that'll slow you down."

Halfway up the mountain, she took a break on a fallen tree, swigging water and wiping the salty sting from her eyes. Cool sprinkles from above dotted the ground and her clothing as the atmospheric rumbles intensified.

"Oh, no. Not again. Ugh, move your butt, Isabella."

She traipsed up the mountain until she found the hidden path that led to the village as the massive white clouds splintered, releasing their moisture.

Her confidence was over the moon. Who could have guessed a rich girl from Malibu could find her way through the Amazon rainforest and survive? A year ago, she would never have imagined it.

She expected to hear the voices of children as she neared the village, but the forest was silent except for the static rhythm of the rain. When she broke through the trees and entered the village, she dropped her backpack and stared.

"Oh, my gosh. Where is everyone?"

FOURTEEN

The Lost Village

August 17, 2026, Late Afternoon

The village was a ghost town. Someone ransacked the field lab just like the base camp. No fires for cooking, no sign of the villagers, and no Quinn.

"The grove," she whispered. "Oh, jeez."

Izzy dashed through the trees along the path to the sacred grove and ducked through the archway. When she gazed across the desolate grove, she hit her knees and groaned.

"How could this happen? Who could do such a thing?"

Before her lay the fresh-cut stumps of the ancient grove. Trees thousands of years old. Murder victims of a grotesque assault against nature. Not a branch, twig, or a single leaf left behind. Innocent lives plundered by an unseen evil. Chills ran up her spine as she struggled to catch her breath. Grappling to grasp the meaning of the devastation in front of her.

She pounded the ground with clenched fists and wailed, tears gushing down her cheeks, her heart shattering.

"Why? Why would they do this?"

She wiped her eyes and squatted on a nearby stump. An overwhelming sadness cast a cold, dark shadow over her. The ancient spirits cried out, their anguish coursing through her veins. Mayuma was a living, breathing being, and she was crying—Izzy felt it in her bones. The Ancients' murmurs filled her soul, whispering, "Nahuari," through the drone of the rain and the groans of the wind.

But who was she? An entitled girl from Malibu? A spoiled rich kid. An above-average gymnast and an average college student. She couldn't fix this. Where would she even begin?

Izzy wandered back to the village and sheltered inside the remnants of the field lab. Scavenging a blanket and mattress, she laid down her head, closed her eyes, and cried herself to sleep to the rhythm of the pounding rain, allowing the cool, tranquil darkness to embrace her.

August 18, 2026

Amber light filled the tent with a soft morning glow. Birds chirped, monkeys squeaked, and crashed through the trees, gliding effortlessly across a vast web of branches and vines. The rainforest stirred as living sunlight filtered through the canopy and bathed the forest floor with life.

She lay in silence, mourning the devastating loss of the Yarumaya and the Kawirén tribe. Where does she go from here? Home? What happened to the village? And to Quinn? Her thoughts and fears raced through her mind on auto-repeat, starting and stopping in the same place, like a broken clock.

Izzy finished the last of her food and was down to her final water bottle. She submerged the empty bottles in Quinn's miniature rain catch.

A bitter crossroad lay ahead, and she must quickly decide which path to take. She squatted on a wooden stump and rested her chin in her palms.

"Where would they go? Where would Quinn take them, assuming they're still alive?"

A sudden realization charged her senses, raising her pulse.

The young grove Quinn revealed to her. "Oh, my goodness. That's it. It has to be."

She strapped on her backpack and marched into the forest, following the hidden trail where Quinn led her to the newly planted grove of Yarumaya. She marched at a steady pace and couldn't get there fast enough.

"Please be there. Please, please."

As she exited the forest, the young Yarumaya grove came into view with several thatched-roof structures butted against its edge. The smoke of a single fire filled the air. But there were only a handful of villagers she could see.

When the women saw her approach, they shrieked and raced towards her, embracing her, kissing her hands, and laying beads around her neck. They sang and took her by the hand, guiding her to the center of their new village—a scaled-down version of the old.

Tarenu greeted and blessed her. The realization that Tarenu and the villagers' eyes had changed from blue to a deep nutty brown saddened her.

Izzy greeted Tarenu and pointed to the band around her wrist—the one that bonded her to Quinn. His eyes lit up as he hugged her and waved for her to follow him.

Tarenu led her to a small hut, giving her a reassuring nod as he turned and walked away.

Her heart pounded into her throat; her insides twisted with nervous energy. She pulled the wooden door half-open and stepped inside.

A mature man lay sleeping on a small cot, holding a gourd that smelled of fermented bananas and citrus. His hair had grayed; his eyes creased with age. She tapped his shoulder. "Quinn? Is that you? It's me, Malibu."

His brows rose before his watery eyes popped open and gazed at her. He smiled and took her hand. A light shade of emerald green stared back at her. The crystal blue was gone.

"Izzy. Why'd you come back?" Tears welled and rolled down his cheeks.

A cramp at the base of her throat stifled her words. She heaved a breath, squeezed his hand, and whispered, "For the Yarumaya. For my tribe, the Kawirén. But mostly, for you, Quinn. I told you I'd return."

She laid her head on his chest and sobbed. He ran his fingers through her thick locks and gently clung to her with trembling arms. The thumping of his heart brought her to tears.

"What happened, Quinn? Who destroyed the village?"

"Poachers. Sent here by a pharmaceutical corporation to steal and harvest the Yarumaya. I-I pleaded with them. Told them that the effect of the resin is unique to this area. That it won't work in the outside world. I should know. I tried and failed."

"How did they find the village? Who told them about the Yarumaya?"

"They found my notes."

"Who?"

"The man funding my research. A powerful and very wealthy man. A man named Ian Bragg."

"I know about your wife, Quinn. I know what happened. It wasn't your fault."

He grew silent for several moments, then whispered, "Everything's my fault."

She sat upright and locked eyes with him as her tears flowed. "Why didn't you tell me?"

"Tell you what?"

"Why didn't you tell me the truth before I—"

She paused and bit her lip, wiping her cheeks.

"Before you what, Izzy?"

"Before I *cared.* Alright? How could you do that?" She stood and turned away from him, petrified that her eyes might reveal the depth of her affection for him.

His eyebrows formed a sharp peak as he pursed his lips. "I should have trusted you, Izz. I'm sorry," he replied in a gentle voice.

"Yes, you should have. This is so unfair."

"I'm old enough to be your great-grandfather. I'm aging fast, Izzy. Nothing is slowing it down, and all the old resin samples are gone. None of the new samples contains the correct compounds to create the longevity effect. The villagers will have normal lifespans now. The ones who are ancient will rapidly age and die."

"Does that include you, Quinn?"

"I'm afraid so, kid. Don't feel bad for me. I've lived a noble life. Accomplished much and met the most amazing young women I've ever had the pleasure to work with."

He took her by the hand and squeezed. "I fell in love with her. No apologies. It just happened. But you're right. It isn't fair to you. We're generations apart … what would a beautiful young woman with so much promise and such a bright future want with a tired old man like me?"

"Don't you give up, Quinn. We can start again. Restore the resin. Save the Kawirén and save you. There's still hope."

"That's what I admire about you most, Izzy. You're too young to give up and too naïve to know better … and so goddamn stubborn. I almost want to believe you. You've inspired places in my heart I forgot existed."

"Then get your ass out of that bed, Dr. Quinn, and help me figure this out. There's work to do, and our tribe is depending on us to get it done. Help me, Quinn."

"They destroyed our lab. Confiscated all of our research and all of our equipment. It's all gone, Izzy. Finished. I depended on the wrong man to fund my work, and I've paid a heavy price for it."

"Do we still have a radio?"

"That's the *only* thing we have left. The only thing they didn't take."

"Then I know someone who will fund our research and rebuild our lab."

"Who could you possibly know with enough money to fund our research, Izz?"

"Me."

"You?" His chuckle turned into short hacks and coughs.

"Yes, me. I'm from Malibu, remember? My father is wealthy, and I'm going to ask for an early inheritance."

"Izzy, you can't do that. Never use your own money to fund research. I'm sorry, I can't let you."

"It's not up to you. So, Dr. Quinn, you'll be working for me, I'm afraid."

He shook his head and forced a feeble grin. "God help me." He gulped a swig of lakira.

Quinn sucked in a sharp breath and extended his hand towards her.

"Why are you standing there, Malibu? Help me up."

"That's more like it, Quinny. What should we do first?"

"We're going to get you back to base camp and get on that radio. You have a boat to catch. I hid the radio beneath the floor."

"Get your shoes on, Quinn."

"I can't make the trip, Izz. I've gone from 30 to 70 in a matter of weeks, and I'll never make it up that cliff. I'll send a tribesman with you and make a list of everything we need. And Izzy, I'm going to pay you back the money."

"You're not paying me squat. But you will owe me. Low-key."

"Low-key?" He chuckled. I need a dictionary of all your Gen-Z terms.

She hugged his neck and kneeled in front of him. "Promise me you'll be alright. I'll return as fast as I can."

Quinn kissed her on the crown and cradled her face. "I'll do my best to stay alive if that's what you're asking. No guarantees."

"You'd better. I'll pack my things. You make that list."

FIFTEEN

An Act of Congress

August 19, 2026

"Daddy, I need the money. It's *life or death* important. Please."

"That's an enormous investment for something with so many vague details, pumpkin. Where is my return on investment? Is this a loan or a gift?"

"It's neither. It's doing the right thing. Write it off as a donation to charity. For the environment."

Her father relaxed on a lounge chair, crossed his legs, and lit a cigar. His den was the only place he smoked in the enormous mansion, and he only smoked when he was seriously considering a transaction.

"I need to know more about this tree you're studying. And the natives. Is there a product to be marketed? A profit to be made?"

"Dad, can something not be about money or a bottom line for once? Can it be about saving people? Saving a precious piece of the rainforest before it's destroyed forever?

"My entire life has been about doing what you and Mom wanted me to do. Pleasing both of you instead of focusing on my dreams. I've found my purpose, Dad. All I'm asking is that you support me. Help me save the lives of innocent people and protect a priceless resource."

He sighed and puffed, blowing a silent stream of cherry-laced smoke towards the ceiling. "I'll have to run it past your mother."

"No … please. Mom doesn't need to be part of the conversation. Let this be a pact between you and me. She worries too much, Dad."

"I don't like keeping secrets from your mother—"

"It isn't a secret. It's, uh … a bond between you and me. A partnership. Please, Dad. This means the world to me."

"I'll give you the money, Mija. But I need the details. I won't partner with you unless I know the full details and every aspect of what I am partnering in."

"All right, all right. I'll give you the full detes and when I'm done, I need a huge favor."

Isabella spent the next hour and a half explaining everything. Her father's expression turned from analytical to compassionate.

"And what is this huge favor you're asking, sweetheart?"

"Your congressman buddy … I need his help."

He nodded and picked up the phone.

"Julio? Can you meet me for lunch tomorrow? I have an important proposition I'd like to bounce off you. Actually, my daughter Isabella does. It'll be worth your time, I guarantee it."

He set the phone down and winked. You have your audience, sweetheart. 1:00 p.m. tomorrow at the club.

She hugged his neck.

"I love you, Dad, and I have a lot of shopping to do … soooo, can you write a check?"

"I've already transferred the funds into your bank account. Buy what you need and send me an inventory of your purchases."

Frederico fiddled with the glittering gold golf charm he wore around his neck. She glared at him and shook her head.

"Dad, that little *lucky* charm of yours won't help your golf game. It never does."

"It brings me luck in business. I'm rubbing it for your success today with Julio."

Izzy and her father watched as Congressman Julio Ortega strolled up the hill, followed by his young caddy.

"How's your game, Mija?"

"A little rusty. But I'm sure I'll beat the crap out of your score today."

"That's because I always let you win, which you are going to do with the Congressman if you want his help."

"Seriously, Dad?"

"I know how competitive you are, Izzy. But this isn't the time or the place. Do you understand?"

She shook her head and rolled her eyes. "Whatever."

He nodded, took a step towards Julio, and extended his hand.

"Are you ready for another golf lesson, my friend?"

Julio snickered. "Always willing to provide a lesson for you, amigo."

Julio turned towards Izzy and beamed. His teeth were as white as his slacks, and his dark-brown eyes were level with hers.

"And this must be Ms. Isabella I've heard so much about."

He offered a weak handshake.

"Pleasure to meet you, sir. Um, your shirt is blinding me, by the way."

He guffawed. "Ah-hah. You're on to my strategy, Ms. Delgado. I bought this shirt in Sint Maarten last summer. It's my secret weapon. Please. Call me Julio."

He gestured towards the first hole. "Shall we play? Ladies first."

"No, I think you should go first, Julio. I want to see how much effort I need to exert today to humiliate the two of you."

Julio chuckled and pointed at her. "You are no doubt your father's daughter, Chica. Watch and learn."

THWACK! Julio's shot drove slightly left around 200 yards. He glanced at Izzy and nodded.

"Not bad for an amateur," she quipped.

Izzy teed off and launched a 225-yard shot that landed near perfect, setting up her second shot.

She strolled to her golf bag, wriggling her hips, and gracefully slid the club into her bag. "M-hm. Not bad for a girl, huh?"

Frederico whispered in her ear. "Izzy, don't piss him off. He hates to lose, and you might be the biggest loser here today."

"Whatever, Dad. Your turn."

At the ninth hole, Izzy led with a score of 38 strokes. Julio was a close 40, and Frederico lagged at 43. The game came down to Izzy's final putt. Julio finished with a 45, and Izzy readied a final 8-foot putt sitting at 43. Frederico scowled at her, scolding her with his eyes not to sink the putt.

Julio looked on with a furrowed brow and a slight frown.

"Don't choke, Isabella. This is where we separate the men from the boys … or the girls, in your case."

His taunt changed her intention of following her dad's advice. He pissed her off, and she was laser-focused as she lined up the final putt, determined to take him down a notch, which would make him shorter than her.

She heaved a breath and slowly exhaled, tapping the ball. It hit the hole, rounded the edge, and dropped.

"Oops," she declared as she leered at Julio.

Frederico rolled his eyes, glanced towards the sky, then glared at her.

She shrugged and smiled.

"Sorry, *boys*. Who wants to buy this *woman's* lunch?"

Julio's face reddened, then he burst into the forced laughter of a nervous dolphin.

"I love this girl, Frederico. Lunch is on me, Hija. You were the best man today. But I want a rematch soon." His face flushed nearly purple.

They sat in a secluded section of the members-only dining room near a bay window with a scenic view of the hills and the golf course.

"Frederico, where did this young lady learn to swing such a mean club?"

"All those lessons growing up. If she hadn't been so dedicated to gymnastics, she would have been an excellent golfer, which is what I wanted for her. But her mother insisted she follow in *her* footsteps and become a gymnast."

Julio opened his napkin with a flick of his wrist and laid it across his lap. "So, young lady. What can I do for you?"

"I need your help with a tribe in the Brazilian Amazon and a rare, sacred tree that is not only a huge part of their religion but vital to their very existence."

"Wow, that's a mouthful. I see. Go on."

"Their livelihood is being threatened by a powerful corporation that hired wood poachers to harvest and steal their holy trees. They butchered their entire sacred grove. And they kidnapped some of the tribal members."

Julio leaned back and locked eyes with her in an intense gaze. After a few seconds of silence, he leaned forward and laid his palm flat on the table. "I can help you, Hija. I'd require the names of the perpetrators to begin with. Details of their crimes."

Izzy slid a sealed envelope across the table. "Everything you need is in there. The corporation, the man responsible, and the location of the poacher's activity."

"I can steer some USAID funds toward addressing this issue, and we'll investigate these crimes against nature and indigenous people. And we will prosecute them to the fullest, Isabella. We'll cut off their funds and finance local law enforcement to run down and arrest the poachers."

"And what about the trees they harvested? Is it possible to recover the wood and return it to the tribe?

"That's a possibility. No guarantees, but we can monitor imports and try to locate where the wood is being imported and sold. Once recovered, we return it to the tribe."

"The wood is unique. It shouldn't be hard to identify. Everything you need to know about it is in that envelope."

"Very good, Hija." He narrowed his eyes and locked eyes with her. "You care about these people and the rainforests?"

"I do. It's very personal."

"Be assured, Isabella, that I am very active in the preservation of our rainforests and climate issues. You've got a friend in me. I'll do everything in my power to help you, these people, and their sacred trees."

"Thank you, Julio. I'm going to hold you to that promise."

"Oh, I bet you will, Hija. I bet you will." He chuckled.

A server leaned into the table and asked, "Are you ready to order?"

Isabella collapsed on her dad's brown leather recliner and sighed. Her knee throbbed, and her muscles twitched. "I need a hot bath."

"I broke the lease at your apartment, Izzy, now that you've graduated. You'll stay with us until we find you a home you like. I have an excellent realtor ready to work with you."

"That won't be necessary, Dad. I'm leaving for the Amazon in a few days. There is still so much to do."

"Mija, I would be lying if I didn't tell you how proud I am of you. But the Amazon is a dangerous place, and all this talk of poachers and criminals has me deeply concerned."

"I understand, Dad. But I'll be fine. I can take care of myself."

"I can see that, Mija. Something has definitely changed in you."

He hugged her tighter than he had in years. "I don't know what I'd do if something happened to you, pumpkin. I'd never forgive myself."

"I love you, Daddy. Thank you for everything. And for not telling Mom."

"It's our little secret. I'll take it to my grave, pumpkin."

"What secrets are you two keeping from me?"

She didn't notice her mother enter the room with a bag full of Asian pears in one hand and her keys in the other.

"Nothing, my darling. If we told you, it wouldn't be a secret, now, would it?" Frederico replied.

"Izzy, dear. Put these in the fridge downstairs. Oh, did I tell you I'm going with you and our realtor to look at houses? And we're throwing you a big graduation party this weekend. Isn't that exciting?"

She gazed at her dad and frowned. His eyes reassured her, and he whispered, "You need to tell her."

"Um, Mom … I'm not going to be here."

She dropped the bag of pears on the counter and rested her hands on her hips. "What? Why not?"

"I'm catching a plane this weekend back to the Amazon."

"No, you are *not*. You're done visiting that awful place. I don't want to hear another word about the Amazon. I have a baker coming this evening to bring us samples of cakes, and I've invited Marsha's son, Stewart." In a melodic voice, she sang, "He's your age and single."

Izzy replied in a mocking melodic voice, "I'm not interested in Stewart Sobrato, Mom. He's a cree-eep."

"Oh, he is not. He's a handsome and promising young man who was just accepted into dental school at UCSF. You would do well with a boy like him instead of that Tommy boy you were seeing."

"Teddy, Mom. Teddy. That's over, and I'm done with relationships at the moment. I'm leaving Saturday morning."

Flo glared at her husband. "What has gotten into your daughter, Frederico? She's turned into you. I have to talk to the caterer in fifteen minutes. I'll be back shortly. Talk some sense into her while I'm gone, will you, please?"

"Flo? Did you hear what she said? She's headed back to the Amazon this weekend. It's important to her, and she's working on a critical project. She's making a difference in the world. We need to support that, sweetheart."

"Alright! Both of you! I have had enough of this nonsense. Isabella Bryn, you are not going to the Amazon or anywhere else. Do you understand me? You've earned your degree, and now it's time to settle down into an actual job. You will attend your graduation party and enjoy it. And you will give Stewart Sobrato a chance and treat him politely. His family is worth billions in the real estate industry."

"I don't care about the Sobrato family or their billions! Don't you understand that by now? I'm tired of you trying to control my life, Mother. I'm a grown woman, and I can make my own decisions, and it's about time you dealt with it. You don't have to agree with my choices, but you *will* respect them. I'm not tolerating it anymore. Have your party and say hi to Stewart for me."

Izzy headed for the door, then stopped and turned. "What really bothers me about all of this, Mom, is that you didn't even bother to ask me what *I* want. You just plan it all out like you always do."

Flo huffed and glared at Frederico. "Are you going to let her talk to me this way?"

"Yes, Flo. I am. Because she's right."

Flo's lower lip trembled. She grabbed her keys and paused. Her eyes filled with tears. "Izzy? Please don't go."

"I'll be all right, Mom. Don't worry."

"Oh, but I do worry, dear. What am I to do?"

"Trust me, Mom. *That's* what you do."

Flo lowered her head and slipped out the door, closing it behind her.

"Do you need a ride to the airport on Saturday, pumpkin?"

"No, thanks. I'll Uber. I'm really sorry, Dad—"

"Ut-tut-tut … You have nothing to be sorry about, Izzy. Your mom needed to hear that, and it's been long overdue. You needed to get that off your chest. Just don't leave without talking to her first. Promise? As controlling as she is, she's deeply concerned and afraid for you."

She nodded as her cell phone rang.

"Julio. Hello … Yes, I can talk."

SIXTEEN

A New Lab, A New Grove

August 20, 2026

She wriggled into her first-class seat on the Delta flight and pushed off her sneakers with her toes. She tried to talk to her mom, like she promised, but her mother was too emotional to listen. The silent treatment, the guilt trips—they no longer worked. Izzy outgrew them. But the sadness in her mother's eyes as she said goodbye hurt her heart. Izzy hugged her tight and told her she loved her as she boarded the plane.

Izzy tapped on her iPhone, flipping through her text messages. A message from Congressman Ortega's office caught her eye.

Dear Ms. Delgado, we have located and recovered the Yarumaya wood stolen from the rainforest. It is stored in a warehouse in the Philippines, being prepared for return to the Kawirén tribe. We've frozen funds being laundered by the corporation named in your documents. I will keep you informed as the case progresses.

Sincerely,

Julio

Izzy reclined in her seat after takeoff as her eyes grew heavy from the drone of the aircraft's engines. Her final thought before she drifted away into twilight was of Quinn.

When she reached the Rio Negro, Chucho was waiting on the pier, carving slices of apple with a hunting knife. The bright yellow bandana around his forehead made him easy to spot.

"Hola, Chica! You're late."

"I apologize, Chucho. Long story. Do you have my supplies?"

"Sí, señorita. That's why we're taking a bigger boat."

He pointed at the large duffel bag she rolled and snickered. "Ay, I think that one will be the anchor that sinks our boat."

She rolled her eyes and shoved the bag toward him. "Funny."

He exaggerated the weight of the luggage by grunting, swinging it into the boat, and dabbing his face with a cloth. "I should charge you extra."

"Chucho, I need help transporting the supplies and equipment to the village. Do you know anyone I can hire?"

He hollered, "Pancho! Chuy! I have a job for you, hombres."

He glanced at her. "How much are you offering?"

"I-I dunno. Uh, what's the going rate for something like that?"

"Give them each a hundred U.S. dollars."

"Done."

"¡Ándale! Let's go, muchachos. Before the rains come."

By the time they reached base camp, it was nearing 2:30 p.m. They unloaded in twenty minutes and packed everything into two medium-sized crates with wheels. The men strapped hunting rifles around their shoulders, and each grabbed a crate. The trip was slow. A three-hour hike turned into six—an extra hour added from lowering the crates, along with her bag, down the cliff to the river.

When they reached the base of the mountain near the lumber graveyard, it was dark as pitch and pouring rain. The men erected a small tent, and the three of them huddled inside. Neither man spoke English, but Izzy was fluent enough in Spanish to communicate adequately. It was going to be a long night for Izzy, cramped inside a cramped four-man tent between Pancho and Chuy, who weren't the slimmest hombres she'd ever met.

❧

Golden rays lit up the inside of the tent. She could barely move; her neck stiffened. Pancho's snoring and Chuy's gas forced her swift exit. Izzy stretched, twisted her spine, and massaged the kinks out of her neck. She gently kicked Pancho and Chuy in the boots.

"Hey. Vámonos, hombres. ¡Venga!"

They lumbered up the mountainside, grunting and resting every hundred yards. Ninety minutes later, they entered the village. Kawirén warriors bull-rushed them and held spears to Pancho and Chuy's throats.

"No, no, no. They're with me," she pleaded.

The warriors shouted at them and pointed to the forest with a firm gesture anyone could understand. Izzy whipped out $200 from her wallet and stuffed the bills into their shirt pockets. "Muchas gracias, amigos. Vámonos." She waved frantically, shooing them away.

They nodded and dashed towards the cover of the trees. Izzy coaxed the warriors to deliver the crates to Quinn's jungle bungalow.

Izzy strolled to the hut, pulled the door open, and found Quinn relaxing on a stool smoking his pipe. He rose, shuffled toward her, opened his arms, and smiled.

"I was afraid you'd changed your mind, Izz."

"And why would I do that?"

"An old man isn't as attractive as the younger version of himself."

"What makes you think your younger self was attractive?"

His head jerked, and his brows furrowed. "The way you made gaga eyes at me when you thought I wasn't looking."

"Oh, you are so full of it. Whatever, dude."

He hugged her. "Welcome home, Malibu."

"It's nice to be back, Junior. And hey, I'm attracted to older guys."

She ran her fingers through his hair and smirked. "I love the gray. But we need to do something with this beard. Gettin' a bit shaggy there, buddy."

He squeezed her tighter and cradled her head against his chest. A whimper escaped her throat as she closed her eyes and savored the moment. Even as an older man, Quinn was handsome and gentle behind his gruff exterior. She missed his younger self, and in a bizarre sort of way, it seemed she'd known him for a lifetime. Or maybe the rapid aging phenomenon was throwing her off.

"I have something for you, Quinn. Something for us, actually."

"Well, let's see what you've got, Malibu. We have a lot to do and little time to do it."

She flipped the latches, swung open the lids, and inventoried the equipment and supplies.

"What are these?" he asked as he held them up.

"That is an ACR Bivy stick. It transmits a GPS signal so we can never get lost."

"I don't like it, Izz. I don't want people to find us."

"Only one person is on the other end, and we can trust him. That other thing in your hand is an Iridium Extreme satellite phone to replace that dinosaur of a radio. We can call Chucho on the *phone* now."

He glanced at the microscopes, analyzers, and the rest of the equipment like an orphan staring through a Macy's window on Christmas

Eve. "This is expensive stuff, Izzy. State-of-the-art. How did you afford all of this?"

"Don't worry about it, buddy. I've got us covered. Time to unpack and rebuild our lab. You up for it, Grandpa, or is it nappy time?"

He chuckled. "The joints are a little stiff, but I can hang, kid."

She pulled a small package from the bottom of the crate and handed it to him. "A little token from me."

He tore it open and grinned. "Mac Baren. Where'd you find this?"

"I stole it from my dad's reading room stash. There's plenty where that came from, so don't worry about it."

"Your dad has great taste in tobacco. Thank you."

They worked the rest of the day converting Quinn's small bungalow into a working lab.

"This is quite impressive, Malibu. I couldn't ask for a better lab partner."

She placed one hand on her hip and wagged her finger. "Uh-uh, mister. Remember, you work for me now. I'm the boss. La jefa."

"Suit yourself, Izz. Whatever blows your skirt up. Let's get to work."

Isabella spent hours analyzing soil and root samples from the ancient grove and the new grove.

"Look at these samples, Quinn. Tell me what you see."

"Well, the old sample seems to have some sort of fungal rot or contamination compared to the new sample."

"That's what I thought at first. But what if we're not after what the tree creates? What if we're after what it hosts?"

"I like where you're going with this, Izzy. What are your thoughts? You have a hypothesis?"

"What if the ancient soil contains a microbe the trees require to complete the puzzle? Another symbiosis besides the one with Microbe X."

"Okay, good. That raises the question of what the difference is in the soils? What's in the ancient soil that's missing in the new?"

Something clicked in his eyes. "There's an old saying Tarenu once shared with me. *The trees are not alone. They drink from the bones of the old gods.*"

"Quinn, are you thinking what I'm thinking?"

"Yeah. Tarenu won't like it. We'll need permission."

Izzy shadowed Quinn to Tarenu's hut, asking permission to enter. Quinn explained their theory to Tarenu, to his angst:

"Wise shaman, the ancient Kawirén custom of burying elders beneath the Yarumaya trees created a closed-loop ecosystem. As the bodies of the Ancestors decomposed, unique endophytic fungi and bacteria from their microbiomes entered the soil. These microbes became symbionts, thriving in the roots of the trees, and in return, enhancing resin biosynthesis. Microbe Y. Over centuries, this became an ancestral microbe lineage, unique to the sacred grove."

Tarenu's face went blank. He shook his head and held up his hands like a student ill-prepared for a final exam.

"Quinn. Whatever you said just confused the heck out of him. In layman's terms, buddy."

Quinn continued. "The new grove lacks the 'sacred inoculation.' Without centuries of ancestral burials, the soil is biologically sterile in comparison. Even with the new trees, rainfall, and sunlight, the resin lacks potency because the microbial catalyst isn't present."

Tarenu's eyes creased at the corners, and he placed his hand on his forehead.

Izzy smacked Quinn's shoulder. "Speak in simpler terms, *professor.* You've completely lost him."

Quinn inhaled a deep breath and nodded. "We need to extract the microbe from the ancient soil to inoculate the new soil. Transfer some Ancestors to the new grove."

Tarenu responded, "No. The ancient burial grounds cannot give up the Ancestors. The forest is alive with their spirits. They must not be violated or awakened."

"What's he saying, Quinn?"

"He says body samples of the ancestors must not be removed."

"Quinn. I have an idea. Ask him if we propose to the council a ceremonial soil sharing—a return to the cycle, not a theft of it."

"Worth a try," Quinn conceded and asked the question.

Tarenu lowered his head and replied, "You wish to override my authority with the council once again?"

"No, great chief. We wish to convince you to choose life for your tribe, which will please the Ancestors. Life and death must nourish the next generation. True longevity isn't just biological; it's intergenerational. The tribe's survival depends on honoring its dead, not just saving its trees. The trees and the Ancestors are truly one. They live within the trees, as you believe, and together, they give back long life. We must join the new generation of Yarumaya with the old generation of Ancestors."

A tear welled in Tarenu's eye. "You speak with great wisdom and understanding, Tupakaí. Our people are dying. Let us perform a ceremonial soil sharing, bonding the Ancients with the young Yarumaya."

Quinn spoke softly, trying not to show too much excitement in front of Tarenu. "He's agreed to do it, Izzy."

"Oh, my God, yes. Fist pump, dude. You got through to him. I knew you could do it."

Quinn and Isabella returned to the sacred grove to test the areas where Microbe Y was in the highest concentration. They marked these areas for ceremonial digs to be transplanted in the new grove.

As evening fell, a council of three men and three women was sent to remove the samples designated by Quinn and Izzy. They ignited a huge fire in the village, prepared a robust meal, and dug holes around the new trees where they would deposit the Ancients to bring life to the young Yarumaya. The elders held hands and chanted as the council returned with the samples and filled the holes of the new grove.

Izzy whispered, "Now we wait. It'll take a few days for the microbes to find their new home in the roots. Then we'll know if we're right."

Quinn handed her his gourd of lakira. "Take a hit, Malibu. You've earned it."

Izzy wandered back to the lab and broke open a brand-new journal she had brought from home to document the science behind the "magic formula" for longevity she and Quinn discovered.

How the Longevity Resin Is Activated-Summary

Fertile yarumaya resin appears deep amber, has a thick viscosity similar to maple syrup (170 centipoises), and emits a strong citrusy scent similar to lemons.

Simplified Process

- *The yarumaya tree excretes healthy resin on its bark containing the longevity molecule.*
- *Microbe X, which lives on the bark, absorbs into the resin. When filtered sunlight reaches the resin, Microbe X metabolizes the longevity molecule.*

- *Microbe Y absorbed from decaying bodies in the soil beneath the tree finds its way into the resin through its roots. These microbes stabilize the longevity molecule, but the molecule remains inactive and locked in an inert state.*
- *When the resin is burned during rituals, the stable, metabolized longevity molecule enters the body via the lungs and is stored in the fat cells and liver of the host. This becomes a cumulative process over several years.*
- *The Piritayá tea contains the yarumase enzyme that unlocks and activates the longevity molecule, which provides the body with the health benefits and longevity effects, and changes the eye color to blue. When the tea is consumed, the process is complete.*

SEVENTEEN

The Morning Sun

August 21, 2026

In the four days since the ceremony, three villagers have succumbed to old age and died. Tarenu buried them in the new grove to begin a new era of ancestors. A knot churned inside Izzy as she prepared to test the new samples of resin.

The satellite phone rang. She snatched it and pressed it against her ear. "Hello? Julio?"

"Yes, Hija. I have three helicopters en route, each carrying a load of lumber from your Yarumaya trees. We've tracked your Bivy stick so we can home in on your GPS location and drop it off in the village."

"Wait. I haven't told anyone yet … I need to get permission."

"Too late, I'm afraid. Their ETA is in about 15 minutes."

"Oh, God. Quinn? Quinn! Come quick."

"Calm down, Izzy. Why the panic in your voice?"

"Good news and bad news. They recovered all the Yarumaya wood from the poachers."

"That's great. What's the bad news?"

"It'll be here in about 15 minutes via helicopter. Well, more like 13 minutes."

"What? That'll scare the shit out of everyone in the village. Are you out of your mind? They've never seen helicopters, Izz."

"No. Yes. I don't know. All I know is there are three choppers and they're going to drop the logs off in the middle of the village."

"Ah, hell. I have to warn Tarenu and the elders."

He dashed out of the lab with Izzy close behind and paused halfway from Tarenu's hut, resting his hands on his knees and pressing his hand against his ribs.

"Quinn. You can't run like that anymore. Slow down."

"You don't understand, Izzy. I have to reach them."

Before he could say another word, the low thump of helicopter blades grew louder in the distance. A few moments later, the village was engulfed in a whirlwind that scattered every object not tied down to the wind. Screams rang out, panic ensued, and children fled for their lives, hiding in the forest, their families close behind. The choppers lowered their cargo and dropped the logs into huge piles, like emptying a box of gigantic Tinker Toys. They disappeared as quickly as they came.

Nearly an hour later, villagers gradually emerged from their hiding spots and approached the logs with caution and awe. As the village gathered around the log pile, the villagers fell to their knees and wailed tears of mourning. Some rested their palms on the ancient wood, chanting. Wood that represented their ancestors, carelessly dumped like somebody's trash.

Tarenu kneeled next to the woodpile and chanted prayers, tears flowing down his cheeks.

Quinn lowered his head and sighed. "How could you allow this to happen? They're devastated by the treatment of their sacred trees. Their history and their ancestors lie in that pile of wood, Izzy. You should have talked to me first. You should have known better."

"I'm sorry, Quinn. I forgot to warn you. It just … slipped my mind. I feel so terrible."

"Well, the trees are back. I just don't know what they'll do with them. But we'll leave that to the village to decide and stay out of it. I'll pass your apologies on to Tarenu and the elders and try to explain."

"I'm so sorry, Quinn. That was stupid of me to think…"

"They'll never be able to use all this wood in a thousand years. It'll rot and become infested. It would have been better and far more humane if the wood had remained lost to them."

"I've let them down. Let you down. It won't happen again, I promise." Her body trembled as the tears gushed.

Quinn's eyes narrowed; deep creases formed at the corners. He took her in his arms and patted her back. "What's done is done, Izzy. The elders will decide what to do with the wood, and everything will work itself out. Your intentions were sincere. You just didn't understand their customs and beliefs well enough to see the consequences."

"I would never have allowed such a thing had I known…"

"Don't cry. The Kawirén are a very forgiving and loving people. Me? Not so much. So, if I forgive you, they will too. I need you to stay focused on the plan. Wipe your tears, keep your chin high, and shake it off. And before you do anything else like that, check with me first."

"Spoken like a true coach. I promise. Thank you."

Quinn was right. She stayed focused on the goal: creating a fertile resin that would bond with the tea and heal the tribe. Izzy buried her head in her work and remained unavailable for the next two days. Bragg and his thieves stole the tea samples they worked so hard to extract from Tarenu in the field lab raids, so they'll need to convince Tarenu once again to give up samples of the brew to test the new resin's potency.

Quinn and Izzy had spent weeks brainstorming, trying to recall and record lost notes and data stolen from the raid to recreate their results. Time will tell whether they missed anything.

August 23, 2026

As dawn crept through the window, she introduced Microbe X and Microbe Y into the new resin sample and set the Petri dish in the nourishing sunlight. She stared at it like a pot waiting to boil. Her heart palpitated as she wiped the moisture from her palms across her khaki shorts and continued to observe with patience and resolve.

Was it her imagination, or was the resin turning a rich golden brown? It could be a trick of the light. Her breaths grew shallow, waiting for the right moment to test the chemical fingerprint of the sample.

She dissolved a drop of resin in ethanol to extract the organic compounds and placed the liquid sample into the solar-battery-powered instruments. Her eyes closed as she waited for the mass spectrum results to appear on the screen as a pattern of spikes—hoping for the correct chemical fingerprint.

Izzy heaved a breath and slowly opened her eyes. She squinted, her face inches from the screen.

"There you are. Got you. Oh, my God!" she shrieked as she leaped from her seat.

"Quinn! Quinn? Wake up. I have a major surprise for you."

She shook him. No response. An empty gourd dropped from his fingers and rolled across the matted floor. She rolled him over and gasped.

The face of an eighty-year-old man peeked at her through reddened eyes, wrinkled with time. He reached for her with a trembling hand, barely able to speak. "Izzy? Did we find it? Did we do it?"

She coddled his hand and kissed his knuckles. His skin was cool and fragile like crepe paper. "Yes, we found it. We have it, Quinny. Now, we need the tea as a catalyst. We did it."

He sighed and wheezed, nodding his head slightly.

"Continue our work, Izzy. Save the tribe. Everything I have is yours now."

"Everything you have is mine already, because I paid for it, dude."

He managed a feeble grin and a slight chuckle that turned into a garbled cough.

"You always make me laugh, Malibu."

"I need the tea, Junior. You're going to be the first to take it."

He shook his head and wagged a tired finger. "No, no…"

"Yes. We need to save the tribe. Together. And we need a test subject. Any volunteers?" She glanced around the room and focused her stare on him. "I guess you're it."

"He won't give up the tea a second time."

"Then I'll take it from him."

"They'll banish you."

"Then I'll find another way to get it from him."

"It's … it's hidden in the old village somewhere. Or in the sacred grove. Look there. Look for symbols. If you get caught, Izzy…"

"Rest, Quinn. I'll find the tea. I promise. And I won't get caught."

"I don't have much time, kid." He took her hand.

"Don't you do that, Quinn. Don't you dare give up, damn it."

"I believe in you. I trust you. Save the people, Izzy."

"We'll save them together after we save you first."

"I love you, Izz."

"Save those sentiments for when you're on your feet and can do something about it. You hang on. You hear me? Don't you go anywhere until I get back."

She slid her backpack over her shoulders and sprinted out of the lab towards Tarenu's hut.

EIGHTEEN

All the Tea and Honey

Izzy had been studying the Kawirénian language in depth over the past few weeks and had made steady progress, but wasn't fully fluent yet. She must make Tarenu understand her need for the tea of the Piritayá flower, despite her limited use of his language.

When Izzy reached Tarenu's hut, she found him cross-legged on a mat outside his door, praying and burning incense that smelled of cinnamon and vanilla. She tapped his shoulder and plopped down in front of him. His eyes opened, and upon seeing her, a shy grin formed across his face, missing several teeth that were present the last time she saw him. His eyes seemed dark and troubled.

They missed the Ritual of the Halfmoon in August. The next half moon will occur in twelve days on September 4th. Quinn didn't have twelve days.

She folded her hands and asked for a tea sample in Kawirénian, the best she could.

"Need tea. People die with no. Quinn dies with no. Please, Tarenu."

He shook his head and closed his eyes.

He replied in broken English, shocking Isabella. She never knew he could speak a word of English. "Tea in short supply. Cannot spare. Cannot risk. Seedpods planted in treetops. Five years, harvest."

"Tarenu, Quinn is dying. Must save him. Need him to save the village. Why won't you help?"

"It forbidden."

"I don't understand why your beliefs prevent you from saving your people."

"Mayuma has chosen those destined to be ancestors of the rainforest. She chooses death for some, life for others. We await her judgment."

"Well, she's not choosing Quinn to die. Not on my watch."

Izzy hopped to her feet and marched toward the field lab. She gazed towards the Yarumaya treetops and did a double-take. An epiphany burned a hole in her brain like cherry-red iron. *The seedpods. Maybe…*

"Ugh. I know it's wrong, but I'm not going to let Quinn die."

Izzy nursed Quinn the entire day, waiting for darkness to fall and the rains to roll in. She needed cover. If she's spotted, they'll banish her, or worse.

Izzy reached into the supply crate and removed a climber's rope, a harness, and a weighted throw bag attached to a thin line. She borrowed Quinn's hunting knife, threading the scabbard with her belt, and slipped a small flashlight into her pocket. She slung her backpack over her shoulders and tiptoed next to Quinn's bed, making sure he was asleep. There was no way she'd tell him about this brilliant idea. He'd lose it for sure.

A light rain fell. The moon was nearly full, dipping in and out of massive purple clouds and the inky silhouettes of Yarumaya trees. She scurried through the grove, carefully stepping over branches and small rocks, aiming to reach the center for maximum cover.

Shining the small flashlight into the treetops, she spotted a small cluster of Piritayá seedpods. Holding the flashlight between her teeth, she tossed the weighted throw bag, catching an 8-inch branch 30 feet off the ground. She sent the climbing rope over the branch and created an adjustable loop with both ends on the ground, then attached the harness and shimmied up the tree like a squirrel. Quinn would be impressed.

When she reached the 8-inch branch, she was halfway up. From there, she climbed the ladder-like tentacles to reach the pod clusters.

The pods were the size of figs, deep mahogany in color with golden speckles that lightly shimmered. The texture was waxy and veined, like polished leather, and hung from thread-like stems. She snatched one and stuffed it in the side pocket of her khakis. A momentary twinge of greed overcame her, so she snatched another.

Izzy slid down through the branches in stealth mode, stepping onto the roped branch 30 feet up. She refastened her harness and zipped to the ground in seconds, like a thief pulling off a jewelry heist. She pulled the rope free and stuffed everything into her backpack. Izzy raced back to the lab, her heart pounding in her throat with adrenaline.

Wasting no time, she lanced the first seedpod and analyzed the viscous amber gel surrounding a pearl-like seed, quickly isolating the enzyme within the gel.

Quinn snored and struggled to breathe. His time was short, she feared, so she combined the fertile resin with the yarumase enzyme from the gel and created a crude vaccine, filling a syringe. Izzy opened his shirt, swiped his shoulder with alcohol, and injected the life-saving medicine.

She whispered, "Hang on, Quinny."

There was nothing to do but wait. She kicked off her boots and crawled into bed next to him, caressing his forehead and running her fingers through his thinning hair as he slept. He'd aged so much it broke her heart. Her eyes grew heavy, her arm flopped over his chest, and she dozed to the rhythm of his breathing.

Soft fingertips brushed her hair from her face and caressed her cheek. Warm lips brushed her forehead. She opened her eyes to Quinn's dimpled smile. It was hard to tell if he looked younger, but that boyish spark was back in his eyes.

"What are you doing in my bed, Malibu? You have grandpa issues you want to talk about?"

"Don't say that. Ew-wah."

"What did you do to me, Izz?"

"What? I don't know what you're talking about."

"I'm not coughing. My fever has broken, and my joints don't hurt nearly as bad as they did yesterday."

She bolted upright and climbed out of bed. Filling another syringe, she pointed at his trousers. "Pull 'em down to the hip."

"Why? What have you got there?"

"A vaccine. Pull 'em down, gramps."

"Is this some kind of payback, Malibu? Did I do something to piss you off?"

"Not at all."

"Put it in my arm, then."

"Nope. This one's going right in your ass, sweet cheeks."

She rolled him over, yanked his trousers down, jammed the needle in his butt, and grinned.

"Ah … shit. Does that make you feel better? Do you feel vindicated?"

She inhaled and patted his bottom. "Definitely. Nice booty, by the way."

He sat upright and braced himself against the wall. "Wanna tell me where you got that? Did you have a breakthrough while I slept?"

"I, uh, got a tea sample from Tarenu."

"Bullshit. Look me in the eye and say that again."

She crossed her arms, heaved a nervous breath, widening her eyes. "I got … a tea sample from Tarenu."

Quinn's gaze burned a hole through the back of her head.

"Okay. Okay. I lied. You were dying, Quinn."

"Izzy? What did you do?"

"You were right. Tarenu wasn't about to give up any of his tea stash, and I had no idea where to look and no time to waste. You were running out of time…"

"Slow down. Take a breath and tell me what you did."

She grimaced and nibbled her thumbnail. "Promise you won't be mad."

"From the look on your face, I know I can't promise that."

"Promise you won't yell."

"I can't promise that either."

"Tarenu said something that didn't click until I was walking back to the lab."

"Isabella, spit it out already. What did you do?"

"I climbed a tree. No big deal."

"And did what?"

"Um, stole two seedpods?"

"Piritayá pods?"

"M-hm. Why are you looking at me like I peed in your coffee?"

"Do you understand how much trouble you're in?"

"I don't care. I wasn't going to let you die, Quinn. I needed you, and I still need you." She burst into tears. "I want you back. I want you by my side again. Looking over my shoulder and questioning everything I do. I want your sarcasm, your wit, the way you stare at me when you think I don't notice. The way it felt when you washed my scalp in that beautiful waterfall. The touch of your hands on my bare shoulders. I … I have feelings for you, Quinn. I'd steal the Hope Diamond from Rose's fiancé if it meant saving you."

"I think you mean the Heart of the Ocean. The Hope Diamond is cursed. But thanks."

She glared at him, speechless, for several seconds. "I'd steal that too."

He moved toward her and cradled her face. She pushed him away.

"I'm not ready for that yet."

"What? Why? Because I'm old?"

"Well, yeah, kind of. Let's give it a few more rounds of vaccines and then revisit that little moment."

"Well, that killed the mood. You really had me going there for a minute."

"I meant every word. Quinn, I don't know how many injections it's going to take to get you healthy again, but we'll need more tea—more of the yarumase enzyme if we're going to save the dying. Tarenu is going to let them die. He was going to let *you* die."

"We can't interfere with their customs and beliefs, Izzy. Whatever Tarenu and the elders decide, we must comply with."

"That's so unfair. So sad for them. And it could have sucked for you."

He pointed an accusing finger at her.

"And no more seedpods. You'd better hope Tarenu doesn't notice them missing. He knows exactly how many he planted, and he checks on them regularly."

"Oh, God. I didn't think of that. Maybe I can replace the used pods when we're done with them."

"Bad idea. I think I can convince him that an animal or a bird ate them. You can't be caught climbing a Yarumaya tree. Understand?"

"Alright, alright. But I'm using what I took to get you back to being you. I mean, it's already taking effect. Although I may end up regretting my decision."

"Well, you're going to regret jabbing me in the ass with that needle, I can promise you that."

"See … you're almost back. A simple thank you would have sufficed."

He rolled his eyes and glared. "Sure. Thank you, Izzy. Now, if you can keep from dropping any more trees on our heads, upsetting the natives, and stealing forbidden fruit, we'll be on a roll again, Eve."

"Wow, Quinn. You're definitely back to your old form. Can we get back to work now? I have some things I need to show you."

She stepped close to him and squinted. "Uh…"

He frowned and stepped backward. "What? Why are you looking at me like that?"

"Your eyes. I swear I see a tinge of blue. But I'm not sure."

He stared at his reflection in the GC/MS instrument glass, pulling his lower eyelid down and rolling his eye around.

"You're bullshitting me again. Come on, man."

"I'm not kidding, Quinn. I see a glint of blue. Now, if you're feeling up to it, you haven't made me breakfast in a while."

"Tapir or turtle eggs?"

"Yuck. How about some fruit and a power bar?"

The thump of rotor blades rumbled in the distance.

"What the hell did you do now, Malibu?"

"I-I didn't do anything…"

Quinn snatched a pair of binoculars and marched from the lab to the center of the village. Izzy trailed him, carrying the satellite phone and pecking at the keys to raise Congressman Ortega.

"Hola, Ms. Delgado. I'm guessing your company has arrived."

"What company? Julio, warn me before you send helicopters near the village. It terrifies the people."

"I'm very sorry, Isabella. I had little notice."

"Well, why the hell are they here?"

"Your missing villagers. We brought them home. We're dropping them off at the base of the mountain, hoping not to alarm anyone."

"Too late for that. But thank you, Julio."

"Anytime. I want that rematch at the club, Isabella."

"Izz? What's that chopper doing over there?"

She heaved a breath and hung up the phone. "The missing villagers. They're home."

Within the hour, they escorted them from the old village to the new and reunited them with their families.

"I hate your methods, Izzy. You need to stop bringing helicopters near the village."

She shrugged and grimaced. "Sorry. I didn't know."

Quinn laid a hand on her shoulder and winked. "But thanks for bringing them home."

August 31, 2026

A week passed. Five more villagers succumbed to old age, but Tarenu refused to give up the Piritayá flowers reserved for the sacred tea. Izzy filled the last dose of vaccine and set it on the edge of the lab table.

"It's time, Quinn. Roll up your sleeve."

"Ah, in the arm this go around, I see? Thank you."

She gazed at him as she jammed the needle into his shoulder and injected the precious liquid. Only his temples were gray now, and his skin was near flawless once again. He glanced at his shoulder, then fixed his bluish-green eyes on her.

"We need to test other plants. Flowers. Even the fruit of the Yarumaya. Maybe the yarumase enzyme isn't solely unique to the Piritayá flower," he said.

"Brilliant minds think alike, Quinn. I've been doing that for three days now. No luck."

"I spoke to Tarenu yesterday, Izz. His stock of Piritayá tea is depleted, which is why he's refusing to share. We have to find an alternative."

"What do you suggest?"

"You're the botanist. Figure something out. Villagers are dying every day. We need answers."

"Wow. No pressure there."

He brushed several strands of hair from her face and caressed her cheek.

"Okaaay," she said with a nervous quiver. "You're giving me chills. Why are you teasing me?"

"I think we need a … sabbatical, Izz. To clear our heads."

"What'd you have in mind, Doctor?"

"A little hike in the woods. A day trip. Whenever I struggle with a problem I can't resolve, a walk through the forest often gives me the answer."

She shrugged. "It couldn't hurt. I'm down."

"Throw some water bottles into that backpack, and some of that deer jerky. Put your boots on and follow me."

"Ooh. Sounds exciting. Where are you taking me?"

"You'll see."

Quinn and Izzy made their way down the mountain and through the logging graveyard.

"Is this where we're going, Quinn? The lumberyard?"

"Not exactly. Let's keep moving."

They stepped over logs and debris and reentered the rainforest, traipsing along a small familiar trail. Chirps and whistles filled the trees; the air was warm, moist, and filled with a stagnant scent of wet vegetation. A trickle in the distance echoed like nature's music.

"Hey. I know this place," she whispered as she kicked off her boots, yanked off her socks, and dipped her toes into the cool, clear water.

"It's my secret, personal space. The place I come to recharge."

"And the waterfall where you washed glyphosate from my hair."

"Yep."

A nervous tingle crept down her spine as her heart palpitated. Her voice quivered. "Why did you bring me here, Quinn? Why *this* place?"

His gentle gaze pierced the deepest, most secret places in her soul. His silence had her heart racing with anticipation—a whimper rose in her throat as she bit her lower lip.

"Izzy. You saved my life and gave me back my youth. I never realized how empty my life was. How badly I want to finish what we started here."

Her heart was pounding out of her chest. She gulped, then sipped a nervous breath. "What did we start here? What are you asking, Quinn?"

"For another chance."

"At what? Washing my front this time?"

His boyish grin brought a twinkle to his eyes. "That too."

"Say it, Quinn. Just … say it already, will you?"

He glanced at the ground, then locked eyes with her—eyes that misted China blue.

"Quinn?"

"Since, uh, I lost my wife. I haven't been with another woman. Didn't think it was possible. Never thought I could find love again."

"Oh my God," she whispered, her pulse throbbing inside her neck.

Quinn stepped towards her and cradled her chin. Without a word, his lips were on hers, moist and gentle. For the first time in her life, she trembled in a man's arms. He slowly unbuttoned her shirt and tossed it over a rock, removing his shirt and laying it across hers. He set his boots neatly on the bank.

She sucked quick breaths as she unbuttoned his trousers and gently slid them over his stocky thighs. He slipped off her shorts and unfastened her bra.

"You've been dying to do that, haven't you?" she hushed.

He bumped his forehead against hers and grinned. "From the moment I met you."

Quinn removed a bar of soap from the backpack, swooped her off her feet and waded into the translucent pool, creating of rush of soft, shimmering ripples. The cool, crystal waterfall drenched her hair, prompting giggles as he set her down on a natural stone bench beneath the waterfall and lathered her scalp.

"You have no idea how good that feels, Quinny. Please don't stop."

He pressed his lips to her ear and whispered, "I don't intend to."

His words created shivers along her spine and neck that invigorated her senses. He rinsed her hair, slid the bar of soap across her shoulders and into the small of her back, and kissed her neck with such a gentle brush of his lips that it moved her to tears.

She faced him. No longer able to restrain the hunger he'd ignited in her soul—an unfamiliar desire she had never known. Wrapping her legs around his waist, she clung to his neck and kissed him with a feverish passion. This is what love felt like. An experience she never knew existed.

Its tenderness touched the most secret places in her heart, and in that moment, bound her spirit to his.

"You're definitely not a 20-minute man, Quinny. I underestimated you. I'm literally out of breath."

Quinn spread a blanket on the shore and fed her bits of passion fruit and deer jerky, chased by lakira as they lay in the fragmented sunlight, listening to the primitive songs of nature around them.

"Does my age bother you, Izzy? I understand if it does."

"Here's a little secret tidbit. I'm attracted to older guys. Even as a girl. I don't know why I wasted so much time with silly little boys. And I have to say, buddy, you don't look or act your age."

Quinn chuckled and ran his finger over the contours of her face, and gently kissed her forehead. "I love your humor … most of the time."

"Quinn? I meant to ask you. *Titanic*? Really?"

"You went through my DVD collection, huh? I always loved ships. History."

"Seriously? Not the love story?"

"I'd rather create my own love story in the rainforest with you."

She giggled, unable to hide a shy grin. "Clever. I think you're full of it, but go on. You have my attention."

"*Do* I now?"

"What are we going to do about the village?" she whispered.

"Uh-uh. Right now, at this moment, the village doesn't exist. Only you and me. Like Eden, where time is irrelevant."

"I never realized how poetic and romantic you are. I'm pleasantly surprised. Shocked, actually."

"I never thought I was either until I found my inspiration."

"Oh, really? And what is that?" she playfully replied.

"You already know. I'm gazing into her adoring hazel eyes, and I really don't want this day to end."

She rested her head on his heart and sighed. "Me neither." She pressed her lips to his ear and whispered, "Take me again, Quinn. But slower this time."

"Got it," he chuckled. "A waltz instead of a tango."

As they lay on the edge of the pond wrapped in each other's arms, an enormous splash drenched them.

"What the hell?" she shouted.

Swimming towards them was a stout jaguar that climbed the shore and flopped between them like a grown child in its parents' bed. Izzy and Quinn stared at each other for several seconds, stunned, before bursting into laughter. Quinn rubbed the big cat's ears and hugged her. "Bessie, you're still my best girl."

He glanced at Izzy and grinned. "She gets jealous."

The ground rumbled like a tremor, and the faint roar of engines approached from the distance. Bessie leaped to her feet and scampered into the safety of the rainforest.

"Shit. Get dressed, Izzy."

"What is it? Quinn? What's happening?"

"I think our friends are back."

They crept along the edge of the rainforest and peered through the brush towards the logging field. The poachers returned to claim a new crop of illegal timber. Stripping another piece of the precious rainforest of its dignity, like shearing the mane from the mighty lion. Or plucking the tail feathers of the majestic eagle. It infuriated her. Blood flushed her face, and her neck prickled as she clenched her jaw.

"We need to stop them, Quinn."

"Another day, Izz. We'll pick our battles when the time is right."

They dressed quickly. Quinn led her through the forest and up the mountain through an alternate route to reach the village. As they entered, a ceremony of life was taking place at the edge of the grove for the recently deceased.

She shook her head and sighed. "Oh, no. Not another one. We need to figure this out. It's so sad to watch them suffer. I mean, they're so amazing and so pure in heart, and their spirits are free of greed and hate. Our society breeds so much evil back home with its social media and politics. But here, society breeds love and forgiveness. They all have each other's backs. When life is simple, good exists in the world. I want to save them, Quinn."

"I know you do. I want to save them too. We'll figure it out, Izzy. As much as I hate to admit it, you've inspired me to believe in miracles again."

"Wow, I've never seen this side of you. Didn't realize I was so inspirational."

"Well, don't get too used to it. It's just the lakira talking."

She slapped his shoulder. "You're so annoying. I need more soil samples from the grove. Wanna come with me, Quinny-poo?"

"I have nothing else going on at the moment. Sure. As long as you never call me that again."

She grabbed her test kit and led him into the center of the grove. He leaned against a tree and watched while she gathered samples.

"Dude, stop staring and put these samples in that bag, please."

"I, uh, am just observing…"

She flinched. "Ouch! Oh, my God. Something just stung me."

Quinn pointed towards the sky. "You're working under a large nest of bees, Izz. You should move your operation a few yards away."

She glanced upward. Sheets of honeycomb hung like an amber-gold stack of buttered flapjacks from a branch 50 feet up.

Quinn yanked the stinger. "We need to get some mud on that."

The cool slime numbed the sting as she focused on the worker bees flying in and out of the hive.

"Quinn? Look."

"Look at what?"

"The bees. They're darting in and out of the Piritayá seedpods."

"You're right. They are."

"You said you believed in miracles. We may be witnessing a miracle right now. Do you think the bees are—"

"Extracting nectar from the pods and making honey? I'll be damned. There's only one way to find out. Let me grab a rope and my climbing gear."

"What? No, they're going to swarm you. Like, ninety-five percent of bees in the rainforest are Africanized. Don't be stupid."

"Stupid is as stupid does. I'll round up some protection. I think you're onto something, kid. Let's find out exactly what."

Quinn bound every inch of flesh with cloth, binding his pants and sleeves with duct tape. He slipped on rubber gloves and goggles from the lab and covered his head with a poorly wound turban.

She covered her mouth and snickered as he approached the tree, lugging his climbing gear. "Dude, you look like you stepped out of a Mad Max movie."

He pulled a glass jar from his pocket and nodded. "Wish me luck."

"Good luck. Better you than me. And hey, don't piss them off."

Quinn scaled the tree in less than two minutes. The hive grew angry, buzzing around him in an agitated frenzy. He scraped a sample of honey, capped the jar, and zipped to the ground in seconds.

"Let's get the hell out of here, Izz. I underestimated these little boogers. They're way smarter than me." He swatted at the swarm dive-bombing them as they raced for the safety of the lab.

Izzy cut the duct tape and helped unravel his homemade bee suit. Several bees fell from the bindings to the floor, buzzing, spinning in a death circle before curling into a ball.

"I think they got me three or four times," he said.

He handed her the jar of golden honey and grinned. "Go to work, Malibu. I want good news when you're done, so I didn't have to take those stings for nothing."

She pointed at his nose. "Um, your face is swelling."

NINETEEN

Tarenu

Quinn took a seat next to her at the lab table and glanced at her journal in silence. She crinkled her nose and covered her notes.

"Why are you looking over my shoulder with your professor eyes? I had an instructor in biology class who loved to do that. It bugs me. Go away."

He chuckled. "It's been a few hours. I'm just curious about what you've found. Guess I'm praying for that miracle."

"Well, Doctor, you are not going to believe this. The numbers are off the charts."

His eyes glinted with intrigue. "Really. Explain."

"The bee isn't just processing the nectar. She's upgrading it. Bee-processed yarumase arrives pre-tuned: glycosylated for stability, wrapped in protective sugars, co-activated by microbial messengers, and primed by trace phytochemicals. The honey is a biological amplifier. If Tarenu's tea was the catalyst, the honey is the catalyst on steroids."

Quinn's stare was intense. He processed her revelation in silence.

"Let me see your data. Show me the readings."

She slid him her notes and turned the instruments towards him so he could view the CRT screen display.

"Holy shit. It looks to me like the bee saliva is modifying the yarumase enzyme with its own enzymes. Invertase, glucose oxidase, small salivary peptides…"

"My thoughts exactly. The bee-derived proteins are attaching their sugars to the yarumase enzyme and associated proteins, which—"

Quinn finished her sentence. "Which increases the yarumase's structural stability, protecting it from denaturation. It improves substrate binding by subtly changing its active site environment, enhancing catalytic efficiency."

"Wow, buddy. That's a mouthful. Spoken like a true scientist. Let's just say the bee's saliva makes the yarumase stronger and keeps it from breaking down. It makes it easier for the enzyme to grab the molecules it needs—the miracle you wanted."

Quinn mixed Yarumaya wood dust with tobacco and stuffed it into his pipe. His breath drew in the crackles of a cherry flame, then blew out a puff of bluish smoke. He stirred a teaspoon of the enhanced honey into a cup of hot tea and sipped.

"What are you doing, Quinn? Experimenting on yourself?"

"M-hm."

He took a deep drag and gazed at her. "Yarumase on steroids for sure. I'll test it on myself for the next six days before the festival and use my blood as a baseline."

"You sure you don't want to use Tarenu or one of the elders?"

"No. But I need to talk to Tarenu … make sure we have the Ritual of the Rebirth of the Halfmoon set for September 4th. We have plenty of wood to burn, and we'll replace the tea with a dose of your super honey."

"High five, Quinny. Teamwork, old man."

"Izzy, I could kiss you right now."

She raised her eyebrows. "What's stopping you?"

"Urgency. Let's go speak with Tarenu."

"Quinn? Last chance to create a test group. The honey may affect the villagers differently than it affects you."

"I know I should listen to you, but we don't have time. Let's roll."

Tarenu lay dying. He barely opened his eyes when Izzy and Quinn entered his hut. His lips formed a peaceful grin as he reached for Quinn and whispered, "Tupakaí."

Izzy was mortified when she glanced at the wall to see her ceremonial mask hanging over his bed, staring at her. Mocking her. She shook her head and huffed. "Why is that thing hanging there? And why does he call you, Tupakaí?"

"It's there because it gives him pleasure. Tupakaí means 'white ape'. Don't ask."

Quinn sat next to Tarenu, having an emotional conversation in Kawirénian. Izzy eavesdropped, but they spoke too fast for her to understand more than a word here and a sentence there.

Tarenu pointed to Izzy and spoke in English. "Tell Nahuari my words, Tupakaí. Make her know truth."

"What does he mean, Quinn?"

"Tarenu says he's dying. Mayuma is calling him home as an Ancestor and Guardian of the Yarumaya. He says his time has come and that he's weary of life and ready to escape his clay form."

"Quinn, we can't let him die."

"It's what he wants, Izzy. He says all the elders are ready to give up their spirits as well. Tarenu wants me to interpret for him. He has something he wants to tell you."

"Seriously? What is it?"

"I don't know. He hasn't told me yet." Quinn pointed to a chair carved of Yarumaya wood. "Sit … please."

Tarenu pointed to Izzy's ceremonial mask and chuckled.

"He says your mask has brought him great joy and taught him how to laugh again, like when he was a boy."

Izzy leaned back in her chair, crossed her arms, and rolled her eyes. "Great. So glad I could help."

"Tarenu wants you to know that upon his passing and the passing of the elders, you will take over as Chief Shaman of the village."

"What the heck? No way … I-I can't do that …that's cra-cra."

"He says the youth will look to you for wisdom. You are Nahuari, who has come home to us. You must take your rightful place."

"Quinn. You know I can't do that."

"Oh, and Tarenu says he knows you stole two seedpods. But he understood your need to save your husband. You're forgiven."

"Oh, jeez."

"Here's what's weird, Izz. Tarenu finally admitted, after all these years, that he believes he and the elders have lived over five centuries. My DNA testing indicated they were roughly 130 to 150 years old. Maybe the readings were skewed by the active longevity molecule; I'm not sure. I'm going to take a blood sample and see if I have a different result with the molecule now dormant in his system. That would be insane if true."

Izzy took Tarenu's hand and scooted her chair next to him. "You must live, Tarenu. The tribe needs you. I need you," she said in Kawirénian.

His entire face beamed, and tears leaked from the corners of his eyes. He squeezed her hand and shook his head. "No, daughter, my time is broken. Must transform like butterfly. Will miss big party, if stay." He snickered.

Quinn tapped her shoulder. "Izzy?"

"What?

"He wants you to place your lips on his."

"Wait, what? That's a bit weird, don't you think?"

"He says he needs to pass his dying breath to you so you can inherit his knowledge and wisdom."

"Quinn, I…"

"Please, Izzy."

She pressed her mouth to his as his icy fingers cradled her face. Tarenu exhaled a feeble breath into her mouth, as his body relaxed and his spirit departed in peace.

"Oh, God. No, no, no. Quinn? Do something."

"It's too late, Izzy. He's gone. We need to prepare him for burial in the sacred grove."

Her eyes blurred as she laid her head on Quinn's shoulder. "Isn't there something we could have done for him?"

"It was his time, Izzy. He was tired of living, and his body was racked with pain. He wanted to move on. Keeping him here against his wishes would have been selfish and cruel. We don't have that right."

"It's not fair. We can save them all. They don't have to die."

"Maybe people die to allow the next generation to have their time—their turn to create the world they want to live in. If we're always here, how can they spread their wings and find their own way? How can the younger generations create new ideas and be innovative or find their independence if they're always told what to do? How to think?"

Izzy nodded. "Hm, I can totally relate."

She grasped Tarenu's hand and sobbed. "Thank you for being so kind to me, even though you made fun of my mask."

Izzy's ceremonial mask slid from the wall and fell harmlessly onto the bed. She yelped and held her hand over her breast, almost hearing the snickers emanating from the wood. "Jeez! I'm so glad I could make you laugh, Tarenu. Hilarious." She snatched the mask and tucked it under her arm. "This thing is going in a box."

September 1, 2026

Quinn, Izzy, and the village gathered for the burial ceremonies of Tarenu and the elders who had passed. They buried the elders in the new grove, but Tarenu requested his burial be with the Ancients in the old grove.

Quinn asked the villagers to prepare Yarumaya wood for the bonfire for the upcoming Ritual of the Rebirth of the Halfmoon in a few days. Izzy would administer the doses of enhanced honey in place of the tea and act as Chief Shaman. Young men climbed the Yarumaya and gathered honey for the celebration. The time had arrived to save the youth and preserve the future generations of Kawirén.

Izzy flopped onto the bed in the field lab and exhaled, blowing raspberries. She glanced at Quinn, who was laser-focused on analyzing Tarenu's blood sample.

"Quinn? … Quinn! Take a break."

"I can't."

"Why? What's wrong?"

"I've completed this DNA methylation four times now with the same result."

"And?"

"Tarenu was telling the truth. Without the effects of the longevity molecule, his DNA indicates an age of roughly 475 years old."

"Are you for real? No flipping way."

"Makes you wonder what the potential lifespan actually is. How long can they live in ideal conditions?"

She sat upright on the edge of the bed. "Indefinitely? Immortal even?"

"I'm not discounting anything at this point, Izz. I'm just flabbergasted by the data. All those stories of the Fountain of Youth throughout history, and we've found it in an obscure tree and a rare flower in the Amazon."

"What about the children, Quinn? The ones under 13 who have never drunk the tea."

"They're the correct biological age. They carry the longevity molecule in their fat cells and liver, but it isn't activated until they're exposed to the yarumase enzyme through the tea or the honey."

"Shouldn't we have the children eat the honey at the festival to activate the molecule?"

"I'd caution going against their tradition. It's been my experience that traditions derive from history or events. There's usually a good reason behind it."

"Yeah, but the honey doesn't contain any opioids like the tea. Maybe that was the reason."

"True. But I've never run a control group of children for the yarumase enzyme. I don't know what effect it would have on a child under 13. Tarenu never allowed it, and I won't risk it."

"But we *did* test it on a child."

"That child died, Izzy. We never got the chance to give him another dose. It's inconclusive, and I wasn't able to perform an autopsy."

Quinn snatched a hand axe from his toolbox and polished the blade across his khakis.

"Whoa. What are you going to do with that thing?"

"I'm gonna help chop wood for the fire, while you work on preparing the honey. And hey, don't forget your little shaman costume for the ceremony."

"Ugh, whatever. I'm creating new wardrobe rules for all females."

"Hey, don't mess with their traditions. They don't have a Western view of the world with all its restrictions. They're a society free of inhibitions."

She tossed him his jug of lakira. "Have another drink with your bros, dude. Leave the women's issues to the women."

TWENTY

Restoration and a Dagger

September 4th, 2026

Smoke billowed. A powerful citrusy scent filled the air. Izzy stood at the center of the Circle, clutching a smooth wooden spoon in her right hand, peering through the eyes of her ceremonial mask at the crowd as it gathered for the ritual. A honey pot sat to her left, filled with sweet golden super honey. Drums rumbled in a powerful rhythm, vibrating up through her sandals and stirring the butterflies in her stomach.

Quinn planted himself in a seat in front of her, spoke to the villagers, and translated for Izzy. He honored Tarenu and all the elders who transitioned to the Great Yarumaya Grove in the heavens. He explained that the time had arrived for the youth to assume their place in the village.

"A new tradition has begun," he said. "Sacred honey will replace the Piritayá tea, and Nahuari will administer the sacrament."

The villagers whistled and cheered as they lined up to receive the honey amid a heavy cloud of wood smoke. As the chants grew stronger, Izzy heard the whispers of the Ancestors. Or was she fantasizing? Could the village finally be saved and fulfill the unlikely prophecy of Nahuari's return? Her spirit was elated as she dribbled amber honey onto the tongues of these amazing people who adopted her as family. How could she ever return home to a concrete world filled with iPad screens and social media propaganda? Life here was simple. Easy. Every soul was precious, and the love and respect these people had for one another were divine and unconditional. They're bonded in ways the outside world could never understand.

She loved and missed her parents, but perhaps she no longer belonged in that world. This world opened its arms to her in a way that humbled her and awakened her spirit in the deepest of places. She was small in the scheme of the universe, but her purpose was immense.

And then there was Quinn. A man she never dreamed she'd find. One who pushed her to the limits of her sanity, but caught her in his arms in her weakest moments. Love isn't about games like the ones Teddy played. That relationship seemed so superficial now. Meaningless. The rainforest with Quinn by her side was her home, and these were her people.

After the ceremony, they ate, drank, danced, and shared stories. The teens played a game where they competed to see who could walk the farthest across a three-inch-thick, twelve-foot-long pole set on two four-foot-high stones without falling. Three of the boys made it to nine feet before bailing. Only one boy made it all the way across, albeit shakily.

Izzy couldn't resist. She climbed the stone and glanced at the skeptical teenage boys laughing and jeering at her. Taking two steps, she feigned losing her balance before grinning. She raised one foot and pointed her toe in front of her. The teens grew quiet. She turned and walked backwards across the pole to the other side, then stepped forward, performing an aerial front walkover before returning to the start. The teens gasped as Izzy leaped off the stone and bowed. She glanced at Quinn and grimaced, aggravating her knee again.

The stunned boys stood with mouths agape and the whites of their eyes glaring. The girls cheered and pointed at the boys, taunting them as they surrounded Izzy and chanted her name.

Quinn sat inside the Circle, sipping lakira and chuckling. He shouted something in Kawirénian, causing the crowd to roar with laughter.

"What did you say, Quinn?"

"I told them you're a showoff."

Izzy plopped into his lap and whispered into his ear, "Only for you."

"No, I think what you did there to humiliate those boys was all for you."

She giggled. "I was performing."

He raised an eyebrow. "Uh-huh."

"Whatever." She kissed his cheek and smiled. "We did it, Quinn. I honestly believe we did it. We saved them, didn't we?"

"Let's not get ahead of ourselves, Izz. We'll monitor them and run test groups to ensure our methods are solid."

"Then what?"

"What do you mean?"

"Then what happens?"

"They, uh, all live happily *forever*."

"That's not what I mean."

"Well, what *do* you mean, Izzy? Spit it out. I'm not a mind reader."

"Us? What happens to us?"

He swigged a gulp of lakira and grinned. "That is yet to be determined. Do you want to live forever?"

She punched his shoulder. "Be serious. What's going on here? Between you and me, I mean?"

"Izz, for once in your life, can you let your hair down, relax, and live in the moment?"

He handed her the gourd of lakira. "Take it."

She tightened her lips, snatched from his grasp, and chugged.

"That's my girl. Now, isn't that better?"

"Am I your girl?"

"Izz, what exactly do you want … a ring?"

"No. I want an answer to my question."

"Yes, you're my girl. But I don't know what happens or where it goes from here. Maybe you'll get tired of me. Tired of the rainforest, and go back home. Maybe you marry some lucky guy who buys you a Mercedes and a mansion on the West Coast, and you have six kids and teach botany at the university."

"I don't want that, Quinn. I thought I did once, but not anymore."

"Then what *do* you want? To live here where there's no internet, no cars, no cafés or restaurants, no banks, no salons to fix your hair or paint your nails?"

"I want to live here with you and the Kawirén. Continue our studies. Fight the wood poachers. The animal poachers. Save the rainforest before it's too late. Can't you see how much my life has changed?"

He tightened his jaw and focused his stare beyond her, towards the darkness. "Yes, I see you. But there are things about my life I can't change, Izzy. And it isn't fair to you. You have a mother and a father who love you, and I'm sure they miss you. You have a life in California. Not here. I can't take that away from you."

"You're not taking anything away from me. I'm a big girl and can make my own decisions. So, what's the problem, Quinn?"

"I don't know if I can give you what you need … I'm not sure if I can let go of the past. I want to be fair to you…"

"You mean Brey? Your wife? Quinn, have you ever considered that she might want you to move on with your life? Maybe instead of masking your pain in lakira and hiding your guilt in the middle of the rainforest, it's time you accepted the fact that you can't change the past. You can only plan for the future while you live in the present."

"I can't live with the guilt, Izz. It eats me up inside. I failed her. It was my fault. I'll fail you, too. I can't be trusted. Not when it comes to the ones I love." He swigged lakira. "You wouldn't understand."

He pinched the bridge of his nose and set the empty gourd on the ground next to him.

"What don't I understand? Haven't you punished yourself enough? Drowning in that gourd and your own tears of self-pity? When is it enough, Quinn? When will you make peace with the devil and choose to live your life again? Because I'm here waiting for you. Out here in the cool darkness of the night, while you bash your wings like a moth to a flame. Come find me, Quinn. Close the door and let Brey find peace from your self-inflicted torment. Do you think she wants that? For you to sacrifice yourself day after day…"

Quinn rose and stumbled away into the darkness.

"Where are you going? Come back. Quinn?"

She followed, but he disappeared into the trees and the darkness.

September 5, 2026

The chitter of insects, the chirps of birds, and the monkeys crashing through the treetops roused her from a restless night. The glow of amber light warmed the lab. She slept alone all night, tossing and turning from the ache in her heart and the cramps in her calves.

Izzy sipped the last of the hot tea she brought from home and sat at the lab table studying Quinn's notes on the feasibility of creating an immortal vaccine using the resin and super honey.

If the activated longevity molecule could be injected directly into the bloodstream, the effects might be compounded and assimilated quicker than with the traditional methods used during the rituals. A viable vaccine would be worth trillions of dollars and change the world and life as we know it forever. It is imperative that this knowledge remain hidden and never fall into the hands of big corporations. The Kawirén and their secrets must be protected at all costs. The reverse is also true and must never see the light of day.

The last sentence puzzled her. What did he mean by "The reverse?" Izzy closed the journal, wandered to the center of the village, and asked if anyone had seen Quinn this morning, speaking in broken Kawirénian. She got the same answer every time. "No."

She strolled through the grove of Yarumaya trees and walked the perimeter of the village. No Quinn.

"Quinn? Quinn, are you out here? Look, I'm sorry about last night. I-I shouldn't have pushed you into a corner. Hello? Please answer me."

Shouts and shrieks echoed through the trees. Izzy bolted through the grove back to the village, where armed mercenaries pointed automatic rifles at the villagers and ordered them to put their weapons down.

Her pulse raced as the mercenaries pushed a battered Quinn towards the front of the line and forced him to his knees.

"We will kill the good doctor here unless you drop your weapons. Comprende?"

Izzy marched toward them, frantically waving, flaming ire rising in her throat.

"They don't understand what you're saying, morons!"

"Izzy, no," Quinn pleaded.

"And who is this little wildcat, Dr. Quinn?"

A tall, slender man dressed in fatigues and combat boots emerged from the group of armed men. His dark blonde hair was combed straight back, sheened with oil, and his bright green eyes pierced hers with defiance. He wore diamond studs in his earlobes and a heavy gold chain bracelet.

"She's a student. My intern. She knows nothing. Leave her be."

"What do you psychopaths want? How'd you find this village?" she shrieked.

"I want the good doctor's notes. The formula that allows this tribe to live so long, and the other formula. Hand them over and I'll release Dr. Quinn, and we'll be on our way."

"You already stole his notes when you decimated the Yarumaya grove, you bastard."

"Those notes were inconclusive. It seems you've been busy with a breakthrough in your research. I want *those* notes. Do hand them over, please. I won't ask twice."

Izzy heaved a breath and glared. "No."

Her disgust of these criminals and their flagrant disregard for the village and the rainforest made her skin burn.

The man nodded to one of his henchmen. The henchman stepped forward and jammed the butt of his rifle into Quinn's neck, knocking him to the ground face-first.

"Stop it!"

"That is entirely up to you, little wildcat."

"Alright. Let him go, and I'll give you what you ask."

Arrows whistled through the air and thumped into the bodies of their targets, spattering blood and dropping several mercenaries. The rapid fire of AK-47s rang out in response, drawing screams from the villagers and leaving several warriors squirming on the ground or dead.

The mercenaries scattered like rats and took cover behind the brush, while Kawirén warriors scaled the trees like ants, disappearing into the branches, volleying waves of arrows toward the invaders.

Izzy helped Quinn to his feet. "Run, Quinn! We have to run!"

They raced in the opposite direction of the battle, gathering the children and their mothers, and aiding their escape. Quinn paused.

"Go with them, Izz. I'll be right back."

"What? No! Where are you going?"

"To grab my notes. Our research. We can't let them steal it a second time. Run, Izzy. I'm right behind you."

The crackling pops of rifle fire and the pings of bullets continued, while arrows swished from the treetops in return. Izzy guided the group to the edge of a nearby river. Speaking in broken Kawirénian, she directed them to follow the river to safety. She then split from them and raced back to the village. Her heart was in her throat, and her thoughts screamed.

The satellite phone, she thought. If she could reach the phone, she could call Congressman Ortega for help. As the battle raged on, she crawled to the rear window of the lab and peered inside. Quinn's voice was deep and angry. He was arguing with someone.

"Call off your dogs, Bragg! You have no business being here. Our contract is null and void. I didn't cash your damn check, so you have no claims on my research and no right to hurt these people."

"How many more times do we need to go over this, Dr. Quinn? I own all rights to all discoveries made through your research. Now turn over your journals and all your samples. You'll be well compensated, I assure you."

"I don't want your damn money. I want you to stop this assault on these people. They're innocent."

"They're collateral damage, Quinn. Don't be such a bleeding heart. I paid you in full for the bioweapon. Now deliver it."

"All you're after is a billion-dollar bank account."

"Well, that too. But hey, you'll be a rich man yourself. And you'll receive all the credit."

"Go to hell."

Izzy crept around the outside of the lab and slipped inside the front door.

"Ah, the wildcat returns. Maybe you should convince your mentor to—"

"Shut up, Bragg," he snapped.

"Why? Oh, wait. She doesn't know."

"What? What don't I know? Quinn?"

"Should you tell her or should I?"

"Don't listen to him, Izzy."

Izzy glanced at Quinn, glanced towards the satellite phone, and back towards Quinn. She kept repeating her glances until his expression changed. She nodded slightly and glanced at the phone again.

Quinn bull-rushed Bragg and shoved him against the wall. "Get the hell out of this village, you son of a bitch." Quinn grabbed Bragg by the shoulders and twisted his body away from Izzy, allowing her to snatch the phone unnoticed as she dashed out the door.

A fistfight ensued behind her as she disappeared into the brush. On her third attempt to phone Julio, he finally answered.

"Hija! What a pleasant surprise."

"Julio, we need your help. A man named Ian Bragg is here in the village with soldiers. They're murdering the villagers and trying to steal our research."

"Whoa, whoa, slow down, Isabella. When did this happen?"

"Just … um, like thirty minutes ago. They're still shooting. The uh villagers are fighting back, but they don't have the weapons to match the soldiers. What do we do? Please help us."

"Okay, calm down. Put Bragg on the phone."

"What? Why?"

"So, I can speak with him."

"What good is that going to do?"

"Just trust me, and allow me to speak with him."

Izzy raced to the lab and kicked open the door.

"Stop! Stop fighting. Please!"

The two men paused, both sucking air and bleeding at the mouth. Quinn raised his eyebrows and shrugged, dumbfounded that she had returned.

"Mr. Bragg. This phone call is for you."

Bragg's eyes darted from Quinn to Izzy and back to Quinn. "What is she up to, Quinn? What kind of nonsense is this?"

"I have Congressman Julio Ortega on the phone. He wants to talk to you. He's probably going to send the Army to kick your ass, so you might want to take this call."

Bragg reached for the phone and chuckled. "Julio? Yes. We're here now. No, Dr. Quinn hasn't surrendered his research, but we're discussing it."

"Wait. You two know each other? What the hell is happening here?"

Bragg waved an impatient hand towards Izzy. "Sh. We're trying to have a conversation."

"What was I supposed to do, Congressman? They were shooting arrows at us." Bragg glanced out the window. "They're still shooting arrows."

Izzy swiped the phone from Bragg's clutch and marched outside. "What the hell is going on here, Julio? Are you in on this?"

"Now, calm down, Isabella. We only want the research. We don't wish to harm anyone. Please cooperate with Mr. Bragg—"

"You asshole! You sold me out? All this time, you pretended to support me, waiting for the chance to fuck me over? Innocent people are dying, you idiot!"

"I always win, Isabella. Even when I lose, I win."

"Are you kidding me? You're doing this because I kicked your ass at golf?"

He snickered. "Of course not, Hija. This has nothing to do with golf. This is the real world, and Dr. Quinn's research is revolutionary. You stand to gain tremendously, Isabella. The discovery of a new species of tree, credited with the greatest medical discovery in history. You'll be wealthy beyond your wildest imagination. Work with us. Convince Dr. Quinn to give up his research, and we'll make both of you full partners."

"You're a liar and a disgusting excuse for a human being."

"Isabella, you need to consider—"

CLICK.

"Call off your men, Bragg, and we'll talk," she conceded.

"Call off yours first."

Quinn stepped outside and hollered into the trees in Kawirénian, "Cease your attack, noble warriors. Allow us to discuss a peaceful solution. Stay ready in case the talks do not go well."

The arrows ceased. Bragg exited the lab and whistled. "Hold your fire. Dr. Quinn and I are going to discuss terms. Stand by."

The Kawirén warriors retreated from the trees, recovering their dead and wounded, and taking cover in the forest.

The mercenaries emerged from the brush cautiously, keeping their distance and clutching their weapons. Several of the men tended to their wounds, while others zipped body bags around their deceased compadres. A few others erected tents, canopies, and tables equipped with gas burners for cooking, organizing a small camp just outside the village.

Three tree stumps circled a roaring fire.

"All of this was unnecessary, Bragg. You've murdered innocent people and cost the lives of your own men."

"What's done is done, Doctor. We need to move past it and discuss our terms for the delivery of your biotechnology."

"There are no terms to discuss. I'm not turning over my research to you or anyone. So, pack your shit and get the hell out of our village."

"That isn't going to happen, Quinn. We're not leaving here without your research—my research. I want your documentation, your samples, and I want you and your pretty little sidekick here to accompany me back to the States. We'll provide the most sophisticated labs and equipment available, along with a competent staff to assist you."

"That's not happening. You can't reproduce the science behind this phenomenon in a lab in the States. It's unique to the Amazon. You're wasting your time and mine."

"Which of your technologies are we referring to? I will write you a check for any amount you like. Name your price and it's yours, my friend."

"We're not friends, and there is no price I'd ever accept."

Bragg turned toward Izzy. "How about you, wildcat? I'll offer you the same deal. Come back to the States with me and head up my department of research at the largest pharmaceutical company in the world. You can name your salary."

Izzy chuckled. "You can forget it, asshole. I'd never work for a scumbag like you, especially after what you've done here today."

"Scumbag, hm? Disappointing."

"Take your men and leave, Bragg. There's nothing here for you," Quinn demanded.

"My men and I are going to stay the night. In the morning, more men and equipment will arrive to disassemble your lab and move it to my offices in New York, where it belongs."

"What do you mean, 'more men'?" Izzy asked.

"Your friend, Julio, will send a crew to assist in the extraction and relocation of your research lab." He shrugged and smirked. "Didn't he tell you?"

Bragg rose, straightened his cap, and hollered towards his men.

"Gonzales! You and Spencer escort the Doctor and his girlfriend to one of our tents. Ensure they're comfortable and that they stay put."

"You're holding us hostage? That's illegal, you know?" Quinn said.

"No laws in the jungle, Quinn. It's just a precaution until our guys arrive tomorrow. Then you're free to go."

One of Bragg's men pointed his weapon at Quinn and Izzy, directing them to one of the tents in their camp, then took a seat outside the tent flap.

Izzy plopped next to Quinn on the floor.

"What do we do now?" she whispered.

"We have a couple of options. We destroy our samples and erase all our data, and do not allow them to take anything. Or we escape into the rainforest with everything and live to see another day."

"What do you mean, 'live', Quinn?"

He narrowed his eyes and squeezed her hand. "Izz. They're going to kill us once they have what they're after. Bragg has no intention of letting us go."

"Are you joking right now? Oh, my God. This can't be real. We have to escape then."

"They'll eliminate the villagers, too. We have to save them, Izzy."

"How? I mean, this is crazy. I-I need to get my satellite phone to call my dad."

"We're on our own. We have to figure this out ourselves. I care about you, Izz."

"No, no. Don't you do that. We're not saying our goodbyes, Quinn. We're smarter than they are. We'll figure something out. Just … just think of something. Come on, help me think."

Quinn shouted through the front of the tent. "Hey! We're sweating our asses off in here. We need water."

Two men dragged Quinn's rain barrel next to the tent.

"There, asshole. Drink up. Then shut your mouth."

Quinn and Izzy stepped out of the tent and guzzled several cups of water. She cupped her hands and washed the sting from her eyes.

Hours passed slowly. Rumbles in the heavens warned of an approaching storm.

"Quinn? What was Bragg talking about back there? The other biotechnology. What did he mean?"

"Nothing. Just something I was working on before you arrived."

"Okay, that's evasive and very sketch. What's going on?"

"Izz, we'll talk about it later. It's not important. We need to figure out how we're getting out of here first."

Izzy poked her head out of the tent and nudged the guard. "Hey. Hey dude. I have to pee."

He rolled his eyes and huffed. "Pee behind the tent."

"Gross. I'm not doing that. Let me do my business in the woods."

The man rolled his eyes and shook his head. "Come on. Make it quick. And no screwing around."

Izzy slipped out of the tent and scurried through the brush into the forest, trailed by the guard.

"Do your business and keep talking so I know you're there."

"Sure thing, buddy."

Izzy scanned the forest for a familiar plant common in the village. She noticed a robust bush three feet away—a green bush with white trumpet-shaped flowers hanging downward.

"There you are," she whispered. "Brugmansia suaveolens. Angel's trumpet. Thank you, Mayuma."

She tore a piece of her shirt to snatch a handful of the flowers and stuff them into her sock, making sure they didn't touch her skin.

"I'm finished. Coming…"

Izzy heaved a breath, traipsed up the hill, and headed back to the tent, closely followed by the guard.

As the afternoon faded into early evening, heavy rains pounded the village. The mercenaries huddled beneath a heavy canopy while a man in an apron lit a gas stove and dumped cans of beef stew into a pot.

Izzy nudged Quinn. "Ask them if we can have some stew."

"You hungry, Izzy?"

He tapped on the guard's shoulder. "Hey, man. How about a bowl of stew for the girl, huh?"

The guard nodded and pointed towards the stove. "One of you can go."

Izzy grabbed Quinn's sleeve and whispered. "Quinn, after you fill my bowl, drop this in the stew." She handed him shredded bits of the trumpet flowers.

"What is this? What are you up to? Is this what I think it is?"

"Trust me."

Quinn guffawed and shook his head. "You scare me, Izzy. I hope I never find myself on your bad side."

Quinn returned with a large bowl of stew and two hard rolls.

"Eat up, kid. Then explain your secret ingredient to me."

"Shhh. Keep your voice down."

They took turns passing the bowl between them and scarfed the rolls.

"Mm, this is so good," she mumbled.

"So, what did we add to the stew?"

"Angel's trumpet," she whispered.

"Holy shit. You didn't."

"We did."

"Oh, man, this is going to get interesting. That was a heavy dose, Izz. In less than an hour, they'll be having tea with Alice and the Mad Hatter. When that happens, we need to get the hell out of here as fast as we can."

"That's the plan, Quinny. They'll be tripp'n so bad they won't know who's who or where they are. Once they fall down the rabbit hole, we're gone."

TWENTY-ONE

Go Ask Alice

Forty-five Minutes Later

Inhuman shrieks and wails echoed through the rainforest. Men groaned like animals. Others shouted frantic orders. Chaos had erupted in the camp. Izzy poked her head outside the tent. The guard lay face down in the mud, writhing and foaming at the mouth. Gunshots rang out as the mercenaries turned on one another. Bullets ripped through the tent and whizzed over their heads.

"Move, Izz! Stay low."

They escaped and scampered across the village into the lab. A half-naked man covered in blood rushed towards them, his eyes wild and rabid. Quinn snatched a stick from the ground and bashed his head like a softball.

Inside, another man lay in a pool of blood. Quinn grabbed the AK-47 lying next to him and checked the magazine. He glanced towards Izzy and nodded.

"It's loaded. Grab the laptop and all the drives. I'll get the samples and my journals."

"What about the villagers, Quinn?"

"They've already fled the village. We have to take care of ourselves now."

He tossed her a backpack. "Put everything inside."

"Wait," she said. "Let me grab the satellite phone and the GPS tracker."

"Izz, they'll track us. Leave the GPS."

"No, I have an idea."

He scoffed. "Of course you do. This should be interesting."

Izzy fastened the GPS tracker to a rotted branch and tossed it in the river. The branch caught a swift current and traveled in the opposite direction.

"I see what you did there, Malibu." He pointed to his temple and grinned. "Clever girl."

They moved along the river, then entered the densest part of the rainforest.

"Where are we going?" she asked.

"We're going to take the long way around the mountain back to the tree shelter. We can hide out for a day or so until things die down, or until Bragg and his men kill each other."

"What about the congressman's men? Bragg said they'd be here tomorrow. How long do we hide?"

"We should stay mobile for the next couple of days, then make our way back to base camp and get Chucho on the horn to pick us up."

"I should call my dad for help."

"I wouldn't."

"Why not?"

"They probably tapped his phone. It's been my experience that politicians, billionaires, and government operatives are the most dangerous people in the world. They won't hesitate to eliminate anyone who gets in the way of a diamond mine like the one we possess."

"Dad has a lot of contacts in the government, Quinn."

"Yeah, I'm sure he does. But does he know whom to trust? Because trusting your congressman buddy didn't exactly work out."

"Ugh. I hate when you're right."

They looped their way around the mountain and crossed the lumber graveyard, staying hidden in the brush. Hours later, they arrived at the tree shelter. Her skin glistened in the cool spray of rain as the storm intensified. Izzy scrambled up the hemp ladder and wrapped herself in a blanket, followed by Quinn.

"Let me see your phone."

She slipped it from a side pocket in her backpack and tossed it to him.

"We have one bar, Izz."

"Oh, crap. I should have turned it off."

"Yeah, probably, we'll save this last bar for Chucho. Let's spend the night here and leave at dawn."

He tossed her a stick of deer jerky and a ripe plantain, then squatted next to her and lit his pipe.

"Oh, I see you had time to salvage your precious pipe."

"Some things can't be sacrificed, kid." He pointed at her food. "Eat your dinner. Do you need me to explain what it is?"

She rolled her eyes. "No … I figured it out."

Izzy snagged the pipe from his mouth, took a drag, coughed, and handed it back to him. "Ew, that's disgusting."

"What's the matter, Izz? Lose your watermelon-flavored vape?"

"Yes, as a matter of fact. I thought maybe a puff of your pipe might satisfy my … impulse … and calm me down."

He chuckled. "Sorry to disappoint."

"Quinn? What are we going to do when we reach civilization?"

"We're going to send you home."

"Send *me* home? What about you?"

"I'm going to hide our research deep in the jungle where no one will ever find it."

"I can't leave you here alone. What about the Kawirén? We have to help them," she insisted as she stretched her legs and massaged her knee.

"I'll move what's left of the tribe to somewhere so remote no one will ever discover them again."

"What about the Yarumaya?"

"Izzy, the government will confiscate the new grove when the feds arrive tomorrow. They'll probably set up their own lab and attempt to duplicate our work. The good news is they'll never figure it out."

"How can you be so sure? All the elements that activate the longevity molecule are present in the young grove."

"Not after I remove the Piritayá seedpods and the bees. They'll have nothing."

"And how do you plan on doing that?"

"In the dark of the night. The same way you stole Tarenu's seedpods."

"Seriously, dude? How are you going to climb your old butt up those trees and remove the hive by yourself?"

"A little thing called *teamwork*, Izzy. I might not be good at climbing trees, but the Kawirén warriors are experts. Did you see how fast they scaled those trees when they attacked the mercenaries? Their agility is inhuman."

He rubbed his beard and narrowed his eyes. "I just have to figure out where they went."

"Quinn, I'm not getting on a plane and going home. I can't leave you…"

He scooted across the floor and wrapped his arms around her.

"I need you to go home and speak to your dad in person, Izz. We need help, and we need to expose your corrupt congressman for who he is and shut him down. *That's* your job now. Mine is to go back and help save our village."

"What does that mean, Quinn? What are you saying?"

"I'm saying we live in two different worlds. The only way we can save our tribe is for us to return to those worlds—me to the rainforest and you to the States.

"What? But what if I never see you again? I can't…"

"You can, Izz. You must. We'll find each other again someday, I promise."

"No … No, we won't. That's an empty promise you can't keep. Without the resin, you'll age again."

"I still have enough samples to keep me going for a while. I'll be alright. Shut them down, Izzy. If you don't, the Kawirén will fade into history forever, as if they never existed. Only you can do this. No one else. I trust you with my life, and I believe in you. So do the Kawirén people. Somehow, you've won their hearts. I still haven't figured out how or why, but they seem to like you."

"Oh, my God. You're such a dick." She chuckled.

She punched his arm and then snuggled into his hug and closed her eyes.

"I'm terrified, Quinn. I don't think I can stop them. Who's going to listen to *me*?"

"I've seen you do things I never thought possible, Izz. You're too goddamn stubborn and naïve to fail. I have no doubt you'll figure it out. That trust thing I'm always preaching? That includes trusting yourself."

"Quinn?"

"Uh-huh?"

"If this is our last night together … then… can we, you know…"

"Yeah."

TWENTY-TWO

A Change of Plans

September 6, 2026

They sat on the bank of the river, a half-mile south of the base camp dock, waiting for Chucho's boat to arrive. Her looming goodbye was stuck at the base of her throat. One second, she was giggling at his sarcastic humor; the next, she was tearing up from the tenderness in his voice. What if this is the last time they'll look into each other's eyes? Their last conversation. Last kiss. The hum of a boat engine in the distance turned her stomach. This goodbye was going to be the worst of all time.

Quinn rose and shielded his eyes as he gazed at the oncoming boat, a half-mile up the river. He kept his eyes fixed on the craft while extending his hand towards Izzy and wriggling his fingers.

"Hand me the binoculars, Izz."

She rifled through Quinn's backpack and slapped the binoculars into his palm. He kneeled next to her and adjusted the focus.

"Shit!"

Quinn stuffed the binoculars into his backpack, slung it around his shoulder, and reached for her hand.

"We need to move."

"Oh, my God. Why?"

"Never mind. Run!"

They crashed into the brush and dashed through the trees, following a narrow creek, until they reached a 150-foot Brazil nut tree—four orange ropes equipped with harnesses dangled from its branches.

"Strap in and climb. Quickly."

"What's going on? Tell me."

"I think your congressman buddy arrived. They've jacked Chucho's boat. Looks like they're forcing him to help track us."

Her biceps and abs burned as she reached the top of the tree and landed on the canopy bridge. She heaved a breath, unbuckled, and stepped onto the landing supported by thick ropes and wooden slats. Quinn yanked on his climbing rope, coiling it until it sat in a pile at the bridge entrance.

"Oh, wow. This is so cool."

"This isn't a tour, Izzy. Help me pull these other ropes up."

Shouts echoed. "They went this way!"

"They have trackers. Follow me. Move!"

Quinn stopped halfway across the bridge. "Gimme the satellite phone."

"Why? You gonna call in a lifeline?"

"I think they're tracking us with it. Maybe a backup to the GPS device they gave you. We can't risk it."

Quinn hurled the phone over the side of the bridge, splashing into the creek below. He led her across two more canopy bridges and down a homemade ladder nailed into the side of a 200-foot kapok tree.

"Where are we going, Quinn? Back to the treehouse?"

"No. Chucho knows most of my hideouts. All but one."

"Why would Chucho help them? I thought you were friends."

"Money."

The foliage was dense. Quinn grabbed branches and hacked them with his machete, slicing a path as they worked their way through the brush.

"Where are you taking us?" she asked.

"To some ruins I found nearly a year back. I believe an ancient culture flourished in the Amazon centuries ago. I've seen the evidence myself. And the way all these rivers and creeks run, the various food trees like the Brazil nut, camu camu, cocoa, acai … a manmade civilization once thrived here. I'm sure of it."

"What do you think happened to the people?"

"My guess? Spanish explorers wiped them out. Probably brought all kinds of diseases. Smallpox being the worst. The natives wouldn't have had any kind of immunity."

"That's awful."

The dense canopy cast an ominous shadow over them as they continued to carve a path deep into a remote area of the forest. Monkeys chittered and crashed through the trees, watching their every move. Birds chirped and whistled nonstop.

"Quinn, there's a pack of mosquitoes following us. It's like a major black cloud of tiny vampires."

"See that nest over there? Azteca ants. Lay your hand on the nest."

"Are you crazy?"

"No, watch and learn."

Quinn allowed dozens of Azteca ants to crawl over his hand, then rubbed his hands together.

"The oil in the ants makes a damn good insect repellent. Rub it all over."

She hesitated and then laid a gentle hand on the nest. "Jeez, this is crazy. They smell like a Christmas tree."

"That'll keep the bugs away. Now, if we can just keep the feds away.

They stepped into an open area bathed in golden sunlight. The forest was tranquil. Almost spiritual. Quinn tugged on vines and small branches until the entrance to an ancient structure revealed itself. A whoosh of cool, stagnant air blew past her.

"Oh, my God." She ran her hand over the cool stones stacked upon each other.

"This looks like something out of Indiana Jones."

"They won't find us here. We'll stay the night and circle back to the village tomorrow. We need to collect the Piritayá seedpods and the beehives before they discover them. First, we'll have to find our tribe."

"What if we don't find them?"

"Then we climb the Yarumaya and do it ourselves."

Quinn whacked two one-inch branches from the ground and pulled some fishing line from his backpack. He attached the line, a steel leader, and a hook to both branches, handing her one and grinning.

"We're going fishing?" she asked with a crooked smile.

"You wanna eat, don't you?"

"Well, ya, but I've never fished."

"A lot of firsts for you in the Amazon, Malibu. It isn't hard. There's a small lake nearby."

"What kind of fish? Can you catch me a big, fat, juicy salmon?"

"In your dreams. We're fish'n for piranha. Well, *you're* fish'n for piranha. Your first fishing lesson."

"Oh, jeez. Don't they have, like, giant shark teeth? I don't wanna lose a finger."

"Sort of. Follow me. You won't lose a finger. A leg, maybe."

She sat on a log near the water while Quinn caught several bait fish near the shore. He set the bait for both lines and handed one to Izzy.

"Piranhas like meat, so keep your toes out of the water. Pay attention. Toss your line like this and count to ten."

"Eek. Are you sure about this?"

The second her bait hit the water, she flinched from a splash and shrieked. The pole jerked from her hand and flew into the lake. She nibbled on the side of her lower lip and slowly glanced at him.

Quinn stared at her, stunned, his mouth half open. He slowly shook his head and rolled his eyes.

"What are you doing, Izzy? Hang on to your pole."

"I'm sorry. I wasn't expecting that."

"You hung a bloody fish on a hook over a piranha-infested lake … and you weren't expecting that?"

"I said I'm sorry. I've never fished before. Jeez. Give me a break."

"Fishing hooks are priceless out here. You just lost one."

"Okay, you know what? I'll jump into the lake and get it back for you. Will that make you happy?"

"That's a start." He pointed at the pole floating ten feet off the edge of the water.

"You're serious? You want me to go in there, risk my life to get your precious fishhook? Walk out of the water on bony feet?"

"Yep."

"Oh my God, you're a creep."

"Your dinner is at the other end of that line. Just step into the water, grab your pole, and step out."

"Okay. I can't believe you right now. Those things will eat my legs."

"They won't eat your legs. Just grab your pole. Stop being such a baby."

"I'm not a baby. Why don't you crawl your butt in there and get it for me?" She widened her eyes and taunted him. "What? You're too scared? Afraid you're going to scream like a little girl and embarrass yourself?"

He chuckled and waded into the lake, snatching her pole from the water and handing it to her.

"Ooh. Now, who's the showoff?" She glared at him and grabbed the pole from his grasp. The pole jerked again. She screamed.

"Pull it in, kid. What the hell are you waiting for?"

"I'm trying, jeez." She yanked a three-inch piranha into the air, dangling it over the water as it flipped and squirmed on the hook.

Quinn roared with laughter. "Stop screaming and pull it in. You got one!"

"Oh, my God … oh my God. What do I do?"

The water beneath Izzy's piranha exploded like a huge vacuum. An enormous, elongated head snatched her fish and crashed into the lake. Izzy screeched and threw her pole in the air, stumbled backwards, and butt-planted on the muddy shore.

Quinn grabbed a 3-foot branch and rushed into the water, stabbing the fish in the gills, fighting furiously to overpower it.

"Quinn! Oh my God, what are you doing? That thing's going to eat you!"

Water roiled as the battle raged on.

"Izz! Gimme a hand!"

"What? No way, dude. Not happening! That was *your* dumbass decision."

An exhausted and battered Quinn dragged a massive olive-green six-foot-long fish with a torpedo-like body, flat head, and upturned mouth to the shore and collapsed.

"What were you thinking, Quinn? I mean, what the hell was that? A freaking Steve Irwin crocodile hunter moment? Are you out of your mind?"

A weary and fully drenched Quinn raised his head and glared at her, sucking deep breaths, and hugging the ground.

"It's an arapaima, Malibu … the best fish you'll ever eat. You're welcome."

"Oh, wow. Better than salmon?"

"Better than a T-bone steak. Help me up."

Quinn spent the next thirty minutes gutting, cleaning, and preparing arapaima steaks for dinner. Izzy gasped when he threw the scraps into the water, watching it boil with piranhas.

"Oh my God, that gives me the heebie-jeebies. That could have been my legs. What the heck possessed you to jump in the water after that fish?"

He slid his arm into the straps of his backpack, grabbed the steaks, and grinned.

"You're about to find out. Tonight, we eat like royalty."

"You're not right in the head, Quinn. No, really. Something is seriously wrong with you."

He lowered his head and snickered. "Shall we?" He offered his arm and led her back to camp, where he gathered wood and prepared a fire. He slathered Yarumaya resin all over the wood like butter and lit it on fire. A huge flame whooshed. Wood crackled, and smoke filled the air. He hung the arapaima steaks over the flames with care and poured a liquid seasoning over them that dripped into the fire and sizzled. A sweet, spicy aroma blended with the smoke, reaching her nostrils and churning her stomach.

"You have marinade in your backpack? What else do you carry in that thing? Besides soap."

He grinned and pulled two steel forks from a side pocket and handed her a giant green leaf. Juice from the fish dripped, and the succulent aroma had her stomach twisted in hunger knots.

"Oh. Oh my God. This is incredible. Mm-mm."

He nodded. "What'd I tell you? Was I right, or was I right?"

"I totally understand why you jumped in. This is so bomb."

She slapped her forearm and winced. "Ow. The mosquitoes are hungry. How are we going to sleep?"

"Like babies in a nursery," he chuckled.

Quinn removed an insect net from the backpack and prepared a bed of branches and leaves over a stone slab inside the ruins.

She giggled. "Why am I not surprised?"

"Let's get a good night's sleep, Izzy, and hit the trail at dawn. We have a lot of ground to cover and little time to cover it."

TWENTY-THREE

The Road Less Traveled

September 7, 2026

They hit the trail early as the skies morphed from a sleepy deep purple to a vibrant spectrum of oranges, pinks, and neon blue. Their research was well-hidden within the walls of the ancient ruins. Quinn whacked branches and vines, clearing a path along a narrow river. Slime and mud slowed their pace in an area where the humidity and heat rivaled a sauna. Her eyes stung from salty sweat, and her calves cramped. The morning air was heavy and rich in oxygen.

"Quinn? I could use some of that yoco bark, there, buddy?"

He took a break from slashing bushes and tossed her the jar.

"Go easy on the chatter today, Izzy. We need to remain stealthy."

"Rude. What's that supposed to mean?"

"I'm simply implying that you turn into a chatterbox and lose your sense of volume with this stuff."

"You're not implying, you're saying it. Maybe I'm speaking louder so you can hear me, Grandpa," she chuckled. Izzy took a shot of yoco bark, glared, and tossed the bottle back at him.

An hour later, they stumbled upon an open area of the jungle where wood poachers had recently struck—the wood smoke from charred timber hung heavy in the air like death's shadow. Her mood turned somber, like the loss of a family member. Mayuma wept.

"This has to stop, Quinn. We have to fight back."

"We will, Izz. Another day."

Two and a half hours later, they found themselves in the shadows of a thick canopy of ancient trees. A family of black monkeys hooted and howled from the treetops, playfully swinging through the branches, staring at them with comical looks of curiosity.

Quinn pointed at them. "Look, Izzy. Howler monkeys. When you see these guys, you know you've entered virgin rainforest."

"They're so beautiful, and too darn cute."

"Their numbers have drastically fallen because of hunters and deforestation, pushing them from their homes. It's a rare sight to see so many. Our lucky day, I guess."

Izzy removed her camera and snapped a dozen photos, zooming in and out and recording video. She zoomed in on a solo juvenile monkey dangling from a low branch, who seemed to be showing off for her.

"Oh my gosh, he's so handsome. I think he's—"

A gray blur crashed through the trees, and the monkey was gone. She looked up from her camera and gasped. A massive eagle snatched the young monkey and disappeared into the trees.

"What? No! Oh my God, what the heck was that? We have to save him, Quinn. That's terrifying."

"Circle of life, Izzy. That big girl was a harpy eagle. They're huge and powerful. We should move along. A little gymnast with a camera and a bad knee might be too tempting for her to pass up."

"Very funny."

She frowned and glanced up at the empty tree branch where the monkey had been playing. She tucked her camera away and moved closer to Quinn.

"You're kidding, right? I mean, they don't attack humans … do they?"

"I wouldn't kid you."

"So, they *do* attack humans?"

"Occasionally, especially cute little girls from California."

She squeezed up next to him, prompting him to lay his arm around her shoulders.

"Don't worry, kid. I won't let her get you."

"Um, can we go now?"

Quinn narrowed his stare and chuckled. "Are you crying?"

She wiped her cheeks and glared defiantly. "No. Why?"

"You're crying. That was simply a mother feeding her family, Izz."

"That isn't helping, Quinn. He was waving to me. I distracted him…"

"That monkey was doomed the second that eagle had him in her sights. It's nature. Toughen up."

"You're so insensitive."

"Monkeys don't wave at the camera, Izzy."

"Well, that one did." She stuck her tongue out and sneered. "Now, his family will never see him again. How's *that* make you feel?"

Hours later, they reached the edge of the young Yarumaya grove just outside the new village. The chatter of English-speaking voices echoed from the distance.

The whistles and hoots of monkeys caught his attention. He grabbed Izzy's wrist and pressed his index finger to his lips. "Sh. You hear that?" he whispered.

"Hear what? The monkeys?"

"Yeah. Those aren't monkeys."

"Seriously? Then what are they?"

"Kawirén warriors."

"So, they're close by?"

"Yep. Probably planning an assault on the invaders."

"So, we should go find them."

"They already know we're here, Izz. They'll find *us*. Let's sit tight for a few minutes."

Moments later, five warriors crept from the forest carrying bows strung with arrows. The leader, a man named Yohami, waved, signaling them to follow. Izzy and Quinn trailed them into the brush, where a party of nearly fifty warriors lay ready to strike. The warriors' faces lit up when they saw Quinn and Izzy. Their presence was a shot of courage to their morale.

Quinn explained to them the critical need to remove the beehive and all the Piritayá seedpods from the Yarumaya trees. Yohami explained their plan of attack, but yielded to Quinn's plea to remove the hive and seedpods first. They would wait until darkness fell before moving.

"Quinn? Where are the women and the children?"

"Hidden deep in the rainforest. They're safe."

Quinn and Izzy spent the rest of the afternoon and evening tending to the men's wounds. The warriors requested a special blessing from "Nahuari" to guarantee their victory as evening fell and the creatures of the night stirred.

Several warriors created a container from large leaves and branches to hold the beehive and all its honey and honeycomb. When the sun crested and dipped below the horizon, the men scurried up the trees and swiftly removed the hive and all the seedpods, using smoke to calm the bees. The task of taking the beehive and seedpods to safety at a secret camp deep in the forest was given to two young warriors.

The stage was set. Warriors drank yoco bark, painted their faces, and tainted their arrowheads and blow darts with the poison from frogs. It was time to move.

"Quinn, where are you going? You're staying here with me, right?"

"Molon labe."

"What is that? Is that Latin for something?"

"It's Greek. It means, 'Come and get them.' King Leonidas said it to Xerxes when told to lay down their arms."

"Oh my God, you're a frickin' cowboy. What am I supposed to do?"

"Those two young men over there are going to stay with you. If this thing goes south, they'll lead you back to the villagers. I'll meet you there. Otherwise, I'll be right back."

"Great. Sure. Catch you later," she replied, exasperated.

She grabbed his wrist. "Quinn? Be careful."

He nodded and winked, then followed the warriors into the darkness with his rifle strapped to his shoulder.

The sky rumbled. She sat with her back braced against a tree and her knees drawn into her chest. One of the young warriors draped a woven blanket over her shoulders and stood guard over her.

A sickening twinge in her stomach had her wringing her hands and tapping her heels. She laid her head on her knees and sighed. What if he doesn't come back? What then? What if none of them come back?

Izzy prayed. Her heart knew the truth because the rainforest touched her spirit so deeply, even though she wasn't raised in a religious home. There is a God of creation. And this God lives in every creature, every tree, and every river in the rainforest. She could feel it—sense the profound love radiating in every drop of sunlight that gave Mayuma life. *Please keep him safe and bring him back to me.*

The shouts began. No ordinary shouts. Shouts of agony and death. The echoing crackles of gunfire rang out, causing her to flinch and squeeze her eyes shut. Her heart pulsed as she squirmed, finally leaping to her feet. She paced. Screams, gunfire, and the swish of arrows raged on for hours.

Izzy pleaded with her two young companions to join the battle with her. She spoke in broken Kawirénian. "Must help. Fight invaders. Please."

They shook their heads wildly. "No, no, no…" Gesturing for her to remain.

Late into the night, the battle noises subsided. Only an occasional gunshot crackled. The screams quieted to low, mournful groans. What could be happening? Why hasn't Quinn come back?

Izzy was exhausted. Her eyes grew heavy waiting, and her head bobbed several times before she dozed.

The thump of helicopter blades roused her, shooting a surge of adrenaline through her veins. Izzy snatched her backpack, raced through the trees, followed by the two young warriors, as rays of filtered light peeked through the canvas.

Bodies strewn everywhere—the ground tinted red. The few survivors squirmed and moaned as they lay dying. Two young warriors dragged the semi-conscious bodies of their tribesmen into the trees to safety.

A small group of government soldiers gathered near the hovering helicopter that was lowering a rescue basket. Two soldiers rushed a homemade stretcher with a wounded man to the basket and laid him inside. It was Quinn! "Oh, God!"

Izzy lost all sense of reason and screamed, "Quinn!"

As she raced towards the helicopter, agents intercepted and restrained her.

She struggled and continued to shout, "Quinn! What did you do to him? Where are you taking him?"

Julio Ortega emerged from the group. "Isabella? Come with me."

"Julio? Why are you doing this?"

"You need to come with me."

"What did you do with Quinn? Is he hurt?"

"He'll be fine. We're airlifting him to a hospital in the States. He'll receive the best of care, I assure you, Hija."

"You bastard! *You* did all of this. You lied to me after I trusted you."

"I promise, Isabella, we are only here for research that could change the world as we know it. Sometimes, sacrifices have to be made for the good of everyone."

"You have no idea what you're doing. You've destroyed these people. Their homes, their lives. You can't duplicate our research outside the rainforest. There's no magic formula. You've failed, Julio."

"We shall see." He pointed at the empty basket. "Get in the basket, Isabella. If you want to see Dr. Quinn, get in."

Izzy glared at him for several moments, then lay in the basket. Her stomach fluttered as the basket spun as it quickly took her up. She rushed to Quinn's side. They had him strapped into a basket with a plastic tube stuck in his arm and attached to a clear plastic bag; his shirt soaked in blood.

Quinn glanced at her with bloodshot eyes that crossed, then closed. She took his hand and kissed his knuckles.

"Hang on, Quinny. Please hang on…"

TWENTY-FOUR

Camp Pendleton Navy Hospital

September 8, 2026

The moment the helicopter landed at Pendleton, they rushed Quinn into the emergency room. Two military police officers escorted Izzy to a secure location, locked the door, and exited. She slumped onto a burnt-orange polyester loveseat and closed her eyes.

A soft tap at the door, followed by a click, snapped her out of her trance. It was Julio. He entered alone, closing the door behind him.

"They've released you into my custody, Hija."

"*Your* custody? Am I some kind of criminal? I've done nothing wrong."

"Oh, I beg to differ, Chica. You're in a lot of trouble."

"I want to call my dad."

"You'll have a chance to call whomever you like when we finish here, little one."

"Little one? You're calling *me*, little one? What do you want from me, peewee, besides some elevator shoes?"

"Answers."

"To what?"

"Well, my questions, of course. Let's start with this: Where are Dr. Quinn's notes, documents, samples … where did you hide his research?"

"Our research. It's mine too."

"Ah, of course it is. And you have much to gain, Isabella. You'll receive full credit for your discoveries and a generous reward for your knowledge. I understand it could be in the hundreds of millions. Do you understand how rich you will be? How much power and influence you will possess? I'm offering you the world, Isabella. It's mine to give."

"Okay, Satan. I'm not interested. Now let me go."

A tap on the door gave Julio pause. He grinned and opened the door.

"This is Dr. Andrew Manucci. He's the leading expert on infectious disease and immunology."

"It's a pleasure to meet you, Ms. Delgado."

"Well, I'm just a simple botanist working on my thesis, Dr. Manucci. I don't think I can help you with whatever you're looking for."

He squatted in a chair across from her, crossed his legs, and narrowed his eyes. The guy looked like Carl Jung waiting to psychoanalyze her.

"Why don't you tell me about the Yarumaya resin and the tribe you've studied for the past several weeks?"

"Uh … I don't think so. You're wasting your time."

Julio laid a folder filled with documents on a small coffee table in front of her. She glared at him and raised an eyebrow.

"What's this?"

"Those are mortgage documents, Isabella. It seems your father has committed a few mortgage felonies over the years. Claiming residency where he didn't live to get lower rates and other little inconsistencies."

"Why are you showing me these?"

"He could face decades in prison. Or we could bury them in some warehouse and move on…"

"Are you trying to blackmail me, little man? Threatening my family to get me to talk?"

"Sí, señorita. You catch on fast, Hija."

"You're unbelievable. A genuine piece of crap."

"How can you turn down such a generous offer? Millions of dollars, recognition in science, a new species named after you, CEO of a huge pharmaceuticals company, and your father safe at home with your mother?"

"Wow, that all sounds great. Let me think, hmm. How about…"

Izzy raised both middle fingers and sneered. "…You shove it up your corrupt little ass, Congressman. You too, Dr. *Freud.* Or is it Dr. *Fraud*?"

He gestured for Dr. Manucci to leave, then slid his chair closer.

"Let me be honest with you, Isabella. My motivation to attain longevity science is personal."

"Personal? Oh, now it's getting interesting. How so?"

"Have you heard of Leigh Syndrome?"

"No. Never heard of it."

"It's extremely rare and painful to witness. It begins in infancy and severely shortens a child's life. They lose motor skills, struggle to learn, and can't remember simple things like who their papa is. It turns a child into a vegetable before it kills them, Isabella."

"Why are you telling me this?"

"One of my twin boys was born with this affliction. I need your research to save him, and I'll do anything to get it. Help me save my son by sharing your discovery."

"I'm deeply sorry about your son, Julio. I truly am. That's tragic. But I can't give you the research. It's too dangerous and untested in the civilized world. It only works in the Amazon among the natives."

Julio's face seemed frozen. His eyes deadened. "I'll give you time to reconsider, Isabella. I can't detain you, so you're free to go."

Izzy paused and studied Julio's expression. "Seriously? I can go?"

He opened the door and gestured for her to exit.

"Then, I'm out of here." She snatched her backpack and bolted down the hallway.

Izzy raced to the front lobby and hovered over the information desk. A middle-aged woman with short dark hair and cat glasses glanced up at her and smiled. "Can I help you?"

"Yes, um. Dr. Quinn. Dr. Dominic Quinn. What room is he in?"

"Let me check."

She scanned her computer screen, squinting, then jotted something on a yellow sticky note.

"He's in room 104, but can't have visitors."

"Okay. What time can I visit him?"

The woman shook her head. "He's in a restricted room. There are no visitors allowed without an approved pass."

"And how do I request a pass?"

"That's all the information I have. I'm very sorry."

"Great. Do you mind if I use your phone to call for a ride?"

The woman pointed to the wall near the entrance. "You can use that one to call out. Just dial '9' first."

"Dad? It's Izzy. I'm at the Navy hospital at Camp Pendleton in San Diego. Can you send someone to pick me up?"

❧

The black SUV dropped Izzy off at her parents' home in Malibu at 6:45 p.m. Her mother rushed down the long driveway to greet her, worry fixed in her expression. Sunken eyes as if she hadn't slept in a week, pasty skin, and her hair in a messy bun, which was extremely uncharacteristic for her.

When Izzy stepped out, her mom hugged her tighter than she had in years.

"Oh, Izzy. I was so worried about you, dear. Are you hungry? Cece has made a wonderful dinner. Your fave. Seafood boil."

"Oh my God, Mom. That sounds so yummy. I'm starving. Is Daddy home?"

"Not yet, dear. He spent the afternoon with his attorneys. Issues with some properties, I think. He's on his way. I know your father is looking forward to seeing you."

"Me too, Mom. It's nice to be home."

"It's nice to have you home, Isabella. Now, do you plan on staying, or are you going to go gallivanting off into the jungle again soon?"

"I'm here for now, Mom. I have a friend in the hospital in San Diego, and I'll be visiting him a lot. Until he's well."

"Very sorry to hear that, dear. I hope it's nothing serious."

"He's in the hospital, Mom."

"Of course. How silly of me."

"Mom, do you think Dad will let me stay at the beach house in San Diego?"

"Your father spoils you. Why wouldn't he?"

Her father's meaty hands kneaded the back of her neck and shoulders as he planted a kiss on the crown of her head.

"Ah, my prodigal daughter returns."

She slid her chair away from the table and wrapped her arms around his waist. "Daddy! So good to see you. I have so much to tell you after dinner."

Flo rolled her eyes and sighed. "Anything I should know?"

Izzy laid her hand over her mother's and smiled. "Yes, Mom. Sorry. I have a lot to tell you, too. But I need to talk to Dad about stuff that would bore you to tears."

"I see. Well, I'll wait my turn, my dear. Now let's eat." Flo twisted her body towards the kitchen. "Cece? We're ready for you, love."

Izzy closed the door to her father's office and plopped into a tall leather chair across from his desk. Frederico stuffed his pipe with tobacco, filling the room with spicy smoke.

"Dad, Julio is a liar and a traitor. I need your help."

He nodded and sucked a deep puff. "What you say is true, Izzy. He's attempting to have me indicted for mortgage fraud. Something about needing research documentation from you and Dr. Quinn. Do you wish to explain this to me, Mija?"

Izzy spent the next two hours explaining everything that had happened to her and Quinn in the Amazon. The onslaught on the Kawirén people, the destruction of the sacred Yarumaya grove, the assault on Quinn, and Julio's betrayal by joining forces with Ian Bragg.

"Dr. Quinn is fighting for his life in the hospital, Daddy. They won't let me see him. He'll age and die if I can't reach him. I have to take him back to the Amazon or he'll die. We hid our research in a place they'll never find. They've slaughtered the Kawirén people and scattered them into the jungle. We have to help them, Dad. Please."

"I see. Are you involved with this, Dr. Quinn, Izzy? Outside of your professional relationship with him? I know that's a personal question, but…"

"Are you asking if I'm seeing him romantically?"

He nodded and narrowed his eyes as he drew another puff of his pipe.

"I love him, Daddy. He's not like other men."

"Love, emotions ... they cloud one's thoughts, Mija ... make it difficult to analyze a situation and take the needed steps."

"I can't help how I feel, Dad, but my mind has never been clearer about the things I want or the things I must do."

"And what do you need from me, Mija?"

"I need to get into that hospital room to see Quinn. Then, I need your help to protect the Kawirén people and preserve their sacred grove of Yarumaya and their customs. We need to prevent Congressman Ortega and Ian Bragg from going anywhere near the Yarumaya and the Kawirén village."

"That is a lot to ask, Mija. I don't know if I have the power to accomplish all of that, but I'll do my best."

Izzy fell to her knees in front of him and squeezed his hand. "Please, Daddy. This is life or death. For Quinn. For the Kawirén, and for the rainforest."

He heaved a breath and rubbed the scruff on his chin. "Let me make some phone calls to some close friends in the government. If they won't listen, we have *other friends* who can persuade and influence. I can't promise anything, Mija. This will be a difficult ask with many strings attached."

She crawled onto his lap and hugged his neck. "Thank you for trying, Dad. I know somehow you'll come through. You always do."

Izzy exited the 405 freeway and sped onto Interstate 5 South towards San Diego, with the top down on her BMW. Her father had bought her the sports car as a graduation gift. More importantly, she had the green light for a supervised visit to see Quinn and wasn't wasting any time getting there.

She didn't even stop to ask her father what strings he pulled or favors he called in. Once he shared the news, she was out the door.

Her mind raced, processing a thousand thoughts, then repeating the process over and over. How bad was he? Will she be able to help him escape? What if Quinn dies? Dozens of red brake lights in front of her blurred as she attempted to process her worst fears.

As she pulled up to the gate at Camp Pendleton, she fished around in her purse for her ID.

"Good afternoon, ma'am."

"Yes, uh, I'm headed to the Naval hospital. I should be on your list … Isabella Delgado."

"Yes, Ms. Delgado." He handed her a pass. "Place this on your windshield in full view. Have a nice day, ma'am."

Her stomach churned as she whipped into an open parking space and rushed to the hospital entrance. An attractive young black woman dressed in fatigues, with her hair pulled into a tight bun, greeted her with a beaming smile.

"Can I help you, ma'am?"

"Yes, um, room 104. I'm here to see Dr. Dominic Quinn … he's a patient."

"And your name?"

"Isabella Delgado."

"Place this sticker on your chest and go through that door."

She should have eaten before she left, but food was the last thing on her mind. The hospital air smelled sterilized, with a hint of alcohol and antiseptics.

Izzy paused in the hallway to calm her nerves before approaching the military guard seated in front of Room 104.

"Sir, I'm here to visit Dr. Quinn."

The guard checked her purse, gestured for her to enter, and returned his attention to his cell phone. She pushed the heavy door and slipped inside. A soft hum and the gentle rhythmic beeps of a monitor were the only sounds in the dim light. An indiscernible voice emanated from the TV as it cast a blue flickering light across the room.

Quinn lay still on a hospital bed set at a 45-degree angle. Tubes wound around the metal bedrails, leading to his arm and nose. His eyes were closed, his face pale and gaunt, and his hair peppered black and white.

A young officer in fatigues with short blonde hair rose from the other side of the bed and whispered, "He's awake. Take my chair. I'll be over here if you need anything."

Her heart ached seeing him aging again. She took his hand and whispered, "Quinn? Quinny? It's me, Isabella. I'm here."

He stretched his eyebrows and peeked, staring at the ceiling, before turning his head towards her and forcing a feeble grin.

"Izzy? Am I dreaming, or is this some kind of nightmare?"

"It's your worst nightmare, dude."

Quinn pointed with his eyes at the camera mounted in the upper corner of the room and whispered in Kawirénian, "They're watching and listening."

She quickly glanced at the camera and nodded. Speaking broken Kawirénian, she replied, "Need to get you out. Must escape to Mayuma."

He chuckled. "I just got out of surgery yesterday morning, kid. Had two slugs removed from my liver and one from my spine. I'm not mobile at the moment. Please tell me you haven't concocted one of your notorious escape plans."

"Not yet, but I will. Quinn, you're aging. We need to get you home."

He shook his head and frowned. "I'm stuck here. They're not going to let me leave."

He switched from English back to Kawirénian. "Izzy, go back to the ruins and recover our research. It won't survive the harsh conditions in the Amazon. Take it somewhere safe."

Then in English, "Understand?"

She nodded, wiping tears from her cheeks.

In Kawirénian, she said, "Go with me, Quinn. I can't do this alone."

"You have to, Izzy. You are Nahuari, and the people need you. The Yarumaya depend on you. Mayuma is calling you home."

"My father knows powerful people. We're going to get you out of here, I promise. But I need you to get better. I'm staying at my parents' beach house, less than five miles from here, so I'll visit every day."

"I'll do my best, Izz. But I'm aging quickly. Exponentially with each day."

They switched to speaking Kawirénian. "Izzy, do you remember how to get back to the ruins?"

"I think so. I-I'm not sure … but I think I can find my way back."

"Give me a pen and paper."

She glanced at the officer, who was busy studying a thick manila folder of documents. Turning her back to the camera and fumbling through her purse, she removed a pen and a bank deposit receipt and slipped them into his hands. Quinn scribbled on the bank receipt, crumpled it, and pretended to drink from an empty cup. He slipped the note inside and handed it to her. She rolled the crumpled note into her palm as she tossed the cup into a garbage bin.

The door opened. A doctor, a nurse, and a man in a navy-blue suit entered.

"Ma'am, I'm sorry, but your time is up," the female officer said.

She caressed his cheek and kissed him softly on the lips, and whispered, "I'll be back."

He squeezed her hand, closed his eyes, and nodded.

❧❧❧

Her throat tightened as she pulled into the beach house and spotted a sleek black limousine parked in front. Her first instinct was to keep driving—call her dad. But her curiosity and agitation got the best of her, so she parked behind them and pounded her horn.

Ian Bragg and Julio Ortega exited the limo and waved, begging her to stop. Izzy stepped out of her vehicle and stormed towards them, their eyes widening at her boldness.

"What right do you have parking in front of my house, huh? How'd you even know I was here?" She pointed her cellphone at them. "I'm recording you. Say hi, boys."

Julio raised a calming hand and smiled. "We're only here to have a friendly conversation, Isabella. Nothing more. May we come inside?"

"Hell no. You step one foot on my property and I'm calling the cops."

"That won't be necessary, Hija. We can speak out here."

"There's nothing to talk about. You both should be in jail for murder."

"Now, let's remain civil, Isabella. We are here to offer a proposal. One that I feel you should listen to. Can you please stop recording?"

"No, I'm going to continue recording for my own safety."

"No one is going to hurt you."

"Yeah, tell that to the Kawirén villagers you slaughtered. Tell it to Quinn, who had multiple bullets removed yesterday."

"Isabella, I know you care deeply for Dr. Quinn. Which is why you should listen to me."

"You'd better not hurt him. You stay the hell away from him, you hear me?"

"Dr. Quinn is in no danger from us, Hija. But as you know, he appears to be aging at an alarming rate. Why is that? Did Dr. Quinn discover the Kawirén's secret to longevity? Is he now aging from a lack of its source?"

"That's none of your damn business."

"I think it is. Look, Isabella, we are here today to make you an offer that will benefit us both."

"Oh, I can't wait to hear this."

"If you care about your dear amigo, Dr. Quinn, then you should consider our offer. Are you at least willing to listen?"

"I'm listening."

"I will have Dr. Quinn released to your care immediately. His time may be short, so you can act quickly in helping him restore his *youth*, shall we say?"

"And what are you asking in return?"

"You know already. Your research—notes, journals, samples, everything."

"You might as well jump back into your fancy little limo, because that ain't happening, buddy."

"You will receive a one-hundred-million-dollar award. Untraceable, tax-free. They'll credit you with the discovery of a new genus of tree. You'll share the credit for the greatest medical discovery in history. Think about it, Isabella. Think of how many doors that will open for you. You could have everything you ever dreamed of. The possibilities are limitless."

He handed her a contract attached to a clipboard.

"Just sign. Simple as that."

She heaved a breath and crossed her arms.

"There was a time I would have jumped at this opportunity. But that time has passed. I'll make you a counteroffer. Release Quinn to me, leave the Amazon and never return, and I won't pursue criminal charges against you and your partner for murder, extortion, blackmail, theft, and a hundred other crimes. Do that, and I won't go to the press with this recording."

Julio's eyes narrowed and darkened. He stepped close and sighed.

"This is a dangerous game you're playing, Chica. One you cannot win. One that could cost you more than you can ever imagine. Tread lightly, or you might lose your precious boyfriend, and your padre will spend 20 years in a federal prison. I'll make sure you are left with nothing. What happened to your villagers in the Amazon will pale compared to what I do to you and your family. Comprende?"

"You underestimate me, Congressman."

"Give me your phone, Isabella."

"I've already sent the video to my father. So much for prison, Julio. You threaten people the way you play golf. Now leave before I call the cops."

Julio sneered as he backpedaled and slipped back into the limo. Bragg pointed at her and winked. "We'll be in touch."

Izzy sucked a deep breath to slow her pounding heart. She raced up the porch of the beach house, slammed and locked the door behind her, and collapsed onto the sofa.

She tapped on her cellphone and held her breath.

"Daddy? Did you get the video I sent?"

TWENTY-FIVE

Reunited

September 9, 2026

Izzy and her father sat on the porch swing of their San Diego beach house, gazing into the vast Pacific. Tanned, half-dressed teenagers slapped a volleyball back and forth, kicking up sand. Children screamed and giggled as they darted across the beach, splashing in and out of the gentle waves. Sunbathers worshipped a blazing white sun cast against a neon-blue sky, slathering sunscreen across their arms and focusing their attention on their cellphones. Mission Beach was in full swing.

"What do we do, Daddy? How do we stop these creeps from destroying an innocent tribe and a sacred species of trees?"

"The video you sent is useful, Mija. I have my attorneys working on it, and I've spoken to a good friend in the Senate. But these things take time, pequeña rosa."

"Aw, you haven't called me your little rose in years." She rested her head on his shoulder and slipped her arm inside his.

"Dad, I have to get Quinn out of that naval hospital as soon as I can. He has to go back to the Amazon before it's too late."

"I'm acquainted with the head of the hospital, Mija. We're having breakfast tomorrow. Keep your bags packed."

"And here I thought you came all the way down here to visit me. I should have guessed." She tittered.

Izzy spent the morning packing a suitcase and her backpack. She sliced a triangular piece of a Nutella-topped, half-burned crepe and washed it down with a shot of syrupy acai juice. A salty, gentle breeze teased the tiny wind chimes hanging above her head as she relaxed on the porch swing, snapping photos of gulls swooping across the empty beach, scavenging the creamy beige sands for scraps and shellfish.

The vibration of her cellphone tickled her thigh.

"Hola. Daddy? How did breakfast go?"

"I think you'll be pleased, Mija. Captain Burnes signed the order to release Dr. Quinn of his own accord. As soon as they discharge him, I'll deliver him to you. Muy bueno?"

"Gracias a Dios, Papa. You're amazing."

"I'll text you when we're leaving the hospital."

She shrilled. "Ooh, I love you, Daddy!"

Izzy made her bed, cleaned the kitchen, and took a shower. She sat cross-legged in front of the bathroom mirror and applied light makeup, painted her lips pink, and blow-dried her chestnut locks into bouncy curls. Quinn had never seen her at her best, and she was dying to surprise him.

Her jeans fit loosely. The jungle diet must have stolen a few pounds, she thought as she stepped on the scale and sighed. "118? Seriously? Ugh."

The jeans landed on the floor as she slipped into a pair of denim shorts, posing in the mirror and glancing over her shoulder at her behind.

"Okay, at least the booty is still there," she whispered.

A summer floral half-top and a pair of straw flats completed the fit.

"Wait." She draped a white linen button-up over her shoulders and smiled. "Perfecto mundo."

She paced. The anticipation sent her stomach into knots, glancing out the window and checking her phone every ten seconds. *What's taking so long?*

Izzy heaved a breath, slipped on a pair of Versace sunglasses, and strolled onto the beach. A soft breeze inflated her linen button-up and tossed her hair. Warmth bathed her skin, and the scent of barbecue wafting in the air prompted thoughts of where she'd take Quinn for lunch.

Her phone buzzed. She snatched it from her back pocket and checked her messages.

Your package is in route, Mija (Fist emoji, red heart emoji)

She wandered back to the beach house and plopped on the swing, legs crossed, checking her makeup in the reflection of her phone. She tilted her head, puckered, and blew herself a kiss. Her pits were sweaty, so she lifted her arms to allow the breeze to dry them. This was worse than waiting on a prom date.

The crash boomed. Less than a mile away. Her phone buzzed, and her heart skipped a beat.

"Mija. There's been an accident. An intentional accident. Two men have attempted to kidnap Dr. Quinn, but he escaped. I don't know where he is."

"Oh, my God! Daddy? Are you okay?"

"I'm a little banged up. The PD is on the way."

"What direction did Quinn go?"

"He ran toward the old rollercoaster park. The two men chased after him. I've called in a favor from a business associate who lives nearby. We'll do our best to find him, Mija. Stay where you are. I'll keep you posted."

"Daddy, please find him."

Izzy hopped into her convertible. Tires screeched, leaving a cloud of white smoke and the stench of burnt rubber as she whipped onto the road, headed for the old rollercoaster. She scanned the sidewalks, darting in and out of alleys and side streets, honking her horn and shouting, "Quinn! Quinn!"

Izzy parked in the lot outside the old rollercoaster and sprinted towards the entrance of Belmont Park. She dashed through the crowded aisles, scanning the area for any sign of Quinn. Two men dressed in jeans, Hawaiian shirts, and sunglasses blew past her. Something looked out of place, so she followed them.

Her cellphone buzzed. "Hello?"

A subdued voice whispered, "Izz. It's me."

"Quinn? Where are you?"

"Not sure. I ducked into a place called 'Tiki Town'. Kid's golf or something."

"I know where that is. Stay put; I'm coming. Quinn. Two men are running around the park—"

"Dressed in Hawaiian shirts?"

"Yes. You saw them?"

"Stay away from them, Izzy. I'll be inside."

She raced to the front of the Tiki Town building, then slowed to a steady walk. Quinn emerged one step at a time—a limp in his gait and more gray in his hair than yesterday. The creases at the corners of his eyes had deepened.

When his eyes connected with hers, his lips curled into that old boyish grin that accented his dimples and melted her heart.

"Where's Malibu?" he asked tongue-in-cheek.

She nibbled her lower lip and pointed. "About 150 miles that way."

He nodded. "M-hm. And who might you be?"

"Your worst nightmare."

"Now that's a gross understatement."

She threw her arms around his neck and planted a hard, wet kiss on his lips.

"No time for that, Izz. Try to control yourself."

"Very funny. I'm parked over there. Follow me."

She grabbed his hand and led him into the crowd, pointing toward the roller coaster.

"Slow down, Izz. I can't keep up."

"You have to, Quinn. Please."

She darted inside a clothing shop and purchased two floppy hats and a large San Diego T-shirt. "Here, put this on."

They detoured towards the beach, where Izzy snagged a free wheelchair near the lifeguard station.

"What are you doing, Izz?"

"Sit, Quinn. We need to get the hell out of here."

Izzy wheeled Quinn along the streets and back to her convertible, where they sped away. She hit the contact shortcut for her father on her cell and drew a deep breath, waiting for him to answer.

"Mija?"

"I have him. We're headed to the airport. Can you pick up my car later?"

"Izzy, be careful. Yes, I'll have someone pick up your car later. Just text me the info. Call me when you reach your destination."

"I love you, Daddy. Please be safe."

She raced through the streets, zipping in and out of traffic with the top down. Quinn tightened his seatbelt and gripped the door handle with whitened knuckles.

"Izz, can you please slow down? I think I'm having an out-of-body experience."

"Don't be a wuss, Quinn. I'm not going that fast."

"It's not your speed; it's your terrible driving. I think I see a tunnel … with a bright white light at the end…"

"Hey, I'm a fantastic driver, buddy. I've never had a ticket, so chill, drama queen."

"Where are you taking me?"

"Back to LA to catch a flight to the Amazon. I have the tickets, but it's going to be a couple of hours before we can leave. I know a secluded place where we can eat lunch. A tiny hole in the wall on the beach called The Blue Fin. Their sushi really slaps. You're gonna love it."

"I don't eat raw fish, Izz. Parasites, man."

"Nah, this place is legit. No one I know has ever gotten sick here. We'll order you a crispy fish taco or some shrimp ceviche. Fully cooked. I'm literally dying here, watching you squirm. We're here, so relax."

"Well, I'm happy to entertain you. Can we park? You've circled the parking lot four times now, and each time a new space opens up."

"Sure. Say less." She whipped into the next open space.

"This place is really giving. You're going to thank me."

"Giving? Giving what?"

"Uh, giving good vibes. Great food and drinks. It's right on the beach. Very romantic, so I expect your full attention."

They sat facing the ocean; the beach stretched before them like a 3D movie across a gigantic screen. She patted his knee and smiled.

"Isn't this gorge? I knew you'd thank me."

"I have to admit, this is pretty nice. Breath-taking scenery and not so bad company. I'm nervous, Izz. Are you sure we're safe here?"

"Yes, Quinny. Relax. No one knows about this place. Only the locals. From the outside, it looks like someone's beach home."

"Questions about the menu, folks? You ready to order?"

"Yes, please. Can I have the sushi, an order of lobster rolls, and a Mai Tai?"

"And for you, sir?"

"Uh … how about a … crispy taco? And a shot of bourbon, please."

She wrapped her arm around his and rested her head on his shoulder.

"I love this, Quinn. I could do this for the rest of my life."

"What? Run from thugs or this?"

"You're so funny." She quipped.

"Izzy. I'm aging quickly. Each day compounds the last. I'm not sure how long I have."

"Quinny, I didn't want to talk about it just yet. I wanted us to have this moment together. Like a real date. I want to know what it's like to share something so beautiful with someone so special. Does that sound stupid?"

He chuckled. "No. Not stupid. Risky, but not stupid. I've never seen you this calm."

She slapped his arm. "I'm scared shitless, Quinn. I'm just trying not to think about it until we board the plane."

"I am too, Izz. But this lunch date idea of yours is crazy enough that I think it's going to be alright."

Her Mai Tai was sweet. Tart. Heavy on the rum. She sipped with her straw and nibbled on the maraschino cherry, squeezing his hand and staring into the vastness of the ocean.

Quinn slurped his bourbon and draped his arm around her shoulders.

"I kinda don't want this date to end."

"Aw, that's sweet."

Her cell buzzed. She glanced at the screen.

Mommy Dearest

"Mom? What's up?"

"Izzy, have you spoken to your dad?"

"Yeah, earlier this morning."

"He never came home. I'm worried."

"Oh, I'm sure he's fine, Mom. Don't worry."

"No, Izzy. He's not answering his phone. He always takes my calls."

"Mom. He does that sometimes. That's normal for him."

"No one knows where he is. I've called his office, his assistant, the chauffeur who picked him up…"

"He said he'd call me tonight, Mom. I'm sure it's fine."

"Call me if you hear from him, dear. Please."

"Kay-Kay, I'm getting another call. I'll talk to you soon. Love you."

"Hello?"

"Isabella. It's Julio. You have a minute to talk?"

TWENTY-SIX

New Beginnings

"What do you want, Julio? I told you to fuck off."

"I'm going to ignore your bad manners, Hija. I'm sitting across from your padre. We were discussing you and your situation. I thought you might want to join the conversation."

"Oh my God, what are you up to? Leave him alone."

"Here's the deal, Isabella. You have seventy-two hours to deliver Dr. Quinn's research to me, or you'll never see your dear papa again. That should motivate you to do what I ask. Questions?"

"Let me talk to him. I swear if you hurt him, I'll hunt you down and end you."

"Ooh, I'm shivering. Say hi to your daughter, Frederico."

"Izzy. Don't do anything they say. Run, Mija!"

"Daddy? Daddy?"

"I'm sorry, Hija. We got cut off somehow. Seventy-two hours. You have my cell. If I don't hear from you by then, well…" CLICK.

"Izzy, we have no choice. He wins. We can't risk your father's life."

"Oh God, Quinn. I'm so sorry. This is all my fault. I-I should never have involved him."

"We don't have time to waste, and I need to find a new boatman. Thank you for the interesting afternoon. It was the *perfect* date."

The flight was long and choppy. Her neck and back ached from the bus ride to the Rio Negro dock. The cabby tossed their bags onto the side of the road like somebody's garbage and sped off.

"Izzy, lend me some cash to buy a new boatman. Bragg cut off my funds, and they've run out, unfortunately."

"Of course. What do you need?"

"Five hundred should do."

She hesitated. "Five? Okay."

Twenty minutes later, they sat side-by-side as a motorized aluminum skiff zipped through the jade waters towards the old base camp. The earthy, moist wind whipped through her hair, and the hum of the engine strangely eased her tension. Quinn rubbed an annoying knot in her neck and handed her a vial of yoco bark serum.

"Ooh, my fave."

"We're going to need the boost. Time is a ticking."

The skiff rounded a final turn towards the dock and coasted to the shore. Quinn slapped the other half of the fee into the boatman's palm as they hopped onto the rickety boat dock. The boat raced off in the opposite direction, leaving them alone in the rainforest.

Izzy adjusted her backpack. It was on the heavier side this trip and stuffed to its limit. She purchased a new satellite phone and a Hasselblad X2D camera to photograph and record every document of their research. Her reasoning was threefold: to keep a record for themselves; to have the ability to call Julio from the Amazon; and to have the ability to send the research to him electronically, if time ran short. Ideally, she wanted to deliver the research in person and ensure the safe release of her father.

Quinn slung an AK-47 over his shoulder and strapped a 24-inch machete to his hip. He handed her his .38 pistol and holster and grinned.

"Strap this on and try not to shoot anything important."

"Amusing. Do you do stand-up comedy too? Seriously. I mean, I can get you a gig for senior night at the lodge."

He chuckled as he hacked through brush, vines, and young trees. They crept through the jungle at a steady pace, headed for the tree bridge. An hour in, Quinn swiped his sleeve across his forehead and plopped onto a log. "I'm sorry, Izz. I need to rest for a minute."

"Quinn, you're pasty white."

"Yeah, I know. I was born that way."

"Can you be serious for a minute? You don't look good, dude. Are you all right?"

"I've been better. My pulse is racing, I'm sweating like a hog, and my head is pounding. I'm dying, Izzy. But I won't leave you until we reach the ruins."

"Don't talk like that! We can rest for as long as you need."

She slid next to him and wrapped her arms around his waist. "Quinn, please don't say stuff like that. I don't *even* want to think about losing you. Or being all alone out here. What can I do for you?"

"Just, uh … give me some water. And a couple of aspirins from my backpack."

She removed the machete from his clutch. "Let me do this for a while. Just tell me where to go and I'll lead."

He nodded and heaved a breath. "I think I'm fine. Let's keep moving."

Izzy hacked and whacked at the brush and vines as they attacked her from every direction, slapping her in the face and knocking her off balance. She wore out after five feet.

"At this rate, we'll reach the bridge by the end of the month," he muttered.

"What am I doing wrong?"

He gently removed the machete from her grip and grabbed a 3-inch-thick vine. "Hack it like this—at a forty-five-degree angle. Let the blade do all the work so you don't have to. Grab, slice, and move. Got it?"

"I think so."

"Show me," he said as he handed her the machete and crossed his arms.

She inhaled a breath of confidence as they picked up the pace. "Okay, I see you. This is working much better."

Quinn grabbed her arm and raised his index finger to his lips.

"Sh. I think we're being followed," he whispered.

"Are you serious?"

"This way. Change of plans."

Quinn took the lead and led them back towards the river, where they moved through the ferns and palms in silence.

"Gonna take an extra hour, but I think we can lose them."

Two hours later, they stumbled into a small clearing. Quinn pushed away vines and branches, revealing the entrance to the ancient ruins, then took her by the hand and led her inside. Flipping on a flashlight, he scanned the chamber for movement and critters and exhaled a breath of relief, collapsing onto the sandy floor and bracing his back against the stone wall. He looked old and tired in the dim light.

She kneeled next to him and kissed his knuckles. "How are you feeling? You need to rest for a while? Please don't leave me, Quinny." Tears erupted, and her body trembled with sobs.

"I … I just need a few minutes, Izzy. You're such a drama queen. Come here."

He opened his arms as she crawled into his hug. They lay in silence, squeezing each other tight as she closed her eyes and sniffled.

"We need to get you back to the villagers, Quinn. They have what we need to get you better."

"We don't have time, Izz. And I don't think I can take another step."

"Don't give up. Please don't give up. I need you. Quinn … I *love* you."

He pointed. "I hid our research behind that stone. Take it. The boatman will return tomorrow at noon. Get back to the airport and go home, Izzy. Don't give them anything until they give you your father."

He gripped her hand and gazed deep into her eyes, forcing a half smile. "I love you, too, Isabella Delgado."

"Quinn? Please. What can I do to help you?"

"I'm so tired, Izz. I'm running a fever, and I think my blood pressure is low."

"Stop diagnosing yourself. You just need to rest. Then we'll go find the villagers."

"That could take days, Izz. Weeks even. We don't have that kind of time. I'd only slow us down."

"Then I'll go find them. I'll bring back the resin. The honey. Just promise me you'll hang on."

"Izz, you're not listening to me. I'm dying. I won't see tomorrow."

"No! You can't. I won't let you."

"We can't stop time, Izzy. We learned to slow it down, but in the end, we all face death."

She wiped her cheeks and whimpered. "But why today?"

She laid her head on his chest and wept. Quinn ran his fingers through her curls and kissed her on the crown.

"I've never met anyone like you, Izzy. Headstrong, overly optimistic, and so naïve. You gave me my life back, kid. I was dead inside when I found you sleeping in my lab. I wanted to send you home, but I needed you. Needed your expertise. I probably could have fixed the radio anytime."

"So, you lied."

"I did."

"I knew it."

"You remind me of her."

"Who? Your wife?"

"Who else, Izzy? Yes."

"Oh, well…"

"She was the ultimate idealist. No one could tell her what to do. No one would dare. And just like you, Izz, she never gave up. Always saw a way out of every situation, no matter how impossible it was. Never gave up on me. Trusted everything I said. I didn't deserve her, and I don't deserve you."

He sucked in a ragged breath and sighed. "She cared about people, Izzy. About the rainforest and all of God's creation. Just like you. You restored my faith in what I was doing out here. For years, I was hiding. From myself, from losing Brey, from the world. Until you showed up."

"You're scaring me, Quinn. You're going to be okay. Just rest."

"Izzy, the Kawirén need you. You're the only one who can save them now. Besides, what would you do with an old man like me as your boyfriend?"

"I told you, Quinn. I'm attracted to older guys. Always have been. So how do I save them? How can I do that without you?"

"Edit the research. Don't give them everything. They'll never figure it out. Get your father back, then return to the rainforest. Restore our people, Izz. Save the Yarumaya, *Nahuari*."

"I'm not Nahuari, dude. That's silly."

"I'm starting to think that it isn't so silly."

"You're delusional, buddy." She squeezed his hand and hugged him tighter.

"I'm burning up, Izz. Water. I need some water."

She scrambled to her feet and snatched a water bottle from his backpack, dribbling small amounts into his mouth.

Quinn's eyes glanced toward the entrance. He reached out his arm.

"Brey? What are you doing here, darling?"

She glanced towards the entrance and then back towards Quinn. He placed his hand on her cheek, his dimples deepening.

"I love you, Izzy. I'll always love you. Remember me…"

Quinn's body relaxed as he exhaled.

"Oh my God, no! Quinn! Wake up. Baby, please wake up. No, no, no. You can't leave me."

She wailed mournful cries that echoed off the stone walls, cradling him in her arms, rocking him, and kissing his lips.

"This can't be real … Oh God. Come back to me, Quinn … please, please come back."

Her body shuddered as she held him and sobbed bittersweet tears. Time stood still; the rainforest mourned; Izzy's heart emptied. Its contents burst like an old wineskin.

She whimpered. "It's okay, Quinny. It's been a long, weary road, my love. Go to her. Go to Brey. And know that you always deserved her love. Deserved *my* love. Thank you for teaching me how to love." She sniffled and lay beside him, exhausted with grief.

"I want to die. My heart hurts so bad."

Isabella closed her eyes, lying next to him exhausted, and fell into a twilight sleep. Quinn's voice whispered, "Wake up, Izzy. They're coming. Time to go."

She gasped and sat upright in the dim light, gazing at Quinn's lifeless body. "Oh, my God."

Izzy slid the stone away and lifted documents and journals from the cranny. She began the meticulous process of photographing everything.

She removed key pages that would prevent anyone from duplicating their results. Unzipping Quinn's backpack, she stuffed the research inside a pocket, then popped the SD memory card from her camera, slipping it inside her boot.

Izzy removed the special "blanky" she's kept since she was a baby, tucking it neatly around Quinn's chest and kissing him on the forehead.

"I'll come back, my love. Your place is with the Ancestors, and if I can hear the voices of the Ancestors, then I'll hear your voice."

Shouts echoed in the distance. She slipped her arms inside her backpack, slung the AK-47 over her shoulder, and snagged the machete.

She glanced at Quinn. A look of peace radiated from his face, and oddly, his left arm stretched toward her as if to say goodbye. There was an object in his hand—his pocket watch. Izzy gently opened his fingers and took the watch.

As she exited the ruins, she replaced the natural camouflage to hide the ruins and Quinn's unintentional tomb.

She raced along the path toward the tree bridge, scurrying up the side of the tree like a creature of the forest. She dashed across the wooden planks, and upon reaching the other side, she buckled on a harness and zipped to the ground.

Thick rolling clouds swallowed the afternoon sun, grumbling and threatening to unleash an angry torrent. Izzy wasted no time darting through their earlier path, headed back to the base camp.

As she turned a corner and plunged through heavy vines, she saw a thousand tiny stars spiraling like dying fireworks. Her head exploded with white-hot pain, and she hit the ground, staring up into the trees.

Her vision blurred, and the surrounding sounds muffled. A warm trickle ran down her temple. Two men in fatigues hovered over her, laughing.

"I think you killed her, Stoney, you fucking idiot."

"Nah, she's still breathing. Look. She's staring at me."

"Can you hear me, Ms. Delgado? We're sorry about that, but we need you to come with us. I'm Orlando Mason. You can call me Lando. I'm going to confiscate your weapons so nobody gets hurt. Do you understand?" His voice modulated like the static of a radio inside her ears.

Stoney and Lando helped her to her feet and guided her to a smooth rock where they sat her down and cleaned her head wound.

"We're taking you into custody. Do you have Dr. Quinn's research?"

Izzy heaved a quivering breath and spat blood. "Everything is in that backpack. But I want a guarantee my father is safe before you take it."

"Congressman Ortega is awaiting your arrival in the city. You can work that out with him. Turn around, ma'am. I'm going to cuff you."

Izzy kicked Lando in the balls, doubling him over. Stoney jerked her by the hair and threw her to the ground. His weight across her chest stole her breath. She wheezed, "Let me go!"

"You like it rough, Delgado? You got it. I like it rough, too."

"Let her up, Stoney. We need to take her back in one piece."

"Hey, man. She started it. She thinks she's some badass bitch. Hell, she kicked you in the balls, brother. We should teach her a lesson. No one's around…"

Stoney grabbed her by the throat. "You gonna calm down, bitch?"

A low growl resonated from the brush ten feet away.

"What the fuck was that, man? Lando? What was that?" He pulled a pistol from a holster strapped to his waist.

"I dunno. I told you to stop fucking around and stand her up."

Two hundred pounds of muscle, teeth, and claws exploded from the brush, shredding Stoney's torso in seconds. The pistol hit the ground next to Izzy. He screamed, "Shoot it!"

TWENTY-SEVEN

The Road Back

The cat continued its vicious attack, mauling and clawing Stoney in the slimy mud. Lando unstrapped his rifle, but Izzy was quicker. She snatched the pistol and pointed it at Lando. "Drop it. I swear I'll waste you."

Lando dropped the weapon and disappeared into the brush.

"Bessie, come here, girl."

Bessie hovered over Stoney, panting and staring at Izzy as if saying, "You're welcome." The mud was crimson beneath the thug—his breathing labored. He wheezed, "Help me. Please."

The jaguar chuffed as it brushed against Izzy, plopping next to her and gently bumping her with its head. Izzy massaged her ears and kissed her nose. "Thank you, Bessie. And tell Quinn thanks for sending you to rescue me."

Stoney slithered away, eventually rising to his feet, limping and dragging one leg as he escaped into the jungle, whimpering.

Izzy lay with Bessie for nearly an hour, rubbing her neck and ears as the big cat pinned her feet and savored the attention. Bessie rose, licked Izzy's hand, and ambled towards the dense brush, glancing back for a moment, then dashing into the trees.

Izzy gathered herself, strapping the backpack around her shoulders, shoving Stoney's 9mm in her back pocket, and slinging the AK-47 over her shoulder.

Without a machete, she plodded through the forest for hours until she reached the trashed field lab at the old base camp. She stashed the rifle and pistol beneath the floor. The rains came, flooding the area as she huddled beneath the canvas on her favorite webbed chair with a blanket pulled taunt around her shoulders. She'd made it. All that was left was to sleep and catch the boatman at noon tomorrow.

A wave of emotion crashed over her as she sat with nothing to do but wait and reflect. Quinn was gone. She couldn't save him—couldn't believe it was real.

Izzy searched her backpack for her satellite phone. As she adjusted the contents, a small ring pinged across the floor. She snatched it from the mat and shook her head. "Teddy," she whispered.

For the first time in her life, she knew genuine heartbreak. It was nothing like losing Teddy. Losing Quinn cut deep into the core of her soul. She easily recovered from her breakup with Teddy; she knew the pain of losing Quinn would last a lifetime.

Izzy stood and glared into the storm. She flung the promise ring into the darkness—into the mud and rain, then zipped her backpack and stretched her legs across the old mattress left behind in the raid. Tears streamed down her cheeks as her exhaustion relented to the cool night.

September 10, 2026

Izzy sipped from a water bottle as she gazed across the glittering Rio Negro, awaiting her ride back to civilization. It was nearly twelve noon according to Quinn's pocket watch as she paced up and down the dock.

At ten minutes past noon, the distant hum of a motorboat cut through the air. She sighed and scooped up her gear, waiting anxiously at the end of the dock.

"Hola, señorita."

"Hola. Muchas gracias, señor."

She stepped aboard, set her backpack on the floor, and planted herself on the rotted vinyl seat.

The skiff jetted through a 180-degree turn, leaving a wake slapping the shoreline. The breeze was refreshing, tossing her hair and evaporating the sweat from her temples.

As they reached Manaus, Izzy marched up the dock into the busy streets. She sat on a bench near a park and removed the satellite phone from her backpack.

"Julio? Yeah, this is Izzy. Guess you didn't expect my call today, huh? I'm sure your thugs briefed you on their failure to kidnap me from the rainforest. You lose again."

"Isabella. How nice of you to call. And well within the time limit I set for you. Do you have what I requested?"

"I have everything. Let me speak to my father."

"In time. As you know, I am in Manaus. I intended a little surprise for you, but you ruined the news. We're staying at the Hotel Villa Amazonia. Room 213. I'll send a car for you."

"No. I'll come to you. Meet me in the lobby in thirty minutes. Bring my father. If I don't see him in the lobby with you, I'm leaving."

"A very bold threat, Hija. If you don't deliver the research, you'll never see him again. We have an agreement." CLICK.

Izzy entered the lobby of the Hotel Villa Amazonian. Her chest tightened, seeing that it was empty with no one at the counter. She crept through the entrance, past two stone columns supporting a ceiling of heavy wooden beams, and peered into a lounge area where Julio sat on a white sofa, legs crossed. Between Julio and a muscular man dressed in a bright-blue Hawaiian shirt, linen trousers, and sandals was her father. The man in the Hawaiian shirt pressed a pistol against her father's ribs.

"Over here, Hija. Have a seat."

Izzy sat on a loveseat opposite them and rested her backpack between her feet.

"Let him go," she demanded.

"Let me see the backpack."

"I'll leave the backpack here once you let him go."

"How do I know it isn't full of empty pages, Isabella?"

"You don't. But why would I risk my father's life not giving you what you asked for?"

"Good point. Open the bag and show me."

She unzipped the backpack and removed journals, documents, and samples, one by one, laying them on a glass coffee table between them, and then slipping them back inside the bag.

"Toss me a journal."

She stood and tossed a journal like a Frisbee, landing on Julio's lap. He flipped through the pages and grinned.

"This better be everything, Isabella. If any part of your research is missing, I will hunt you all down. No one will find the bodies."

"Can we go now?"

Julio nodded at the man in the colorful shirt. Frederico stood and rushed towards Izzy. His warm hug squeezed the air out of her in a sigh of relief.

"We need to go, Daddy," she whispered.

Izzy and her father marched towards the exit and away from the hotel arm-in-arm.

"I have a private jet waiting to take us home, sweetheart. A car is on the way to take us to the airport."

"Dad, I'm sorry, but there's something I have to do first. It's really, really important. I'll catch a flight home in a day or two. I have my satellite phone, and I'll call you when I leave Brazil."

"Aye, Mija. It's too dangerous here. Let me help you with whatever it is."

"Trust me, you can't. You can, however, give me a ride back to the docks."

"I'm taking your mother and going away for a while. I'll send for you when you get home. Be very careful, sweetheart. There's an investigation going on at the DOJ involving Julio Ortega. We should lie low while it's in progress."

"I'm safe in the rainforest, Daddy. Don't worry about me."

They climbed into a small limo and drove away. Frederico laid his hand on the driver's shoulder.

"Take my daughter to the docks, then take me to the airport, por favor."

TWENTY-EIGHT

In Search of Quinn

It was a race against the sun. Izzy dashed across the old rickety boat dock to the field lab. She retrieved the weapons she had stashed and wasted no time heading back to the ruins where she had left Quinn. Slicing a fresh path with the brand-new machete she purchased at the market, she pushed through the forest at an exhausting pace.

Storm clouds boiled in the distance as long gray shadows consumed the daylight. The air was heavy with the scent of rotting vegetation and ancient mud. Her eyes stung from sweat, and her skin itched from insect bites exacerbated by heat rash. Izzy paused, resting her hands on her knees, heaving quick breaths. She was close, but her calves were cramping and she needed water.

As she entered the clearing outside the ruins, her stomach fluttered with nervous energy. Her heart pounded from exhaustion and fear. Fear of what she would see when she entered the ruins. Quinn's remains have surely decomposed, and that fact is something her heart isn't ready to face. She'd never witnessed a decaying human body and didn't know if she was capable of it now. That can't be the last memory she has of him. But she owes it to him to give him an honorable burial alongside the Ancestors in the sacred grove.

Izzy set her backpack on a large stone and leaned the rifle against it. She removed a large vinyl bag from her backpack and pushed the branches and vines covering the entrance to the side. *The moment of truth.* Izzy switched on a small lantern, ducked, and entered.

When she held the lantern high, she gasped. All that remained of Quinn was her childhood blanky in a pile. Quinn's body was gone. Did animals find and carry him away? There were no signs of blood or being dragged across the floor. And how would an animal have replaced the branches over the entrance?

Did someone steal his body? Why would they do that? Could Quinn be alive? But how? She watched him die. Held his hand. Said goodbye. That'd be impossible.

She planted herself on a square stone and stared at the ceiling. "How could he disappear like this?"

Maybe several of Julio's thugs discovered his body and stole it to use as a bargaining chip in exchange for their research. *But surely Julio would have mentioned it, wouldn't he?*

Her instinct was to return to the base camp, phone the boatman, and go home. But something inside—a gut feeling, a premonition, or just a curiosity—was driving her towards finding the Kawirén. Or what remains of them.

She brought enough food and water for three days, and Quinn taught her how to survive—to treat water to make it drinkable. She knew which plants were edible. This could buy her time to search for the villagers.

The sky exploded with crackling thunder. Lightning lit up the clouds. A torrent crashed outside the entrance, creating a waft of cool air that filled the cavern. Izzy hunkered down in a corner with her blanky, listening to the storm stretch the trees and pound the ground outside the entrance.

She gnawed on a jerky stick and swigged from a bottle of water. At the moment, she wasn't going anywhere. Resting on the spot where Quinn breathed his last breath brought her comfort and pain. She curled into a fetal position and closed her eyes, waiting for the storm to subside.

September 11, 2026

Izzy opened her eyes and screeched. A green reptilian face glared at her from inches away, rolling its rusty-red eyes and tasting her with its tongue.

She leaped to her feet in a flash and kicked dirt at it.

"Get away from me, you! Oh, my God. What the heck are you? Spawn of Godzilla?"

The large green lizard studied her for a moment and then slithered away to the corner of the chamber and perched on a cornerstone.

She peered outside. Soft golden light illuminated the forest. The rain was light, but the ground had flooded. The air was fresh and heavy with oxygen. Nowhere in the world is the air this pure, she thought.

Izzy stuffed a dried-up biscuit in her mouth, washed it down, and gathered her gear. She was determined to reach the old sacred Yarumaya grove by midday. Maybe she'd find answers there, or at least discover a clue regarding the whereabouts of the tribe.

Hours passed. Every corner of the rainforest looked the same—like she was walking in circles. She knew the standard path to the old village Quinn had taught her, but not the alternate route from the ruins. Her clothes stuck to her. She wrapped a bandana around her forehead to soak up the sweat stinging her eyes. Her breathing deepened, and her heart raced as she realized she was lost.

Izzy squatted on a rock and rubbed her temples. "God, where am I?" she whispered. If Quinn were here, he'd know the way. But he wasn't there to guide her. She couldn't fight her sobs, and she didn't care. There was nobody here to see her cry, so she let it out. Tears dribbled from her chin into the tiny pools of water left over from last night's rain. Her eyes looked puffy in the pool's reflection.

"Oh, Quinn. Why? Why did you leave me? What do I do now? I have no clue what I'm doing. I thought I did when you were with me, but now I see how helpless I am without you."

She wiped her cheeks and dabbed her eyes with her sleeve. As she stared into the forest, guessing which way she should go, she spotted something peculiar several feet up the side of a tree. She squinted. "What is that?"

As she drew nearer, she exhaled and hit her knees. "Oh my God, Quinn. Even now you're looking out for me."

Nailed into the tree was one of Quinn's large orange spikes, screaming at her to follow. Izzy stood and continued her journey. Another spike came into view, then another.

Thirty minutes later, she heard the angelic sound of a familiar waterfall.

"I know this place."

Izzy strapped on a harness and descended the craggy cliff to the river 50 feet below. She reached the familiar trail Quinn had taught her.

It was early afternoon when Izzy strolled into the old village. Quinn's pocket watch showed 2:37 p.m. The emptiness of the village hit her like a tumble from the balance beam mid-performance. It was quiet. Too quiet.

A ghost town in the Amazon. She kicked charred wood in the firepit inside the Circle and could almost hear the laughter of children, the gossip of the women, and Quinn yukking it up with his boys.

In a flash, life in the Kawirén village was gone. Wiped out by the cruel and ignorant outside world that fed on greed and corruption.

She wandered along the trail to the sacred grove and stepped through the ancient archway etched with glyphs from the distant past. A twinge of fear crept over her, wondering if the demons and mischievous spirits were following her without Tarenu's blessing to keep them at bay.

Sprouts and saplings covered the ground in vibrant green. A promise that life will not be denied. The Yarumaya trees were growing. Fighting to return under the loving care of the Ancients. Chills filled her with waves of warmth as a sense of love and protection embraced her. The Ancients. They were alive, and their presence was powerful.

Her eyes squeezed shut as she plopped onto a stump and took a deep breath. She called to them in her thoughts—hoping they'd answer. Praying they could tell her what happened to Quinn. But only the wind answered in hushed, gentle gusts.

Izzy meandered through the forest and returned to the village, resting on a hammock inside the deserted field lab where she and Quinn spent so many hours researching and discovering answers to the most troublesome questions. Side-by-side, they worked day by day. And moment-by-moment, she fell hopelessly in love with him. Life wasn't fair. It was cruel.

Fearful of the condition of the new village, she stayed the night and would head to the new village before dawn. God only knew what Ian Bragg and Julio Ortega had done to the village and the young Yarumaya grove. What horrors would she encounter when she arrived?

TWENTY-NINE

Justice is Blind and Silent

September 12, 2026

Izzy crawled to the edge of the village and peered through the fronds. The village looked more like a small town, complete with a landing pad for a helicopter. The Yarumaya grove expanded into what she could only describe as a tree farm.

"You've got to be joking," she whispered. "You assholes."

Anger prickled up the back of her neck. Overnight, they'd turned the village of an endangered remote Amazon tribe into a pharmaceutical research factory.

She flinched at the crunch of leaves and broken branches behind her. A hand clamped over her mouth and whispered in her ear.

"Shhh." Before she could turn around, a gentle voice spoke in Kawirénian.

"Nahuari? What are you doing here?"

Two Kawirén warriors, Tavera and Orani, sat next to her and beamed with boyish grins.

She replied, "Looking for you. What are *you* doing here? Very dangerous." Her heart leaped with joy at their presence.

Tavera pointed at the helipad and whispered, "Every seven days, a great black bird lands and the murderer of our people visits."

She paused and narrowed her eyes. "But why are you here?"

"To take revenge by stealing the murderer's life as a sacrifice to Mayuma." He raised his blowgun and grinned.

As they were talking, the thrumming of helicopter blades cut through the heavy air in the distance.

Orani placed his hand on Izzy's shoulder and nodded. "Wait here, Nahuari."

"Why? Where are you going?" Fear gripped her as Tavera and Orani split up and crept through the brush to gain a closer vantage point near the helipad.

"Oh, God. Are they out of their minds?"

Izzy hid, watching as the warriors positioned themselves to deal a lethal strike. The helicopter touched down moments later as the whirl of blades and the shrill of the engine faded. Three armed men met the helicopter as the door swung open. Two men exited the craft, shook hands with the armed men, then wandered towards the camp.

One of the men was Ian Bragg, dressed in blue jeans, boots, and an unbuttoned long-sleeve denim shirt over a black T-shirt.

Orani peered above the ferns, aiming his blowgun directly at Bragg. A muffled thump fired a dart that stuck Bragg in the right thigh. A second dart flew from Tavera's position and stuck Bragg in the chest. He yelped, yanking both darts from his body, and pointed towards the brush where the warriors hid.

A firm hand grasped her upper arm and tugged. "We must go, Nahuari. Run."

Izzy hesitated, watching as Bragg hit his knees and fell face-first into the mud. His body convulsed as he foamed at the mouth. Men feverishly tended to him, lifting and carrying him towards a tent.

Orani and Tavera took her by the hands and pulled, urging her to follow them. Automatic gunfire rang out, echoing behind them and shredding the brush like a woodchopper as they fled. She trailed them through thick vegetation to a small river, where they hopped into an 8-foot canoe, frantically waving for her to board. They raced downstream through massive trees and dense brush until they reached a bend in the river.

The bottom of the canoe scuffed onto the slimy beach of the riverbank, where they leaped out and hid the canoe beneath palm fronds and tree branches.

Just like that, Ian Bragg was dead. The Kawirén warriors had exacted their revenge for the murder of their people and the theft of their villages. It happened so fast, Izzy felt robbed of the full satisfaction that justice had been served, swift and silent. Ian Bragg was a monster, and the world will never mourn his loss, she thought.

The warriors led Izzy through dense rainforest, up a mountain, and into a hidden valley where a tiny village thrived with the remnants of the Kawirén people. She estimated a hundred men, women, and children in all.

When they entered the village, children screeched, and the women shrilled as they gathered around her, chanting, "Nahuari, Nahuari…" The men greeted her by kissing her hand, laughing and smiling.

Orani led her to a single hut made of timber with a thatched roof. Inside was a small bed of fronds, a hammock from one of the labs, an empty gourd that smelled of lakira, and a chair constructed of vines and wood. He nodded and grinned.

"Stay with us, Nahuari. Tonight, we celebrate our victory. You are home now. Returned to us by Mayuma."

"Thank you, Orani. I'm honored to be here with you, but I need to ask you a question."

Orani sat on the ground of the hut, crossed his legs, and motioned for her to sit opposite him as was tradition. "Ask your question, great shaman."

"I'm sad to tell you that Quinn … Tupakaí … has died."

Orani crinkled his brow and chuckled.

"Why are you laughing?"

"Tupakaí walks among us."

"I understand. Tupakaí's spirit will always walk among the people and watch over you with the Ancestors."

Orani tilted his head and rested his hand on hers. "Tupakaí awaits you. Said you will go to him soon."

"What? God, I hope not," she whispered in English.

"Orani, Tupakaí's body disappeared after he died. Do you know what happened?"

"Yes. We tracked your presence to the ancient temple. Found Tupakaí alone, and took him home."

"You buried him?"

"Took him home. Here. To the village."

"Where you buried him?"

"No, great one. Where he lies recovering from his wounds after an ancient ceremony and secret medicines, where we rescued him from death."

"What? Oh, my God! He's alive? Where? Take me to him, Orani. Please."

He rose and took her hand, leading her out of the hut and across the village to a larger hut. Orani paused and pointed.

"Your husband awaits you inside. He said you would come."

Izzy burst through the door, her heart pounding out of her chest. She could barely breathe.

Stretched on a bed of banana leaves and bamboo lay Quinn. His hair was as black and as thick as a panther's mane, and his eyes glinted fiery sapphire. The beard was gone, revealing a solid chin that beamed, deepening his dimples. He was shirtless, barefoot, and wore linen trousers.

"What took you so long, Malibu? Shit, I thought I taught you better."

She collapsed on top of him, hugging and kissing his face.

"Whoa, whoa, I'm still not fully healed, kid. You're going to set me back."

"How? You were dead. I watched you die, Quinn. Held your hand."

"I fell into a coma, Izz. The Kawirén search party must have found me shortly after you left. You gave up on me too soon, kid. What the hell kind of partner are you?"

"I must be dreaming. This can't be real."

"I know. It's a curse."

"Oh, jeez. I'm gonna stop you right there. Okay?"

"Izz, it was the Kawirén who were following us."

"No, Quinn. It was two of Ortega's thugs. They attacked me. Tried to kidnap me. You'll never believe this, but Bessie saved me."

"No shit? Always loved that cat."

"My dad is free, Quinn. He took my mom and disappeared while a DOJ investigation into the congressman is underway. They're safe for now."

"That's great news. I guess you'll be sticking around then?"

"Yeah, I guess so. And what about you, buddy? You look swole … jacked … almost like your old self again." She fiddled with his hair near his ears. "You should grow this out. Cover those satellite dishes."

He felt his ears and frowned. "What's wrong with my ears?"

She snickered and ignored his question.

"How did they know what to do? How, Quinn?" she asked.

"I don't know. These people never cease to amaze me. The entire tribe performed a sacred ritual I'd never seen before. It saved my life. Then they fed me the yaru-honey, keeping me locked inside the men's hut filled with Yarumaya smoke. They pulled me out of my coma."

"Well, mystery solved, I guess. Tarzan lives to see another day."

He grabbed her hand and pulled her down beside him. "Izzy, while I was in that coma, I found myself traveling."

"What do you mean?"

"It was like my spirit left my body. I ended up in the treehouse. It was nighttime, and I had a fire lit in the stove. As I sat in the darkness, I heard Brey's voice call to me. I checked outside, but didn't see anyone. But when I turned back around, she was sitting on the floor with her legs crossed, looking beautiful and at peace, like when she was 25."

"Oh, my God, Quinn. Do you think it was real? Were you dreaming?"

"It was as real as you and me talking right now."

"What did she say to you? I mean, why was she there?" she asked, trying not to sound too anxious.

"She told me she would always love me and that she knew how much I loved her and how I've struggled and suffered all these years."

He choked back the words, his eyes misting. "She took the wedding band from my finger and placed it on hers. I asked her why. She said her love for me was too great to watch my pain from a distance and that she was setting me free. Free to love again. She mentioned you. Told me I belong with you now and to let her go—that I was keeping her spirit trapped in this world."

He glanced away and wiped his eyes.

"I don't know what to say, Quinn…"

"She kissed me, faded into a blinding white light, and disappeared."

She hugged his neck and rested her head on his chest.

"The pain is gone, Izz. The weight's been lifted. I can't explain it, but I haven't felt this free in years."

"Can I just lie here with you the rest of the day, Quinny?"

"Who am I to deny you?" he chuckled. "Actually, you're crushing me, Malibu. Could I ask a favor? I'm a tad hungry." He closed one eye and flashed a gentle smile.

"Seriously? What else is new?"

She marched to her hut and removed her half-eaten bag of beef jerky and a ripe apple from her backpack. The satellite phone rang.

"Hello," she said, with a sense of trepidation.

"Isabella. How are you?"

"How did you get this number?"

"I have my resources, Chica."

"Why are you calling me? Shouldn't you be calling your lawyers instead? I understand you're in big trouble, Julio."

"Not as much as you, Hija."

"What do you mean?"

"I regret to report that tribesmen assassinated my dear friend and compadre, Ian Bragg, in the Amazon. Do you know of this?"

"I, uh … hadn't heard. We don't have CNN or Fox News in the Amazon. Word travels slowly here."

"Indeed, it does. Indeed, it does. Then the word that your parents have tragically died in a mysterious car crash hasn't reached you either?"

Izzy dropped the phone and fell to her knees. After several seconds, she heaved a ragged breath and snatched the phone.

"You're a liar! I swear to God, Julio, if you hurt them, I will hunt you down and kill you myself."

"Powerful threat, young one. You have my deepest sympathies, Hija. I expect you'll be returning home soon. Have a safe journey, mi amiga. Travel can be treacherous these days. I'm genuinely sorry for your loss."

"You bastard! You'd better pray this isn't true."

"I'll pray for you, Isabella … because it *is* true."

She was numb, sitting on the edge of the bed with her face buried in her hands, sobbing. "This can't be real. He's lying. Trying to trick me into coming home."

THIRTY

Immortality's Opposite

She raced back to Quinn's hut and paused as she stepped inside.

"Where's my … Izz? What's wrong? You're as white as a porcelain doll."

She knelt by his bed. "My parents. They killed my parents. I have to go home, Quinn."

"What the hell? Who Izzy? Who killed your parents? Julio?"

"Yes. I have to go."

"Not without me."

"You're still recovering. You can't travel."

"Don't tell me what I'm up for, Izzy. I'm fine. I can't let you do this alone. These are dangerous people we're dealing with, Izz. They don't care who they hurt."

"Ian Bragg is dead, Quinn. Orani and Tavera killed him this morning."

"I know. I heard. The world is a better place."

"I'm so scared. Is that the reason they murdered my parents?"

"I don't know. Maybe you should wait before going home, Izzy. It could be a trap to lure you out of hiding."

"I thought of that."

"If it's true, there's nothing you can do for them now. Your parents would want you to stay safe."

"What do I do, then?"

"Maybe we go to Manaus and check the news. Scan the internet for information. Make sure he's telling the truth."

"And if he is?"

"Then we wait, Izzy. Bide our time. Figure out a way to take him down for good."

"Maybe the DOJ investigation will uncover his corruption. Send him to prison."

"The DOJ won't do a damn thing to him. They're as invested in stealing our research as he is. It's a network of corruption."

"I'm going to call my dad's attorney. He'll tell me the truth. And if it *is* true, Quinn, I stand to inherit an obscene fortune. Money I can fight Julio Ortega with."

"Izz, I think a better plan is to move the tribe deeper into the rainforest. Find a suitable area to replant the Yarumaya and seedpods. Far away from any chance of someone finding them again. We'll need to set up and equip a new field lab. Stay as far away from Julio Ortega as we can."

"Then I need to call the attorney. To arrange access to my father's fortune, so I can fund it all."

"I'm deeply sorry about your parents. My heart breaks for you. Let's make sure their deaths aren't in vain."

"And what about Julio? I want to take him down so badly."

"We'll need time for that. We'll wait until he feels safe. Sure, you're no longer a threat. Then we'll strike."

"How Quinn? I mean, who are we kidding? We can't take down a sitting congressman."

"I have some thoughts on that. I'd like to discuss them with you. Something I've been working on for a while."

❧❧❧

Izzy set the satellite phone on the bed. She glanced at Quinn and feigned a half-hearted smile.

"What's the verdict, kid?"

"My parents died in a crash heading to the airport. A semi T-boned them at an intersection two miles from their terminal. Their car exploded like a bomb. There was …" She broke into tears. "There was little left of their bodies after they put out the fire. Our lawyer will handle the cremation and burial. They wanted to be buried together in our family mausoleum. I don't want to visit them there, Quinn. That place has always given me the creeps. Am I wrong to feel that way?"

"Of course not. They won't be there, anyway. Only their remains. You'll have to take your time, Izzy. Grief affects us all differently. I'm so sorry."

He sat upright and laid his arm around her shoulders.

"Is there anything I can do?"

She quietly nodded.

"My attorney is going to meet me in Manaus tomorrow afternoon so I can sign all the legal documents inheriting my parents' estate. He'll manage things and ensure I have full access. I can finance our research, Quinn."

"Good. Because I have something I want to share with you. Something that should remedy your issues with Congressman Ortega. For now, let's get you back to the city for your meeting."

"The suspense is killing me, Dr. Quinn."

She rested her head on his shoulder and sighed. "Are you sure you're up to taking me back to Manaus?"

"Absolutely, Izzy."

She wrapped her arms around his waist and ran her finger gently across his lips.

"I'm getting a room in Manaus, Quinny. Wanna share a bed?"

"I think a nice hot shower and clean linen are just what the doctor ordered. Me being the doctor, of course."

"Good. Now tell me about this secret research of yours and how it can help us take down a congressman."

"Before I explain, I need you to promise that you trust me, and what I'm about to tell you will remain between you and me to the death."

"Oh, my God. So cryptic. It's that serious?"

"Yes. Promise, Izzy."

"Okay. I promise. Continue, please."

"During our research, I discovered that the Yarumaya resin doesn't just slow aging. We can flip the molecule to accelerate the aging process. Under normal circumstances, the resin protects the body's cells and helps repair DNA damage, allowing the body to live significantly longer. But by tweaking the chemistry, I created a version that does the opposite. Instead of protecting cells, it makes them 'burn through' their natural lifespan much faster."

Izzy sat wide-eyed with her jaw hanging. "Oh, my God. What have you created, Quinn? And why? I mean, why would you do that? How does it work?"

"The normal longevity molecule tells cells to stay young by keeping their telomeres—the uh, DNA ends—from wearing out too quickly. The altered version of the resin blocks the signal and pushes cells into overdrive. Their telomeres shorten much faster than normal, so the cells *think* they're old even though they're not."

"I'm afraid to ask, but what are the effects?"

"The effects? The person's body ages at hyper-speed, Izz. On the outside, it looks like years are passing in days, but inside it's because their cells are hitting their 'expiration date' way too soon."

"Why didn't you tell me this? And why were you working on this in the first place?"

"This is what Ian Bragg was actually after. He didn't want a drug to save the world. He wanted a bio-weapon he could sell for trillions of dollars to the highest bidder."

"And you were helping him? Are you crazy?"

"No. I developed it so I could figure out how to shut it down. Deactivate it. I needed to be the expert on the subject so that no one else could acquire this knowledge."

"I'm confused, Quinn. So all this time you had the answers but allowed me to think I was helping to discover the longevity serum?"

"No. All of your work was genuine, Izzy. It gave me the answers to fill in the blanks for this alternate research on speeding up the aging process. I had to keep it from you. To protect you. I'm sorry."

"Oh, Quinn. How could you? No wonder you were so secretive about the work you were doing. I feel so stupid."

"I refused to give it to Bragg. That's why he cut me off."

She crossed her arms and glared. "And is that why he invaded the village and slaughtered innocent villagers? This is your fault."

"Yes! It is my fault, Izzy. All of it. What was I to do? Give Bragg the most lethal biological weapon in history, or face the consequences of refusing to turn it over? It was a no-win scenario. I chose the latter."

"And you've kept this secret all this time?"

"I was going to tell you, Izz. The night in the ruins when we hid our research behind the stone wall. The night I fell into a coma and you left me for dead."

"Don't try to spin this back on me, buddy. You looked and acted like a corpse. I'm not a medical doctor."

"I'm sorry. You're right."

She frowned, ran her fingers through her hair, and paced. "Okay, we don't have time for this. We'll discuss it later. Besides, this is water under the bridge, as they say. Bragg is dead, so it's a moot point. Tell me how we can use this knowledge to take down Ortega."

"The normal resin protects cells like armor—it keeps the telomeres from wearing down too fast. That's why it slows aging."

"And … the serum's evil twin removes the armor?"

"Worse than that. It tricks the cells into burning through their lifespan at high speed. Without protection, the telomeres shorten way too fast. The body thinks it's decades older than it really is. It's a nasty little trick, Izzy."

"So, what happens to the poor fool who's unfortunate enough to be its victim?"

"They will look and feel like they've aged ten years every seven days. Wrinkles, age spots, graying, pissing five times a night, erectile dysfunction—all the good stuff of old age. Eventually, their organs fail, and they succumb."

"And said volunteer would have no clue what was happening to him?"

"Not until it's too late. I have a remedy to reverse the effect. I've just never tested it. Once the serum is injected, it's a dirt nap for the victim. One hundred percent fatal within weeks."

"How do we get him to take it?"

"That's where you come in, Izzy. You'll need to convince him that you've decided to betray me and sell him the research. Promise him immortality. Get him to test the serum himself."

"Get some rest, Quinn. I want to leave at dawn."

THIRTY-ONE

The Pitch

September 13, 2026

They arrived in Manaus and checked into the Tropical Executive Hotel at 1:35 p.m. Quinn dropped his backpack onto the king-size bed and peeked inside the spacious bathroom at the tiled walk-in shower. He glanced at her and winked.

"Take your hot shower, buddy. I'm going to call the attorney and let him know I'm here and give him our room number."

She flopped on the bed, closed her eyes, sinking into the softness of the mattress and the scent of clean linen. The spray of the shower echoed across the tile floors as a moist, warm breeze inflated a set of sheer white curtains, filling their room with an earthy, sweet scent of jungle flora mixed with smoke from recent wildfires.

Izzy allowed her clothes to drop to the floor as she tiptoed across the tile and crept into the shower behind him. Quinn lathered himself in suds and washed his hair. His body was hard and soapy as she wrapped her arms around him, kissing the flesh separating his shoulder blades.

"Is that you, Izzy, or is it room service?"

She spoke with a thick Spanish accent. "Who do you want it to be?"

"Whoa, I didn't know you could do that."

He turned and ran his fingers through her hair, cradled her face, and whispered, "I want it to be you … but with that accent."

She giggled and snuggled into his body and the warmth of the shower spray. A wave of emotion engulfed her—like an unexpected storm. She couldn't face the grief of losing her family, and she dreaded the upcoming meeting with her attorney. Izzy turned into an aggressor, hungering for his kiss and the feel of his body inside hers. She shoved him against the wall and made love to him in a lustful frenzy. He didn't resist.

At five minutes to four in the afternoon, three knocks rattled the door. She rose from the balcony where they sat, taking in the scenic view of civilization cast against primal nature, and swung the door wide.

"Izzy! So nice to see you. I'd rather the circumstances were different."

"Come in, Carlos. We can sit at the table. Oh, this is my good friend, Quinn. He tagged along for moral support."

Carlos nodded, laid his briefcase on the table, and unsnapped the buckles. He laid a stack of papers in front of her and placed an expensive-looking pen on top of the stack.

"Your father left you everything, including his businesses across the globe, his stock portfolio, jewelry, all his properties, and a substantial amount of money in various bank accounts. It's an immense fortune, Isabella. I know it is no consolation, but you are very wealthy."

Her heart pounded, trying to absorb the reality of her new status as the tears streamed.

"Your father left strict instructions to sell all of his businesses and add the funds to your investment portfolio. He didn't want you to have to deal with the headaches of managing them. I'm your executor, Isabella. I'll also act as your accountant to help manage your investments and bank accounts."

"My father trusted you, Carlos, so I trust you as well."

Izzy took a deep breath and sighed. "How much am I worth? Approximately that is."

"Roughly seven-hundred and fifty million."

Her temples throbbed. "What the… I had no idea."

"Just sign where I've indicated, and I'll handle the rest. I'm deeply sorry for this terrible loss, Mija. Your papa and I have been friends since childhood. He paid my way through law school, and I … I loved him like a brother. I promise you, Isabella, I will handle your affairs with the utmost care and detail."

"I know you will. Thank you."

She pushed the stack of signed documents towards him and offered her hand. He placed both his hands over hers and smiled.

"I'll be in touch, Mija. Don't hesitate to call if you have questions."

As Carlos opened the door to leave, he paused. "Oh, I almost forgot."

He pulled a golf ball charm dangling on a golden chain from his pocket.

"Your father wanted me to give this to you. For luck."

Izzy held the necklace in her hand and stared at it for several moments before locking the door. She fastened it around her neck, silent tears streaming before she crumbled and hit her knees.

"Come here, Izzy." Quinn held her tightly and rocked her gently, leading her towards the bed where he laid her down and cradled her until she cried herself to sleep.

❧❧❧

She gasped. Her eyes popped open. Her heart slowed upon realizing Quinn held her as they slept. His snores grew louder, so she slipped beneath his arm and escaped his hug. She must have slept for a couple of hours based on the fiery orange sunset that glowed outside their balcony window. Izzy picked up the phone and ordered dinner for her and Quinn. She wanted to surprise him. Splurge on him. So, she ordered food from the most expensive restaurant she could find on the list next to the phone.

She nudged him. He groaned and rolled over.

"Hey, wake up, Prince Charming. Dinner is here. Are you hungry?"

He lifted his head, his hair flat on one side and his eyes bloodshot.

"You made dinner, Izzy?"

"I *bought* dinner."

She lit a candle and dimmed the lights.

"I've always wanted to do this. A little fantasy of mine. Scoot over so we can eat on the bed. This is like, so romantic, right?"

"If eating on the bed makes you feel romantic, who am I to argue?"

After dinner, she crawled on top of him and pinned his arms to the bed, kissing him hard on the lips.

"Whoa, Izzy? What's gotten into you? Where did this wild woman come from?"

"I-I don't know, I just … I just need you to make love to me again, Quinn. I don't want to think right now. Just hold me. Please."

September 14, 2026

Early morning rain filled the hotel room with damp, cool air. The splatter on the balcony was soothing. She didn't want to move or open her eyes. The down-filled pillow, silky sheets, and fluffy comforter cradled her like a baby in its mother's arms.

Quinn rolled over, propping his head up with his hand behind his ear and his elbow on the mattress, gazing at her with adoring eyes that sparkled blue.

"Izz? Are you ready to initiate operation 'Old Man'?"

She heaved a deep breath and rubbed her eyes. "I don't know. Oh, my God. What if he doesn't buy it?"

"Trust me, he will. The thought of immortality and a mass fortune will be too much for him to resist. It will blind him. He'll never see it coming. Besides, didn't you say one of his sons suffers from a debilitating disease?"

"Yes, that's what he told me."

She sighed and stretched her legs. "What do I say? I mean, how do I present it to him?"

"That's what we're going to practice this morning. By lunchtime, you'll be ready to make that call. You're going to do just fine."

"Quinn, are you sure this is the right thing to do? Isn't it a cruel way to die?"

"Are you having second thoughts? Julio deserves to die. He had no mercy on our village. None for your parents. He's a callous, calculating murderer. Who knows what other crimes he's guilty of?"

"True. But when I think about the son he's trying to save with the longevity formula, it makes me nauseous doing this."

"Sometimes you have to do the wrong thing to do the right thing, Izzy. These choices are never easy. There's nothing to stop us from helping his son afterward."

"I didn't think of that. We should."

At 12:47 p.m., Quinn handed her the satellite phone and smiled reassuringly. His confidence and his dimples encouraged her to follow through with their plan.

"Make the call, Izzy. And don't screw this up."

"Okay … okay. Go into the other room."

She sucked in a nervous breath and nibbled her lower lip as she dialed Julio's number and listened as the phone rang.

"Julio? It's Isabella."

"And to what do I owe the pleasure of your call this morning, Hija?"

"Business."

"Business? Okay. I'm listening. What kind of business?"

"The kind that can make you rich and save your son. The business you've been waiting for."

"Well, you have my full attention, Isabella. Will you be attending your parents' funeral on Sunday? I'm looking forward to seeing you."

"No. I won't be. I'll have a private visit with my parents when I come home. Can we keep the conversation focused on our business, please?"

"Of course. What are you proposing?"

"I'll give you the missing pieces of the research I delivered, in the form of a serum."

"I'm disappointed. You excluded certain aspects of your research?"

"Yes, Julio. What I gave you was incomplete. You and your team of scientists will never figure it out. Vital information is missing."

"Tsk, tsk. What am I to do, Hija? I can hardly hold your father for ransom again."

She ignored the jab. "I have a stabilized and concentrated serum, Julio. One that only requires two injections. I'm offering you immortality and the missing pieces of my research. Think of your son."

The phone went silent for several seconds.

"I'm intrigued. And what do you want in return?"

"Ten million. And your word that you will leave me and Dr. Quinn alone forever."

"And how do you propose we complete this transaction?"

"Meet me in Manaus tomorrow. At the Tropical Executive Hotel. Room 403. Two o'clock."

"And what of Dr. Quinn? Has he agreed to this arrangement of yours?"

"No, he doesn't need to know. This is between you and me. No one else. Come alone, or the deal is off."

"I'm going to consider your offer, Hija. See you tomorrow at 2:00 p.m. Do not cross me, Isabella. I warn you."

"You can trust me, I promise. I just want all of this to be over. And for you to stay out of my life for good."

"Deliver what you promise, and I'll keep my end of the bargain."

September 15, 2026, 2:01 p.m.

The satellite phone rang.

"Hello?"

"I'm in the lobby, Isabella. Meet me at the bar in ten minutes."

CLICK.

"Quinn. He's here. Oh, my God. I'm so nervous I could pee my pants. My pits are sweaty. He said to meet him at the bar in ten."

"Calm down, Izzy. You can do this. Relax and stick to the script."

"Okay. Gotcha. Whew. How do I look?"

"Like someone from Malibu who just inherited a fortune. I think the red dress and heels were a perfect choice. You've got great gams, by the way. The hair looks fantastic, make-up is perfect. You are the bee's knees, kid."

"Gams?"

"Yeah. Gams. Legs, Izzy. Great legs."

"Okay, awesome. I've gotta bounce."

"Bounce?"

"Yeah, bounce. You know, hit the road. Blow this popsicle stand. Leave."

"Got it. I'll be at the restaurant next to the bar. Scream if you need me. Wait…"

He adjusted her dress. "A little more cleavage. Keep him off balance."

Izzy sauntered towards the bar and slid into the seat next to Julio. On the outside, she was as cool as a California breeze. On the inside, she was a train wreck.

"Wow. You dressed up just for me, Chica. I'm flattered. Mui bonita. What would you like to drink?"

"I dress for myself, not for any man. Especially you. I'll take a Caipifrutas."

"Excellent choice. Now tell me more about this serum."

She removed two syringes from her purse and laid them on the bar.

"This is what Quinn spent years perfecting. He calls it Serum L-1. It's not just an extract from the Yarumaya tree—it's the purified compound, stabilized and concentrated so it actually works outside the rainforest. Two injections. That's all it takes. No tea, no resin, no tribal rituals. The enzyme catalyzes instantly, and the molecule integrates with your cells as if it were always part of you."

"Intriguing. Tell me more."

"Your aging slows to a crawl, and your body repairs itself at the cellular level. No more sickness, Julio. This is the culmination of all our work—the very thing your old buddy Ian Bragg wanted but could never have. I'm willing to share it with you exclusively for ten million dollars and the promise that you'll leave me alone for good."

She lifted a syringe. "This is the first dose. Once I receive your payment to my bank account, the second, permanent dose is all yours. Immortality, Congressman. And for another ten million, I'll give you another series of doses for your son."

He lifted the syringe and examined it. "How do I know this will work?"

"You don't."

"Then allow me to sample it before I buy. Twenty mil is a lot of dinero."

"Fair enough. Take the first dose. If you're not satisfied, then walk away. But if you end up feeling like you're 25 again, transfer the money into my account, and I'll send you the second dose. Imagine your golf game, Julio. Or your prowess in the bedroom. Just saying. Imagine watching your child fully recover and live a very long and healthy life."

"And you guarantee this will save my son?"

"Yes. But we should try it on *you* first. To ensure there are minimal side effects before we administer it to your son."

He narrowed his eyes, grinned, and rolled up his sleeve. Izzy's ears swished with a rush of blood from her pounding heart. She drew a breath to settle her nerves and gripped the syringe.

"Are you ready? I really hope this hurts."

He chuckled. "You're a sadistic little bitch, Isabella."

You have no idea, she thought.

She wiped his shoulder with an alcohol pad and jammed the needle deep, injecting every drop of the serum. She stretched a Band-Aid over the injection site and nodded.

"Wow, you took that like a man. The first sign of the drug taking effect will be a blue ring around your irises. You should feel the full effect within a week. I'll be in touch, Julio. Maybe I can meet you on the golf course for that rematch you've been begging for."

"Man, that's a rush. My body is tingling. I already feel younger. I don't need to wait. Give me the second dose."

She couldn't believe her luck. "Are you sure?"

"Sí, give me your account information. I'll transfer the funds tonight after I receive the doses for my son."

After the second dose, Julio stood and extended his hand. She ignored him and sipped her drink.

"Pleasure doing business with you, Ms. Delgado. I'll be in touch."

As Julio left the hotel and climbed into a limo, Izzy chugged her drink, slammed the tumbler onto the bar, and exhaled a ragged breath.

The bartender removed Julio's drink and wiped the bar with a white cotton towel.

"Excuse me? Is Mr. Ortega's tab still open?" she asked in Spanish.

"He said to bring anything you ask for."

"Oh, in that case, I'll take two more of these and a six-pack of your most expensive beer. Oh, and buy everyone in the bar a round."

"Are you staying at the hotel, señorita?"

"I sure am."

"I'll have them sent to your room."

"Room 403. Muchas gracias, amigo."

She left the bar and stepped into the elevator. A hand poked through, jamming the doors and reopening them. Quinn stepped inside and beamed.

"You were amazing, kid. I'm so damn proud of you."

He pressed his lips to hers and ran his hands over her backside. She pushed him away and giggled.

"They have cameras, buddy. Watch your hands. What do you say we go back to the room, get drunk, and have a wild, crazy night of kinky sex?"

"I'd say that's a hell of an offer. Throw in the accent and I'm all in."

THIRTY-TWO

Hijacked in Manaus

September 16, 2026

Her head pounded, and her tongue was stuck to the roof of her mouth. She stumbled out of bed, staggered into the bathroom, and hurled last night's dinner into the porcelain bowl.

"Oh, God. Never again."

"Izz? You alright?"

"No. But I'll live. I need water."

"Open my backpack. I have a couple of bottles in there and some aspirin. Take two and come back to bed."

"It's like noon, buddy. I don't want to sleep all day. Do you?"

"Nah. I just want to lie here for a few more minutes and relive last night. Not sure what the hell has come over you lately, but whatever it is, I like it. You could say, I'm still drunk on your love."

"Hm. How original."

The satellite phone rang.

"Oh, God," she muttered.

"You need to answer that, Izz."

"I know, I know. Okay. Yikes."

"Hola."

"Isabella?"

"What's up, Julio?"

"I see the blue rim around my irises, but my head is on fire and my joints ache. I swear if you've crossed me, I'll have you filleted and fed to the pigs."

"Well, that creates a disgusting image."

"Why do I feel so malo? Like a sick dog."

"It's just a few side effects. They'll go away in a few days, and you'll feel like a teenager again. Give it some time. Take some Tylenol and drink lots of fluids. Did you get the package I sent over?"

"I did. Your money should reach your account today."

"Well, I still don't see it, Julio. You're not trying to screw me, are you?"

"Of course not, but I'll call you in a few days. If I'm not feeling better, there is nowhere you can hide. I will hunt you down."

"Prune juice, Julio. I hear prune juice helps. And maybe a six-pack of Ensure. Maybe invest in a walker and a Miracle-Ear. I'm sure you'll manage."

"I don't understand your jokes, but I'm having my blood tested and running other tests. Pray they turn out normal, Isabella."

"Oh, I'm praying for you, Julio. Believe me, I am." CLICK.

"Quinn, we need to go."

"Where?"

"Back to the rainforest. Julio is suspicious, and by tomorrow, he's going to know. When he wakes up and looks in the mirror, he'll know."

"Give him a few days without answering the phone. He'll panic and grow desperate. That's when we'll tell him about the antidote."

"Oh my God, I cannot wait to have that conversation."

❧❧❧

September 18, 2026-Three Days After Inoculation

The satellite phone has been blowing up for three days now. As much as Izzy was dying to answer, she resisted until this morning.

"Good morning, Congressman. How's your day?"

"How's my day? How do you think my day is? You've ignored my calls for three days, and now I see a much older man when I look in the mirror. What the fuck did you do to me?" he shouted.

"Calm down. I guess you don't always get what you want, Julio. It sounds like you're about to lose everything to the little girl who beat you at golf."

"I will find you, and I will kill you with my own hands."

"You're too old, Julio. I'll kick your ass and embarrass you. How does it feel to know you're about to die so soon? To know that I hold the only key that can save you or let you die? Something you didn't offer my parents when you arranged their deaths."

"Key? What key? Isabella, I can pay you—"

"I don't need money, Julio. I'm wealthier than you and all your friends combined."

"What do you want then? Power? Fame. What? Name it, just sell me the key to stop this insanity."

"What I want doesn't involve money, or fame, or power, Julio."

"Then what? Tell me, Isabella, and it's yours. Name your price."

"Revenge."

The phone went silent. His breath grew heavy and rapid.

"What are you asking of me?" he meekly replied.

"A recorded deposition in front of my attorney admitting all of your crimes. The murder of my parents, the murder of an innocent indigenous people, the destruction of a rare and ancient species of tree, the attempted murder of Dr. Quinn, and all of your corruption as a congressman, laundering money, and siphoning taxpayer funds from government programs. I want it all on tape, Julio. Do that, and I will provide you with the only cure for your ailment."

More silence on the phone.

"You have nothing to say, Julio? That's so unlike you, dude."

"I will admit my white-collar crimes. But I will not admit to murder. Ian Bragg murdered those villagers in the Amazon, not me, and he's guilty of Dr. Quinn's wounds. And I had nothing to do with your parents' unfortunate accident, Isabella."

"Oh, are we negotiating now? Let me simplify everything for you. There *is* no negotiation. You asked what I required of you, and I told you. Nothing less is acceptable. When you are ready to agree to my terms, call me and we'll make the arrangements. Until then, find an excellent nurse and invest in a wheelchair."

"I'll have you killed, Isabella. Tortured. You have twenty-four hours to give me the antidote."

"You're threatening me? I hold all the cards. If I die, nothing and no one can save you. You will age ten years for every week, until you are dead and rotting in the ground, Julio. Twenty-four hours? That's how long you have to decide your fate. Death or prison?" CLICK.

Quinn applauded. "That was spectacular, Izzy. He's shitting his britches right now."

"That felt so good, Quinn. Oh, my God. I can't tell you how awesome that was."

"Let him stew in his own sweat. A few more days and he'll be begging you to send him to prison."

"We should change hotels, Quinn. Just to stay safe."

"You stole the words right off my lips."

September 21, 2026-Six Days After Inoculation

The satellite phone rang. Izzy snatched it off the kitchen bar, glanced at Quinn, and plopped onto a wicker loveseat on the balcony of their new hotel room.

"Have you changed your mind, Julio? You must be what … in your mid-sixties now?"

"Do not play games with me, Isabella. My patience has run out."

"Ah, but this *is* a game, Julio. Like golf. You're 25 strokes down on the 18th hole. Why not concede? You have no bargaining chips."

"And that is where you are gravely mistaken, Hija."

"How do you mean?"

The door to their room splintered and slammed against the wall.

"On the ground! Now!"

Five Secret Service agents stormed the apartment, weapons drawn on her and Quinn.

Cold steel tightened on her wrists as two agents grabbed her upper arms and stood her up. Two agents held Quinn to the floor. The fifth agent mumbled into a cellphone, "They're in custody, sir. Yes, sir, we've confiscated everything. We'll leave within the hour."

Izzy couldn't move. They strapped her to her seat inside a private jet, handcuffed.

"Where is Quinn?" she demanded.

Julio entered the plane and sat across from her, sneering with contempt. His hair was gray and thinning; his eyes sunken and bloodshot. His nose had grown, and his skin showed signs of age spots. He folded his trembling hands and rested them on the small table separating them.

Izzy crinkled her brow and narrowed her eyes. The effect of the drug was staggering. She couldn't help herself. Izzy burst into roaring laughter, tears forming in her eyes.

Julio reached over and slapped her in the face. She paused for a moment, then laughed some more. "Is that it? That's all you got, Julio? You slap like my nana. Did you hurt your hand, buddy?"

"You've wandered into treacherous waters, Chica. You've messed with the wrong man."

"And you have maybe a week or two to live, cabrón. I'm enjoying watching you die. Every day that goes by, you age another year and a half."

"That may be true, but I will enjoy watching your pain when your boyfriend Quinn dies at my hand."

"What do you mean? Where is he?"

"He is on the plane. For now. Where is the antidote, Isabella?"

"I don't have it."

"Then Quinn will die if you don't produce it."

"Really? Because Quinn is the only one who can provide you with the antidote."

"Thank you for sharing that bit of vital information. Maybe Quinn should be in front of me instead of you."

"Quinn will never give it up."

"Then I will torture it out of him. Allow him to watch as I torture you."

"You are a sick bastard. No matter what you do to us, you can't change the fact that you are about to die. Your life is over, Julio, unless you do what I ask. The antidote is in Quinn's head, not written in a journal or in a syringe in someone's fridge. You're screwed."

"Am I?"

"Yes, you are. What about your son, Julio? We can save him."

He pounded the table with his fist. "I should trust you?"

"Yes, you should. I don't let innocent people die the way you do, Congressman. Your full confession will save his life and yours."

Julio whispered into one of the agent's ears. The agent stood and left the cabin. Moments later, he shoved Quinn into the cabin, battered and cuffed, forcing him into a seat next to Izzy.

Tears filled Izzy's eyes seeing how badly they had beaten Quinn. Prickling anger flushed the back of her neck.

"What the hell did you do to him? You assholes."

"Dr. Quinn. Isabella tells me the antidote lives in that head of yours. So, how are we going to extract it?"

"Go to hell, Ortega. It's a pleasure watching you die like a dog."

Julio nodded to the agent. The man grabbed Quinn's cuffed hands, took a pair of handheld pruning shears, waved them in the air, and grinned.

Quinn howled in pain. The agent tossed him a cotton towel and chuckled.

"Oh, my God! You disgusting pigs? Leave him alone!"

"You have five minutes to produce the antidote, Dr. Quinn. Kindly speak into the microphone. Resist, and I'll remove another digit every sixty seconds until they're all gone. Then we'll go bigger."

"Quinn. Give it to them. Please."

He shook his head and grimaced. "They're going to kill us either way, Izz. I say we let the congressman die. Let his son die."

Quinn glared at Julio and snickered. "I failed to mention that after the first week, the pain becomes unbearable. Just thought you should know in case you want to end yourself sooner."

"The clock is ticking, Doctor."

The pilot tapped Julio on the shoulder and leaned in to him. "We're clear for takeoff, sir. Where do you wish to go?"

"Mexico City. We're delivering two drug dealers to the most notorious prison in the country." He leered at Izzy. "Where you'll both rot. I always win, Isabella. The antidote, por favor. Before time runs out for you and the doctor."

Engines whirred, and the aircraft jolted as it moved forward. The jet rolled along the taxiway toward the runway, preparing to take off.

"Sit back, relax, and enjoy the trip. You have only twelve hours of freedom left. Unless you're ready to talk."

The jet rolled to an abrupt stop near the active runway, and the engines shut down.

"What are we waiting for? Take off," Julio demanded.

The pilot turned toward Julio and shrugged.

"We are being told to return to the hangar."

"What? Why? Who is telling you this? I'm ordering you to take off."

"The authorities, sir. We have no choice. They revoked our clearance to depart."

"I don't care what they are telling you. Take off now!"

"Sorry, sir. I can't do that."

Quinn glanced at her with raised eyebrows as he continued to apply pressure to his finger with the blood-soaked towel.

As the jet rested in the hangar, the door opened to three United States government officials, who boarded the aircraft.

The man in the middle stepped forward and asked, "Good morning. I'm looking for Congressman Julio Ortega. Is he aboard the aircraft?"

Izzy screamed, "Help us! They're kidnapping us!"

An agent accompanying Julio placed his hand on a holstered pistol.

The two other U.S. officials pulled pistols and directed them at the agents sitting next to Julio.

"Stand down," they ordered.

Both agents raised their hands as the officials confiscated their weapons.

Julio stood defiantly. "I'm Congressman Ortega, and this is an outrage. I'll have all three of your jobs by the end of the day."

The official in charge stepped towards Julio and scowled.

"You are under indictment, Congressman, and ordered to accompany us back to the United States, where you will appear in court."

"For what crime? I am a U.S. congressman—"

"You may come willingly, or by force. Your choice, sir."

"Hey! Can someone remove these cuffs? My friend is bleeding. They chopped his frigging finger off. He needs to go to a hospital, like, right now. Please."

They removed their cuffs and escorted them off the private jet.

"Ma'am, are you Isabella Delgado?"

"I am. Why?"

"Senator McCreery tried reaching you when we received a tip from your hotel that you and your companion were taken hostage. The senator was a close friend of your father's. My condolences on his passing."

"Uh, yeah, I know the senator. Is he here in Brazil?"

"He is, and he wishes to speak to you and your friend in private."

"This is Dr. Dominic Quinn. Can we get him to a hospital, please?"

"Yes, ma'am. I have a car waiting to take you there, then afterward, the driver will take you to see the senator. Walk with me."

"What's going to happen to Ortega?"

"He'll be returned to the States and brought up on charges of embezzlement, bribery, and a host of other crimes. He's in a lot of trouble, ma'am. The senator requests your assistance as a key witness in the case against Ortega after his last conversation with your father."

Izzy and Quinn left the hospital with Quinn's hand tightly bandaged on their way to meet Senator Wayland McCreery at his hotel suite. She slipped her arm inside his and rested her head on his shoulder as they drove along the crowded streets of downtown Manaus. Her father promised he had powerful friends who could help with their situation. Senator McCreery was a highly respected senior senator with a stellar record and an avid supporter of the Amazon and environmental issues.

"What do you think is going to happen, Quinny?" she whispered.

"Not sure. But one thing we can be sure of is that Julio Ortega is going to die of old age before he spends a single day in prison."

"Maybe we should give him the antidote. So he can rot in prison, like he wanted us to do. Seriously."

"Maybe we should. And once we do, we should destroy everything related to the technology of rapid aging. It's an abomination of science, Izz. And I have such deep guilt in having been involved with it."

"I agree, Dr. Frankenstein, we should."

The limo parked in front of the lobby of the Hotel Villa Amazonia, where they were escorted to the senator's suite.

"Ah, Isabella. The last time I saw you, you were a young'n barely starting high school. Man, you've grown. Thank God I received your message in time."

McCreery glanced at Quinn and grinned. "Dr. Quinn, I presume."

"Yes, sir. I'd shake your hand but…"

McCreery raised his palms and shook his head. "Unnecessary, son. I'm Wayland McCreery. Deeply sorry this happened to you. To both of you. I'm relieved we caught the plane before it took off. Please have a seat. Can I fix either of you a drink?"

Quinn glanced at Izzy and raised his brows. "I'll take whatever you have, Senator."

"Do you have any water bottles, Senator McCreery?" she asked.

"Please. Call me, Wayland. We're all friends here."

He tossed Izzy a water bottle from the bar and filled two tumblers with Scotch.

The white-haired senator took a seat opposite Izzy and Quinn, who sat side-by-side on a leather loveseat. He crossed his legs and sipped his drink, then narrowed his eyes.

"I spent a lot of time with your father before his unfortunate accident, Isabella. I'm deeply sorry for the loss of your parents. Tragic shock to us all."

"Thank you, Wayland. He always spoke highly of you."

"Your father was a firm supporter of my campaign. I owe him a great debt, which is why you are here today."

Wayland sipped his drink and jangled the ice cubes before setting the tumbler on the table next to him.

"We found evidence that Congressman Ortega was involved in your parents' demise. Strong evidence. We have witnesses and whistleblowers who will testify about Ortega's many other crimes of extorting money from government-funded organizations."

He leaned forward in his seat, lowering his gray bushy eyebrows and focusing his piercing green eyes on her.

"Your father explained some of the research you were conducting in the Amazon and the tragic abuse of indigenous people and their resources.

I'd like to call you both as witnesses to those crimes. We can put Julio Ortega away for the rest of his life. He'll never trouble you again."

Izzy swigged her water and glanced at Quinn. "Respectfully, sir, if you have enough evidence to lock the congressman away for life, Quinn and I would prefer not to testify. Our research is delicate and something we'd totally prefer not to enter into a court docket."

"I understand and respect your decision, darl'n, and I hope to earn your support and continue the partnership your father and I had, Isabella."

"I'll continue my father's contributions to your campaign. But on one condition: we need to have a serious convo about the Amazon rainforest and how we can stop the poaching of trees and animals and restore and protect the rainforests. And not just a bunch of political talk and empty promises. We need guaranteed action. I've clocked politicians pretending to be concerned, only to turn their backs when someone slaps a wad of cash in their hand."

"Your father was right about you, young lady. He was very proud of you. I can promise I will use the power of my office to support your efforts in the Amazon. No bullshit promises. I'll show you actual results. The passion in your eyes when you speak of the rainforests inspires me, darl'n. And I'm not easily inspired. You tell me what you need and I'll deliver it."

Izzy and Quinn spent the week in Manaus detailing their plan to help save the Amazon Rainforest with Senator McCreery. Izzy negotiated government funding for a new field lab for her and Quinn in exchange for a generous contribution to Senator McCreery's campaign.

She used some of her fortune to acquire state-of-the-art equipment and supplies. They spent their last night in their hotel room vegging on the king-size bed, drinking local beer, munching on exotic fruit, and watching the international news on the TV.

She jumped when the aged face of Julio Ortega flashed on the screen, pointing the TV remote at the television and raising the volume.

"Oh, my God, Quinn. That's Julio. Let me turn it up."

U.S. Congressman Julio Ortega of California, indicted this week on charges of fraud and embezzlement, is now charged with the murder of a wealthy Malibu couple. The congressman appeared aged and haggard at his recent arraignment, as shown in this recent photo. We regret to report, however, that Congressman Ortega took his own life early this morning before his arrest. He was 44 years old and left behind a wife and two sons. In other news…

"Holy shit, Izz. I guess he took the easy way out."

"That's terrible, but he was a coward and brought this on himself. I feel horrible for his family, Quinn. He didn't deserve them. We need to help his son. How can we do that?"

"Let me make some calls to the hospital providing care for him. Maybe I can arrange a visit, and we'll administer the yaru vaccine when no one is watching."

"I love that idea."

THIRTY-THREE

Two Years Later

August 30, 2028

The new field lab stood at the edge of the original village like a watchtower—the place where Quinn once introduced Izzy to the Amazon rainforest, the sacred Yarumaya tree, and the Kawirén people. The lab was now a solid structure, constructed of brick, wood, and a sturdy foundation. State-of-the-art equipment, supplies, and a powerful solar generator stocked the lab area. A spacious bedroom and a full kitchen completed the structure with a few comforts of home. Izzy added a small gym with a balance beam, mats, and weights, where she has spent hours teaching the youth of the tribe gymnastics and physical fitness. She even roped Quinn into a daily fitness routine.

It took months to gather the remnants of the Kawirén village and return them to their sacred and secluded home on the mountain. They seeded and replanted the ancient Yarumaya grove several years ago, and now the trees flourish in the rich soil beneath the nurturing blaze of the Amazon sun.

Swarms of bees made their homes among the flowering Piritayá blooms atop the canopy, creating a rich and powerful cocktail of longevity.

The old customs returned; women harvested the Earth, prepared food, chose leaders among the elders, and gossiped, while children ran wild playing games and performed daily chores. Men honed their hunting skills and their arrowheads while sipping lakira and swapping stories of old—essentially gossiping like the women.

The mysteries of longevity and vitality in the Amazon will remain a protected secret of the Kawirén and Mayuma (Mother Rainforest).

Senator McCreery kept his promise. Hordes of wood and animal poachers were arrested and prosecuted, saving acres of natural forest and the precious habitats that support delicate life.

Criminals remain in the rainforest, but their activities are under constant attack, reducing their numbers and confounding their efforts. Izzy purchased acres of rainforest to protect and preserve from poachers.

Quinn and Izzy's compassion ensured Julio Ortega's son recovered from his devastating disease. Izzy anonymously provided full-ride scholarships to both sons for the colleges of their choice.

Helping Julio's son raised moral questions with Quinn and Izzy. They grappled with the ethics of their knowledge for months. The power to play God with such knowledge must never tempt them. They concluded the secrets of the Garden of Eden must not enter an evil and self-serving world that would only exploit them.

Izzy finally found the strength to visit her parents' gravesite at the mausoleum. She broke down several times, telling her dad how much she missed them. Apologizing to her mother for being so stubborn and not listening to her concerns. She knew it was too late, but the floral, gentle breeze that blew through the gravesite assured her of their presence and gave her closure.

Izzy slipped on denim shorts, leather hiking boots, a baby-blue T-shirt, and a long-sleeve flannel. Her long, thick chestnut hair pulled into a tight ponytail and a touch of light makeup completed the fit. She stared at herself in the mirror, analyzing how tight her shorts fit and adjusting her top.

A pair of muscular arms hugged her waist from behind, gently kissing the nape of her neck.

"Ooh, you're giving me chills, Quinny. I'm so excited for our date. We deserve a day off, don't you think?"

He gazed into her eyes as they stood side-by-side in the mirror.

"I do, Izzy. I have to admit, blue is definitely your color, kid."

She glanced at her T-shirt. "You like this shade of blue?"

"Your eyes, Izzy. Not the shirt."

She faced him and wrapped her arms around his neck. "So. Where are you taking me, old man?"

"I know of a beautiful, secluded waterfall a few miles away. Just down the hill. I thought we'd pack a lunch and enjoy a little swim."

Quinn dropped a bar of soap into his backpack and smirked.

"Okay … I see you, buddy. Lead the way, Tarzan."

As they glided through the gigantic trees, plush vegetation, thick vines, clear, cool creeks, listening to the orchestra of whistles, screeches, and the buzz of insects around them, peace filled her heart.

The peace of absorbing nature in its purest, most primal state, the peace of knowing and understanding what it is to love with all your heart, and the comforting knowledge that she is loved and accepted unconditionally by Quinn and the extended family of the Kawirén people—the big family she always longed for.

Losing her mom and dad still haunts her dreams and cuts deep into her heart and soul. It's a hurt that never resolves but keeps her grounded in the things in life that matter. Love, family, and trust.

As Izzy and Quinn hacked their way through the dense forest, a familiar roar caught their ear. Strolling out of the brush was a muscled cat. A proud and beautiful jaguar, trailed by two young cubs who practiced their roars that sounded more like playful growls as they romped and attacked each other before turning their attacks on their mother.

"Oh, my God, Quinn! Bessie's a mama. Look at them. Aw, they're so precious." Her eyes blurred.

Quinn kneeled and opened his arms to the big cat. She bypassed him and rubbed her powerful neck across Izzy's thighs, chuffing and introducing her cubs to her.

"What? Hey. She likes you better now?"

Izzy giggled. "We bonded. And besides, she is an excellent judge of character, Quinn. Women stick together and have each other's backs. You should know that by now, Junior."

Izzy sat and rubbed Bessie's ears, hugging her and whispering baby talk.

"Who are these two handsome fellas, Bessie? Can I hold them? I hope their daddy was worth your time, girlfriend."

Bessie seemed to understand, allowing Izzy and Quinn to hold and hug the beautiful cubs that symbolize the Amazon rainforest in their grace, natural beauty, and strength. As they set the cubs down, Bessie nudged her babies, instructing them to follow her into the cover of the dense forest. Her roar seemed to say goodbye and thank you at the same time.

Quinn took Izzy by the hand and led her to the crystal, shimmering pond beneath the flowing 10-foot waterfalls where their love story began—and will continue centuries into the future.

AUTHOR'S NOTES

The Amazon rainforest is dying and under siege. Wood poachers, cattle farmers, agriculture, and land grabbing destroy thousands of acres of forest each day. The destruction of these natural habitats and ecosystems also displaces and destroys the rare and exotic wildlife that thrives within them.

As I wrote this work of fiction, all the stories I encountered researching the Amazon deeply moved me. It is a spiritual place of Eden-like beauty. A delicate environment vital to the health of our planet and to the lives that call this paradise home. I encourage you to open your hearts and learn more about our rainforests. Maybe find a suitable organization to donate to.

As the author, I pledge to donate a portion of my book profits from "Blood of Yarumaya" to organizations supporting the conservation of our rainforests.

I hope you enjoyed this story and felt the power and beauty of the Amazon rainforest. Please share this book with family and friends to allow them to experience this place of primal beauty.

Please visit my website, AuthorKevinMiller.com, for more of my books and more about me as an author, husband, father, and grandfather.

Facts

- The Amazon Rainforest covers a whopping 6.7 million square kilometers, spanning eight countries and one territory in South America.
- It is estimated that the Amazon is home to 10 percent of the world's known species.
- The Amazon is home to over 47 million people. 2 million are indigenous. Over 400 indigenous groups live in the Amazon, with over 300 spoken languages.
- It is estimated that there could be nearly 400 billion trees thriving in the Amazon.
- The Amazon absorbs approximately 150 to 200 billion tons of carbon in the trees and soil.
- Current estimates state that 17 percent of the Amazon rainforest has already been lost.

Want to help conserve the Amazon rainforest, its wildlife, and indigenous people? Many organizations are fighting for the survival of our rainforests. You can reach out or donate to: **The Rainforest Trust**, **The Rainforest Alliance**, **The Nature Conservancy**, and the **World Wildlife Fund (WWF),** to mention a few.

Author Kevin D. Miller

Kevin is an international award-winning and best-selling author who began his writing career after discovering his last name wasn't his real name. Some old, yellowed newspaper articles from the 1920s revealed a terrible and tragic family secret. After his great-grandfather was murdered in his sleep in a small town in rural Ohio, his twelve-year-old grandfather, Stanley, was sent to fetch the sheriff. The story unravels into a tangled web of lies and shocking family secrets so dark his grandfather took them to the grave.

Kevin has appeared on national talk radio shows, network television, podcasts, and newspaper and magazine articles, and his books have won many prestigious book awards.

Kevin was born in Canton, Ohio, and grew up in Tempe, Arizona, where he played a variety of sports. He graduated from college with bachelor's degrees in electronics technology, electronic engineering, and information technology, and served his country in the United States Air Force. Kevin spent years in semiconductor engineering and was a web developer for a major city in Arizona. He and his wife, Annette, have two young daughters pursuing acting careers in Hollywood, and they have a beautiful blended family of nine children.

www.ingramcontent.com/pod-product-compliance
Lightning Source LLC
Chambersburg PA
CBHW021503110726
47899CB00001BA/276
9798993422503